Sergeant Tom 4

Resistance!

Joseph Taylor

Also available:

Sergeant Tom & The Battle Of Crete (2017)

In Kindle and in paperback

Sergeant Tom 2: Return to Crete (2017)

In Kindle and in paperback

Sergeant Tom 3: The Battle of France (2018)

In Kindle and in paperback

Glossary

Brass – Slang term for the highest ranks, the decision-makers in the armed forces.

Bristol Beaufighter – A twin-engine British aircraft, used as a night-fighter, a torpedo-bomber and in ground- attack.

Boche – French slang term for German.

Château – it can be a palace or a fortress or, as in this instance, a country house.

Corvette, Flower Class – A small warship of the Royal Navy. At about 1,000 tons, this ship served mainly as a convoy escort in World War Two.

E-boat – The Allies designation for the German Schnellboot, the fast attack craft of the Kriegsmarine.

Flic – French slang for cop or policeman.

Folboat – Folding kayak.

Gestapo – Abbreviation of Geheime Staatspolizei, the secret police of Nazi Germany and German-occupied Europe.

Kriegsmarine – The navy of Nazi Germany from 1935 to 1945.

MTB – Motor Torpedo Boat, the British equivalent of the German E-boat.

NCO – Non-commissioned officer i.e. Corporal, Sergeant, Petty Officer.

RDF – The early term for Radar.

SOE – Special Operations Executive. A secret British organisation, formed to conduct sabotage, espionage, reconnaissance and to provide aid to local resistance movements in occupied Europe. The London headquarters was at 64, Baker Street.

SSRF – Small Scale Raiding Force. A combined 62 Commando and SOE organisation which conducted raids on Northern France and the Channel Islands from 1941 to 1943.

Unteroffizier – NCO rank in the Wehrmacht, equivalent to Sergeant or Staff Sergeant.

Wehrmacht – The armed forces of Nazi Germany.

Chapter 1

October 1941

As hard as he tried, Sergeant Tom Lane lost ground steadily. The extreme heat was brutal, and six months in the Mediterranean climate of the island of Crete had not prepared him for the stifling, broiling temperatures of the Red Sea. The forward motion of the ship produced some cooling but the air temperature was so high, and the sun so fierce, that the benefit was small.

It had been young Geraint's idea to run laps of the top deck of the 'Queen Mary', as a way to use up an hour of the long, hot day, and perhaps to bring Cape Town that few miles closer. Tom had readily agreed, forgetting that the young German was more than ten years his junior, and carried at least two stone less weight to push around the hot deck. George and Phil, old hands in many ways, had declined the opportunity to participate, and were sitting in the shade, counting off the laps, and trying not to smirk as Tom's complexion coloured more deeply with every circuit of the mighty ship.

The four men, fresh from a successful operation in Crete, under the auspices of the Special Operations Executive, the organisation tasked by Churchill to 'set Europe ablaze', were on their way to Britain to undertake training for an, as yet, unknown operation in the future. They made an interesting grouping, having so recently combined their differing skills and experiences with lethal effect.

Tom Lane belonged to the Welch Regiment of the British Army, but had been picked up by the SOE, as it was known, as a result of the enterprise, skill and sheer fighting spirit that he had shown while escaping from Crete after the German invasion of May 1941. With his three companions, he had returned to Crete several weeks later to give training to the Cretan resistance and to attack the German airbase at Heraklion. The operation had been a stunning success, and to cap it all, Tom had re-met and married Elena, a Cretan woman with whom, in the midst of the Allied defeat and evacuation from the island, he had shared a romantic relationship. It had not been a normal courtship, being pursued by German troops over the high mountain-tops of Crete, but these were not normal times, so proposing marriage to Elena before he left the island for the second time had seemed to be the best solution, and fortunately for him, she had agreed.

So, here he was, a thirty-year old English sergeant in a Welsh regiment, sailing further and further away from his new wife, attached to a still-secret organisation and with a highly uncertain future. The previous two years, encompassing the Phoney War, the Battle of France, Egypt and then Crete had been both exciting and terrifying, more than he could ever have foreseen, and if they were a measure of what was to come, then a little extra fitness would do him no harm.

Ahead of Tom, just turning at the bow to run back down the port side of the main deck, Geraint seemed to be floating along, the brat! The young man had been born Yakob Baumann, a German Jew, whose parents had been arrested by the Nazis in 1938, and who had avoided the same fate by assuming a false name and relying upon his blond hair and blue eyes to convince the Jew-haters of his Aryan descent. He had eventually been conscripted into the Kriegsmarine, the German Navy, as a wireless operator, and had been rescued from the Mediterranean by Tom, as the sole survivor of his patrol boat, which had been sunk by British aircraft. Although a patriotic German, he hated the Nazis, and after interrogation by the SOE, he had joined with Tom and the others in their raid on the aerodrome, and had proven himself to be utterly trustworthy. He hated having to kill and maim fellow Germans, but saw the Nazis and their barbarity as a greater evil that had to be eliminated before Germany could be free again.

He did not know it yet but there were many other German Jews fighting for the Allies, and like most of them, he had taken a British name, in case of future captivity. He was now Private Geraint Williams from Ffestiniog in North Wales, the theory being that his foreign accent could be explained away as that of a native Welsh-speaker, speaking his second language, English! Fortunately, he had been a student of languages in University, so his English was good and his Greek was passable, and with his wireless operator's skills, he was an asset to the SOE and to the Allied cause. It also helped that he was modest and well-mannered, with an inner strength that initially surprised his new comrades.

Corporal George Parry and Tom had known each other for more than ten years, from when Tom had joined the Royal Welch Fusiliers. George already had ten years' service by then, and had taken Tom under his wing, teaching him the principles of soldiering, both official and unofficial, and they had become the closest of friends. He had been delighted when Tom had climbed the NCO ladder, starting at Lance-Corporal, then to full Corporal to Sergeant, with a temporary demotion to Corporal when they were drafted from the Welch Fusiliers to the Welch Regiment after Dunkirk. He had accepted a single stripe himself, when under fire in the Battle of France, but it had not been confirmed, so he had reverted to Private, not that he cared a jot. To his surprise, this had been reversed not long after arriving in Egypt, for his qualities were evident to the officers in his new regiment, and a further battlefield promotion to Corporal had come his way during the Battle of Crete.

The decision to make George's promotion to Corporal permanent may have been influenced by the award of the Military Medal to him, for his action in destroying a German machine-gun nest in Crete. One of his final appointments in Alexandria, after getting a haircut and buying presents for his wife Rachel and their daughters, back at home in Wales, was to attend General Auchinleck for the award of the medal. The honour meant very little to him, but many good men had been killed in that attack, and in the privacy of his own mind, he had accepted it on their behalf. He also thought of Davey Williams, one of the participants in that action and in others, who had escaped the island with him and Tom, until half-way across the Libyan Sea, when he had been killed in the process of shooting down a German aircraft. Dead at eighteen.

Slight of build, greying, and giving more than ten years away to Tom, George did not look, at first glance, like the dynamic soldier that he was. Possessed of great endurance, he was a quick thinker, a crack shot with his Bren gun and set a wonderful example to younger soldiers. Despite the stripes, he simply thought of himself as a professional soldier, but at the same time, he never forgot that he was also a loving husband and father.

Tom had asked him how he could reconcile the two, and his answer had been, 'I do the best I can'.

The fourth member of the party, Phil Watson, with the rank of Petty Officer in the Royal Navy, had been one of the sailors who had pulled the other three out of the Libyan Sea, and what a contrast he was to George. A Gunner by trade, he was built like a heavyweight boxer, with a voice to match, which he used to his advantage. In his naval career, ratings had quivered at his bellowed orders, and he was well known not to tolerate fools or idlers. He would call a spade a bloody shovel, and could never be accused of diplomacy.

But again, there was more to him than met the eye. He had been recruited for the mission in Crete, and his contribution had been immense, delivering the demolition party to the airfield by sea, and helping to fight off German attacks afterwards. Perhaps more importantly for himself, in the long run, he had learned that there was more than one way to skin a cat, and more than one way to fight a war.

He had been scathing in his opinion of the Cretan people and their resistance fighters before he had met them, yet sharing their struggles and hardships had forced him to revise his opinions entirely. Years of naval routine and ritual had conditioned him to a particular way of thinking about himself and others, yet within a few weeks, he had discovered a delight and a talent in irregular warfare, and an open pleasure in the company of these people, mostly untutored, who fought with such fortitude and tenacity for their freedom. His regard for them had been returned, and he had been genuinely sorry to leave the island. Perhaps most tellingly, he had admitted that a quick return to the Andrew was not what he wanted for himself, and he had been a willing recruit for this operation, whatever it might turn out to be.

Together, they were a formidable combination, and 'Smith', their SOE handler, had decided to offer them the option of a further operation together, hence the voyage through the Red Sea and the Indian Ocean to Cape Town in South Africa, where they would leave the 'Queen' for another ship to take them on to Britain. Tom's suspicion was that Smith was using their success to further his own career, but on reflection, how surprising was that? Of course, there would be reflected glory for him in their achievements, and now that they were leaving the Middle East, probably they would be managed by another handler anyway.

Despite his personal reservations about the man, Tom had to admit that Smith had always delivered what he had promised. Training and supplies certainly, but he had also taken responsibility for Geraint's transfer from the Kriegsmarine to the British Army, a feat of persuasion and bureaucratic mastery! He had even secured a separate sleeping cabin for the four of them onboard, on the grounds that their security could be compromised if they were forced to share larger quarters with inquisitive strangers.

None of the four had ever travelled on a gigantic ship such as the 'Queen Mary' before, and even Phil, the only real seaman amongst them, was astonished at her huge size and air of opulence. Although her luxury fittings had been either stripped out or covered over, and her cabins re-fitted with bunks to increase her passenger capacity from two thousand to fifteen thousand, there was still an air of space and scale that was beyond any of their experiences. Stairways were broad and sweeping, and the canteen, where they took their meals, had clearly been a restaurant of elegant yet enormous proportions in the recent past. Fortunately for them, she had delivered a full complement of passengers to Suez, and for the voyage back to the Cape, she was less than a quarter full, so her vastness was not hidden by thousands of bodies.

They had learned, through discreet questioning of the crew, that twelve days should see them to Cape Town, and each of the four had their own way of passing the time.

George, married for the past seventeen years, looked for no great excitement or social whirl, and was content to spend much of his time reading, borrowing books from the ship's library. He was a student of history, right back to Roman times, and had come to the conclusion that mankind, through the ages, had made the same mistakes, over and over again. People put their trust in knaves, were promised the earth and were led into disaster. How else could the rise of Mussolini and Hitler be explained?

It did not get him down though, for another lesson he saw in his studies was that every tyrant eventually fell, without exception. Even Julius Caesar had his come-uppance in time, and so would Adolf, he was sure of it, and if he could help it come a little sooner, then that was all to the good.

There were letters to write, to his wife, Rachel, and separately, to both of his daughters, and indeed, he felt some guilt for not writing often enough in the past months. They were not to know how impossible conditions had been, either under fire or on the move, but Rachel was used to his long absences. Hopefully, there would be some leave when they reached port, and he would be able to make it up to them. Meanwhile, he would write some jolly letters and if he posted them in Cape Town, there was a small chance that they might reach home before he did.

Tom could not write to Elena, living as she was in occupied territory, and he knew that he had to accept that they would be apart until the war was over. Germany was strong, so it could be years yet, especially as the rest of Europe was either neutral or under the Nazi thumb. He had no regrets about their marriage, it was all that they could do for each other under the circumstances, and he had to swallow their separation, in the hope that time would put it right.

He wrote letters, but to his parents on the farm. Censorship and his own discipline discretion ensured that he could include nothing of his activities, but he did manage a reference to his new wife. On his last leave, after Dunkirk, his mother had revealed her anxiety about his marriage prospects, nearing thirty and no girlfriend for years, so at least he could put those worries from her mind.

Tom read too, and went to the ship's cinema, watching the same films over and over again, and there was always conversation with George, or with other soldiers as they took their promenade. He had been warned by Smith that their activities, past and future, were secret, and he was to divulge nothing, even to the most senior officer they might come across. So, he chatted about inconsequential things with the people that he met, and somehow passed the time. He slept enthusiastically too, hoping to put a few hours 'in the bank' for the future, when sleep would become a rare commodity once more.

Phil and Geraint, both unattached and possessed of a roving eye, took no time at all to gravitate towards the females on board. There were WAAFs returning from service in Egypt, and 'Queen Alexandra' nurses, either posted home or out to India or Ceylon from Egypt or Palestine. On the first evening out of Suez, they both disappeared after supper, to make their first forays, and most evenings, one of them, and sometimes both, would be seen escorting a young woman around the less-frequented areas of the Upper Deck. Neither of them was looking for a wife, or so they assured Tom, not that he was concerned. They should make hay while the sun shone, for soon enough, he knew, they would go back to war.

Geraint told him how he fended off questions about his strange accent. 'I tell them, Sergeant, that it is a secret, that I would like to share it with them but I have promised the King that I will not'.

'And does that work, do they stop asking?'

'Sometimes it does, Sergeant, but sometimes it does not. They laugh, and ask me again'.

'What do you do if they keep asking?' asked Tom.

'I tell them that I will walk out with another girl, one who asks less questions'.

'And how do they like that? Not much, I shouldn't think'.

'No, but they stop asking. There are many girls, and they all have time on their hands, and they know that I will soon find another companion'.

Tom had forgotten all about the heartlessness of youth and playing the field, but why shouldn't Geraint enjoy his few days on the 'Queen'? In years gone by, he might have done the same, although he had never had quite the confidence with the opposite sex that Geraint displayed.

Phil, at thirty, the same age as Tom, seemed to appeal to the slightly older women on board, and although he would walk out with a favoured one or two, he was more likely to be found playing cards with a group of nurses after supper, or chatting over a cup of tea with a WAAF. 'I just like women's company', he explained to George one evening, 'I've had years of men on board ship, farting and belching like it was something clever, a few days of civilisation will do me the world of good'.

What a case he was, thought Tom, he might look like Primo Carnera, the giant Italian boxer, but the more he got to know him, the more he sensed that there was more to be revealed.

The 'Queen' was a fast ship, with engines powerful enough to push her eighty thousand tons through the water at an easy twenty-eight knots, making her a difficult, although very desirable, target for submarines. Her constant zig-zagging, to make the task of torpedoing her even more difficult, took a few knots off her forward speed, but still only eleven days had passed when the beautiful view of Table Bay, and the spectacular Table Mountain beyond, opened up in front of her.

Chapter 2

Eloise Beauchêne, twenty-eight years old and a mother of two children, was a widow. The French Mobilisation Générale of the second of September 1939 had taken her husband, Henri, away from her, into the Armée de terre, and other than a few letters, the last posted in April 1940, she had neither seen nor heard from him again. Henri, ten years older than her, was the least likely man to make a success of being a soldier, being studious and peaceable by nature, and Eloise feared for him if he was ever forced to fight the Boche.

Eloise knew that he was in north-west France somewhere, near to the border with Belgium, but after the German invasion, one month after his last letter, he had disappeared. She held out hopes for his return but after six months without a word, she had finally accepted that he was not coming back. Final confirmation was provided by the son of one of their neighbours, conscripted with Henri, who had returned at Christmas, after being severely wounded and in hospital. Henri had been killed by German shellfire as he carried ammunition to his comrades in the trenches, and he had been buried where he fell.

It was heart-breaking. Henri had not even seen his second child, a daughter, born after his departure, and their first-born had no memory of his father at all. When they grew up, it would be as if he had never existed.

Life in Brittany, living in a cottage near to the village of Lilia, within a stone's throw of the coast, was not easy without a husband. He had been a senior teacher, working in the town of Brest, and they had lived a comfortable life, not wealthy but with no real worries. Henri had driven a little car, and they could afford a restaurant meal from time to time, without anxiety about paying other bills. They had loved living here together, with the sea, cliffs, beaches and pretty harbours on one hand, and the fertile farmland and beautiful forests on the other, and it had seemed like the best place in the world to raise a family. Now, all of that was in the past.

The car had gone first, she couldn't drive it and certainly could not afford to buy the fuel to run it anyway. She had sold it for a fraction of its true value, she was sure, but it made sense just to get it off her hands, and the money would pay the rent for their cottage for several months. They had a little silver, and a few small pieces of Sèvres porcelain, Henri's pride and joy, and that had soon followed the car.

Her next task was to find work, for the proceeds from selling their few valuables would eventually be spent, war or no war. Eloise had started work as a very young plongeur in her late father's hotel, washing dishes and peeling vegetables, moving gradually through commis to sous-chef and chef de cuisine could have been hers within a few years, for she had a genuine talent and had learned fast. Her father had been deeply disappointed when she decided to abandon cooking but feeling that there must be more to life than be swallowed up by the family business, she had re-trained as a language teacher, and this was when she had met Henri, in the course of her first job. When they had married, he had insisted that she stopped working and this was the cause of their first, and only, major disagreement, for she knew that she had a talent for both professions, but she had quickly become pregnant, and life had seemed to fall into place. Then came the war.

Teaching was out of the question, for there was no job available now and she had her son, almost three years of age, and her baby daughter to think about. Finally, a friend of her husband's, an elderly gentleman living alone in a nearby chateau, had offered her domestic work and at the same time, a neighbour had offered to look after her children while she worked. It was four hours work per day, preparing food and cleaning, on every day of the week except Sunday, and although it was poorly paid, it would support them for now. Madame Le Roux, a widow, would accept no payment for minding the children, telling Eloise that it was little enough that she was doing, and that she enjoyed their company. Eloise suspected that Madame Le Roux and Monsieur Hervé had cooked the whole thing up between them, but she was gratefully respectful, and never asked.

Lilia was a small Breton community, and in better circumstances, Eloise would have continued to love living there. It was deeply rural in nature, yet bordered by the rocky coast, sandy beaches and the churning waters of the mouth of La Manche, or the English Channel, as their neighbours over the water insisted on calling it. Everyone knew each other, and there was considerable sympathy for Eloise in her predicament. There would often be a knock at the door in the evening, and a few mackerel would be handed over, or a rabbit, or a few eggs. She and her family, although incomers, belonged to the village, and they would not see her, or her children, starve.

The evidence of the German occupation of France was not slow to show itself in Brittany. The largest garrisons were at Rennes, Lorient and Brest, but Germany was wary of the presence of Britain across the Channel, and small bases were placed around the coast, to keep an eye on the fishermen and to deter any incursion by the British. There were patrols, by day and by night, when troops would appear without warning in the village, and would stop and search people randomly.

For several months, this did not cause any problems for Eloise. She would pedal her bicycle to and fro, between home and Monsieur Hervé's modest chateau, enduring wolf-whistles and ribald comments directed at her, which she ignored. No one followed her, and she always managed to get to her work or back home on time. Inside her head though, she churned with indignation that these barbarians had over-run her country, and killed her husband, but she never let it show, or even spoke about it.

Life changed in late November 1941, when one morning, as she was cleaning the chateau kitchen, the old man answered a loud knock at the door, then was hustled back into the room by a German unteroffizier, with a dozen soldiers at his heels.

The NCO barked out some stern-sounding orders, causing his men to scatter through the rest of the house, stamping up the stairs and along the corridors, and before long, Hervé and Eloise could hear the sound of furniture being turned over, objects dropping to the floor and what was probably glass and china shattering.

Turning to the frightened pair, the unteroffizier told them, in poor French, why he was there, 'We have information that you, old man, have been harbouring terrorists. Do you deny it?'

Eloise knew that it was a ludicrous accusation, for Hervé was seventy years old, and could hardly look after himself, let alone hide resistance fighters, for that was surely what the Nazi meant by terrorists.

He answered spiritedly, 'Of course I deny it. I have lived alone since my wife died, and my only visitor is this young woman here, who cleans and cooks for me. You will know this if you have been watching this house. Your soldiers will find nothing, because there is nothing to hide'.

The unteroffizier turned to Eloise, 'And you, woman, have you been hiding bandits for this old fool? Tell me the truth, for it will go badly for you if I discover that you have'.

In the background, Eloise could hear more furniture being smashed, but knew very well that any show of defiance or anger from her would be used as an excuse for more destruction, so, taking a breath, she answered as calmly as she could manage, her heart thumping inside her chest.

'Sir, Monsieur Hervé is correct. He lives here alone. I am here between ten o'clock in the morning, and half past two in the afternoon, on every day except Sunday, and I have never seen any signs of other people staying here'.

The soldier was unimpressed, 'So you are saying that terrorists could be here overnight and on Sundays and you would not see them'.

Eloise was aghast, but forced her indignation down, 'Sir, I am not saying that, not at all. If people were staying here, there would be disturbed beds, mud on the floors, extra laundry. There are none of those things, in all of the months that I have worked here. I think you have been misinformed'. She spoke with an unforced sincerity, and it must have been obvious to the German that she was telling the truth.

As she finished speaking, one of the soldiers came into the kitchen and shook his head, they had found nothing.

The unteroffizier was unimpressed, and turned to Hervé, 'We may have found nothing today, old man, but I believe my source. Had I found any evidence today, I would have had you shot in your own garden! As it is, I will confiscate this house for the Reich. You have one hour to collect whatever clothes you need, and get out. If you are still here in one hour, you will be arrested and taken away for questioning. Do you understand me?'

Hervé understood perfectly, 'I think that the German Army wants my house, Monsieur le Sergent, or whatever you call yourself. You know as well as I do that there are no terrorists here, and never have been'. The unteroffizier was colouring up as the old man spoke, for his ruse had been seen through. The Wehrmacht wanted this chateau, comfortable and with a view of the bay, for a local headquarters, and this was a mere smokescreen to evict the owner.

Before the German could reply, Hervé spoke again, 'I will leave within the hour and Eloise will help me pack. A friend will take me in, and your army may have the house. Now, please, leave us in peace'.

The NCO flushed again, for he was being dismissed, and he knew it. However, he had achieved what the Oberleutnant had ordered him to do, and could afford to be magnanimous.

'Go, old man, before I change my mind and arrest you anyway', then turning to Eloise, 'You, woman, you cook for this man?' She nodded. 'You will continue to work here. Come in at your usual hour tomorrow, and I will give you your orders, ask for Unteroffizier Brauer', and with that, he was gone.

Eloise turned, expecting Hervé to speak or shout a response but instead, he quickly shook his head, pointing towards the corridor where someone might still be lurking, then, speaking to her in a loud voice, said, 'There is a hand-cart in the stable, my dear, please bring it to the front of the house, and you will help me push it to the house of Madame Le Roux, she would not marry me fifty years ago, but now I will become her lodger'.

Hervé's clothing hardly filled two cases, and Eloise could see that the handcart would be easy enough for her to push the kilometre and a half to the Le Roux villa. They were just out of earshot of the guard already placed at the chateau, and she was still grappling with the idea of working for her country's enemy when the old man's quiet chuckling interrupted her thoughts, 'If they only knew, the bastards, if they only knew'.

She turned to him, not understanding, 'If only they knew what?' she asked.

'How stupid are the Boche to suggest that I would allow the Résistance into my house, do they think that I am as stupid as they are?'

'Of course not', she answered, 'you would never do such a thing'. There had been no sign of other people in the house, ever, and that was why she had sounded so truthful to the unteroffizier, because it really was the truth.

'What I want to know is this', he continued, 'someone must have suggested something about the Résistance to them, otherwise why did they even mention it, they could have just requisitioned the place. Who has been talking to them?'

Eloise was beginning to feel confused, 'No one was talking to them, Monsieur, it was just an excuse to steal your house, you said yourself, no one has been in the house, except you and I'.

He smiled, kindly, 'I did say that, and it is true, but I did not mention the stables, did I?'

'What about the stables?'

'Well', he answered, a little hesitant, 'sometimes the Résistance have left weapons there for a day or two, or a fugitive has hidden from the Germans'. He noticed her horrified face, 'This is why I did not tell you, Eloise, so that you could truthfully answer their questions'.

'What if they had looked in the stables and found something?' she snapped, 'would they have believed me then?' He tried to interrupt but she would not allow him to.

'What would happen to my babies if I was arrested, who would look after them? They have no father and you would risk them having no mother either? How could you be so cruel, you foolish man!' She was beside herself with fury, and Hervé stopped, aghast at her vehemence.

'Madame, it was for France', he stuttered.

She stared back at him, disgusted, 'Don't you think that I have given enough for France already?'

They walked on in silence for a while, then Hervé cleared his throat, 'Madame, I owe you an apology, I did not consider your situation, the loss of your husband, and for that, I am sorry. Sadly though, I think that I have left you with another dilemma'.

'And what might that be?' she demanded, still angry.

'You have been ordered to meet that fool Brauer tomorrow, you are going to work for them'.

'I will refuse, I cannot be expected to work for the enemy, that is monstrous!'

'Madame', he explained gently, 'you cannot refuse, they will not allow you to refuse. If they are not aware of your children yet, they will be by tomorrow. They will not threaten them outright, but they will make sure you understand that they know of them, and what more will they need? You will have to work there'.

Eloise was stunned, speechless, how could her life have taken this turn? She was just trying to be a mother to her children, that was all, and now she would have to work for the bastards that had killed her husband. How could life be so pitiless?

'They will have their own orderlies to clean up after them, why would they want me there? I would be a risk to them, surely?'

Hervé shrugged, 'I agree, but they must have their reasons, perhaps they will tell you tomorrow'.

He tried to smile reassuringly, 'Maybe you will be able to bring food home for the little ones, chérie, and perhaps they will pay you more than I did'.

'Will Madame Le Roux still look after my babies, what will I do if she changes her mind?'

He smiled more confidently, 'I have known Clarisse all my life, she will guard your children with her life, as will I'.

'And what about the villagers, Monsieur? What will they think, when they see me working for the Boche? They will call me a traitor!'

'They will not, I promise you. I will make it known that you are working there against your will, and that it was my fault it happened. They understand the Nazis and their ways, they will still help you'.

Madame Le Roux was surprised but welcomed them, saying to Hervé, 'So, you have found your way under my roof at last, you old goat! I hope that it is not for too long', although Eloise thought that she looked secretly pleased. To Eloise's question about the children, of course she would look after them, it was an honour, and now Gilbert, Monsieur Hervé, would help her.

Hervé had told her that Madame Le Roux knew nothing about the Résistance, and that he had no intention of telling her about them, or of inviting them to use her outbuildings. He would pass the message to those who needed to hear it that, unfortunately, he could no longer be of help.

Eloise returned home that evening feeling exhausted and somewhat terrified. What had started out as an ordinary day had suddenly become extraordinary. It was out of her hands, she realised, and she must just keep her wits about her and stay out of further trouble if she could.

Chapter 3

Smith had told Tom that, as long as they arrived on time, they would have three days to themselves, from leaving the 'Queen' to joining a slow convoy back to Britain. Only Geraint had not visited Cape Town before, Tom and George had stopped there going to and from India, and Phil had called in on different Royal navy ships, in peace and in war. They were all agreed though that seventy-two hours to re-acquaint themselves with the town, and to show Geraint the sights, would be a great tonic for the remainder of the voyage, which would be conducted at a funereal pace, at least, compared to the 'Queen'.

Each of the men had one large kit-bag and a small haversack, and they were packed and ready as the huge ship dropped anchor in the bay. She would be collecting a full load of troops for India, with her first stop at the port of Trincomalee in Ceylon, and would be on her way within forty-eight hours.

George and Tom had joined the farewell party on the last night, and had enjoyed a few drinks with the friends that Geraint and Phil had made. Both being married, they were noticeably less interesting to the female company than the two younger men, and they were happy enough to leave them to it. Phil had followed them an hour later but they hadn't seen Geraint until breakfast the next morning.

'You sly dog', teased George, 'I expect she's upset to see you go, is she?'

'I don't know, George, she said that she would treasure her memory of me'.

'No exchanging addresses or promising to meet again?'

'No. She told me that we were ships that pass in the night. I didn't understand what she meant but I thought I should agree, so I said yes, we were, so goodbye and thank you very much'.

'Thank you very much! Is that what you said?'

'Yes. That is polite, surely?'

'I suppose it is, but not very romantic, is it?'

'I thought that it was the British thing to say, you say thank you for everything, George'.

'And what did she say?'

'She didn't say anything, just pushed me out of the cabin and closed the door'.

'There are things we need to talk about, young man', finished George, as Tom and Phil howled with laughter, much to Geraint's confusion.

They had not left the cabin when a rating poked his around the open door. 'Sergeant Lane? The First Officer wants to see you, urgent matter. Would you follow me, Sergeant?'

Tom left with him, and the other three dropped their kit back onto the deck and sat back on the bunks. 'It won't be good news', muttered George, 'it never is'.

Fifteen minutes later, Tom was back, with the rating standing behind him. 'Go on, tell us', pressed George, 'we're going back to Egypt, or maybe off to India, so Geraint can see his young lady, which is it?'

'Neither', answered Tom, 'we're joining a medium convoy immediately, no shore leave, I'm sorry to say. Passage to Freetown, Sierra Leone, we'll be met there. He said the order was from a Mr. Smith'.

The other three, all servicemen and well used to last-minute changes of plan, said little, for there would be plenty of time for that on the voyage, but Smith's name probably meant an operation of some kind. They followed Tom and the rating down through the ship to an accommodation ladder that delivered them into a ship's boat, manned by sailors in a mixture of kit. 'Not the Andrew then', remarked Phil, and sure enough, they were delivered to a merchant ship at anchor in the bay, but one with fixed guns at bow and stern, and what looked like an anti-aircraft mount amidships.

'Armed merchant cruiser', explained Phil, 'there's not enough warships to cover all the convoys properly, so they've converted a few of the faster merchant ships, the guns will be old six-inch, a few Bofors and probably some depth charges'.

'And what do you reckon to it, mate?' asked George.

Phil wrinkled his nose, 'Neither fish nor fowl. Better than nothing, of course, and the gunners will be Navy, so they'll know what they're doing, but she's not heavily armed enough to do much damage, depends what she's up against'. It was hardly a ringing vote of confidence. There was no name or home port painted on the hull, but they discovered that she was the 'Cathay Empress', belonging to Liverpool.

As it happened, there was no need to test her fighting capabilities. The convoy seemed pedestrian after their journey in the 'Queen', but they made Freetown, Sierra Leone, in seventeen days.

Phil spent much of his time on board with the gunners, especially after he recognised their Petty Officer as an old acquaintance from Whale Island, the Royal Navy gunnery school. He joined in their exercises, and even made one or two suggestions that might speed things up, once he was confident that his old pal wouldn't be offended. Shots were fired, but not in anger, and for once, the U-boats left them in peace, although contacts were more likely once the convoy had cleared the latitude of the Canary Islands.

There were no young women on board for Geraint to get to know, so he spent most of his time with Tom and George, improving his English and listening as they discussed the possible reasons for this diversion.

'Perhaps Smith wants us back in Alexandria for something, Crete again maybe?' suggested George. Tom shook his head, 'No, it would have been quicker to send us back to Suez by sea, than waste nearly three weeks getting us to Freetown'.

'The West end of the Med, then'.

'I don't see that either. All the action in the desert is the Eastern end. No, it'll be something local, that's my guess. They need some more bodies for something, and we're to hand'.

Tom turned to Geraint, 'Does Germany have colonies near Sierra Leone?' he asked.

Geraint shook his head, 'No, there used to be Cameroon and Togoland but the Kaiser lost them in the Great War. Now it is Britain and France who control these countries'.

Their imaginations would take them no further forward. A flight back to Alexandria over the Sahara Desert seemed highly unlikely, if not impossible, so they had to sit back and wait. As they neared, and then crossed the Equator, the temperature increased once more, as did the humidity, but it was made bearable by the forward motion of the ship. Nights were stifling in an enclosed cabin, and often they would sleep on deck in a quiet corner.

The morning of the eighteenth day broke over a now silent ship, as she lay at anchor off Kroo Bay, one of the many inlets along the shoreline of Freetown. The heat and humidity, even this early in the morning, was startling, leaving those not used to it feeling weary and unwilling to move around more than necessary.

The remainder of the convoy had moved further into Freetown's enormous natural harbour, leaving the 'Cathay Empress' separated from it by a half-mile of sea. Tom and his companions were told to get ready to disembark, but instead of them being pulled to shore, a familiar-looking sailing boat, a British trawler according to Phil, came alongside, and they exchanged one vessel for another.

They were greeted on the cramped deck of the trawler by a tall, clean-shaven young man, dressed in army-issue shorts and a collarless shirt, with most of the buttons open and both sleeves rolled up. To complete the picture, he was barefoot but wore an officer's cap.

'Sergeant Lane, I presume?' he asked with a grin, 'Captain Pearson, late of the Royal Sussex', introducing himself and returning Tom's hurried salute, 'Welcome to the 'Matron'. Come below and I'll tell you why you're here'.

There was more space below decks than Tom had anticipated, and as Pearson directed them to benches along the hull, the motion of the boat changed as she got under way. A sail had been rigged to direct more air below, and as she picked up a little speed, they started to feel the passage of a cooling breeze.

Tom quickly introduced his three companions and Pearson got down to business, after handing around some water.

'I'm six chaps down for an operation, spoke to London and they told me that you were, ah, en route, and that I might borrow you. They spoke to your friend, Mr Smith, he had no objections so here we are'. So far then, it was as Tom had suspected, SOE wanted them for another operation, and if the trawler was anything to go by, it would be local to this part of Africa.

'Let me tell you about the operation', Pearson continued, 'there's a thought that Jerry U-boats are refuelling on this coast somewhere, there's any number of creeks and inlets they could use, so for the last two months, we've been creeping up and down, trying to find them. Unfortunately, we've drawn a blank, and to cap it all, I've lost six chaps to malaria. You see, we've had to sail right up these rivers, a few miles sometimes, and of course, there's hordes of mosquitoes, millions of the buggers'.

'Now', he continued, 'I was beginning to think they'd be flying us home, tail between our legs sort of thing, but some interesting info came up, courtesy of your SOE boys'.

'Are you not SOE, sir?'

'Good lord, no, I'm SSRF, that's Small Scale Raiding Force, the name explains itself really. Now, this info, have you heard of Fernando Po?'

Everyone looked blank, except for Phil. 'Island, sir, off Cameroon, I believe. Spanish territory, sir'.

'Spot on, ah Petty Officer, spot on. Yes, it's Spanish and therefore neutral, can't be touched, but in the harbour there, ah, your chaps have spotted an Italian ship, about 8,000 tons and a rather large German tug. Now, what are they doing there? Up to no good is my guess!'

'So', he continued, 'the plan is to nip in there one night and cut them out, Sir Francis Drake sort of style, like bloody pirates, what do you think?' Pearson's face lit up, eyes twinkling, as he spoke, and it was impossible not to catch some of his enthusiasm.

Geraint coughed a little self-consciously, he had an observation, 'Sir, Spain, as a neutral country, will not like the British taking ships from their harbour, they will want to kick some arse, I think'. His English really was improving.

'They would, my friend', answered Pearson with a grin, 'if they knew it was the Brits who had done it, and they won't. We'll be going in after dark, and no one from the shore will see us. By the time it's light, we'll be well on the way to Lagos'.

He explained the plan in more detail. They had ten days to sail to Lagos, where they would collect the rest of the men, then transfer to a tug, one of a pair, for the two-day voyage to Saint Isabel, the port on Fernando Po where the ships were moored. He wanted Tom to join the party that would board the Italian ship, the 'Duchessa d'Arpino', with the particular job of subduing the crew, which would not be large, and taking over the wireless cabin, making sure that no messages were transmitted. The other party would deal with the German tug. The two British tugs would then tow the vessels back to Lagos. It sounded simple.

George had a question, 'Sir, I'm guessing this Italian ship will have a skipper and a First Mate and whatever, we would have to secure them first, sir, or they'll organise the crew and we'll have a fight on our hands'.

'Good point, Corporal, good point, but your SOE friends have thought of that. This is going to sound damned ridiculous but the Italian officers, and their German friends, often receive invitations to dinner parties and suchlike on shore, and who can blame them? Shut up in ships that are more like bloody ovens for months on end! Your chaps are going to make sure that there's a party in the town that night, and that they're invited'.

He looked so amused that none of them could avoid smiling along with him. It was a simple plan, only dependent on timing. If the information was correct, then hopefully minimum force would be required, and they could intimidate the crew, rather than have to fight a small battle.

The ten days on board passed slowly, and Tom had everyone working at keeping themselves busy. Phil was a natural to help with the boat, and Geraint helped him, hauling sails, reeving cordage and all the variety of routine tasks that a boat without an engine needed. George, their weapons expert, overhauled all the personal weapons on board, lubricating and adjusting, until he was satisfied that they would all perform as they should.

Tom spent more time with Pearson, trying to learn as much about the 'Duchessa' as possible, although they had no schema, so it was mostly educated guesswork. He soon came to respect the young officer, for behind the light-hearted exterior, he detected an honest soldier.

The trawler, 'Maid Irene' as she was named, had a small crew, some of whom doubled up as part of the assault team, and George was surprised when he heard the accent of one of them. The man in question was like a more heavily sun-tanned version of Tom, tall and strongly built, but without being enormous like Phil. He looked younger than Tom though, with dark hair, somewhat bleached by months of sun, and a ready smile. He didn't say much, but when he spoke, his voice stood out, surrounded as he was by a variety of British accents.

George introduced himself, 'George Parry, mate, Welch Regiment but detached, like. Where are you from then?'

The man grinned and shook his outstretched hand, 'Glad to meet you, George. Bud Wilson, New York'.

'Well, bugger me', replied George, 'I never met no one from New York before, never met an American at all! What are you doing here, Bud? The Yanks, sorry, I mean the Americans, they ain't at war with Germany yet, are they?'

'Not that I know of, George, but I am'.

'How do you reckon that then?' asked George, intrigued that someone should be fighting when he didn't have to.

'It's a real long story, you sure you want to hear it?'

'Course I do, mate, crack on, we got hours'.

'Well', the young man started, 'to begin with, my mother is a Brit, from Seaford in Sussex, and we visited couple of times, and I got relatives there, I really like the place'.

'Enough to join up?' asked George, innocently.

'I said it was a long story, hold up'.

'Alright, alright, I'll keep my trap shut'.

'OK, I'm an amateur sailor, learned from my Dad, plenty of good sailing around New York, and when I finished college, I crewed for folks, delivering boats, up and down the East Coast, went as far as Cuba one time'.

George didn't know where Cuba was but it sounded exotic.

'And they paid you, did they?' asked George, for this was a world so far outside his experience.

'Sure. Hundred bucks, two hundred down to Havana, I remember. Anyway, Spring of '39, I had a chance to crew a boat across the Atlantic, to London, and five hundred dollars on delivery. Who was gonna refuse that, not me! I reckoned to do the job, take a look at London, see my folks in Sussex. The owner had promised to pay my way back home, steerage on whatever ship I could find, but when I wired the guy from London, he wouldn't pay me! Not the five hundred, nothing!'

'Bastard', commented George, 'what did you do?'

'I got a ride down to Seaford, and my Grandad found me some work on a boat, fishing out of Newhaven, I reckoned I could save enough for my ticket home'.

'What happened?'

Bud grinned, 'I met a girl, Mary, a real looker. We hit it off and that kinda slowed me down, no rush to go home. Then the war came. Carried on fishing just the same, and I had enough money to get home whenever I wanted, then everything changed'.

'What changed?' asked George.

'Dunkirk. The skipper volunteered the boat to pick up soldiers from the beach there, and we did three trips. Was you at Dunkirk, George?'

'I was, and Tom. We saw the little boats too, we was on the Mole, come back in a destroyer'.

'You know how bad it was then, I saw sights there I never want to see again, the best and the worst of what men can do to each other, and I knew I couldn't just leave. It looked like the Nazis were gonna be over the Channel in a week, how could I leave my grandparents and skip off home?'

'And Mary, of course, you wouldn't want to leave her in the cart, now would you?' added George.

'And Mary, yeah. So when Dunkirk was done, I volunteered. They was gonna bench me at first, send me home'.

'Back to New York?'

'Yes, but then they said, if I promised to do what your King told me to do, and gave up my American passport, I could be a Brit, so I did, and now I'm as English as you, George!'

It was George's turn to smile, 'I got news for you, Bud, you're more English I am, and what's more, never tell a Welshman he's English, it'd be like telling an American that he's Canadian, it doesn't do!'

Bud chuckled, 'I'll remember that, George. Anyways, I signed up for King George, the Dorsetshires, but somebody heard about the sailing and not long after basic training, I got pushed over to this crew. Got sent to Poole and been training every day until this trip came along'.

George shook his hand, 'I thought I'd heard it all, Bud, my old mate. I'm sure that we're very glad to have you, and if you could persuade a few more of your young chaps to come over, they would be very welcome. Hitler won't stop at Europe, you know'.

Chapter 4

Eloise arrived at Monsieur Hervé's chateau the following morning at her normal time of ten o'clock, feeling anxious and afraid. She did not have to ask for Unteroffizier Brauer, he was waiting for her at the door and took her into one of Monsieur's reception rooms at the front of the house, now a guardroom. He sat down behind a desk, presumably looted from Monsieur Hervé's study, and stared at her. She immediately felt even more uncomfortable, which she guessed that he had intended, but had decided that the best way to deal with these awful people would be to appear docile and a little stupid, so that, after a while, they might disregard her.

Brauer spoke, 'Madame, from today, you will work here under my orders. You have been watched for the past few days, and I am satisfied that you have no connections with this ridiculous Résistance that is springing up across Brittany, but be warned, if you are even suspected of having dealings with these rebels and bandits, you will never see your children again'.

Hervé had warned her that they would take this approach, so it was not a surprise when she heard his words, but they chilled her through and through. However, deep inside herself, where he would never see, a small flame of anger and fury was beginning to burn, for what gave this monster the right to come to her country and then threaten helpless, innocent children? It was abominable!

Nothing of her hidden emotions showed on the surface, and Brauer continued, 'From tomorrow, you will come in every day, and you will come in earlier, at six, and you will make breakfast for everyone in the chateau, to be served at seven. There will be coffee and other refreshments available all day. You will prepare and serve lunch at one o'clock, and dinner at seven. You may go home at nine thirty. You will only work in the kitchen and dining room, you are forbidden to enter any other rooms, do you understand? Oh, and the bathroom, you may use the bathroom, of course'.

'I understand, sir', Eloise replied, looking down at the carpeted floor.

He continued, 'There is no obligation for the Reich to pay you anything, of course, but if you work well, you will get a wage. What did the old man pay you?'

'800 francs, sir'. This was true, 800 francs was very little but it was for twenty-four hours work only, and she was given her lunch too.

'Then if your cooking is good enough, I will pay you the same'.

'Thank you, sir'. It was virtual slavery, but what could she do? She supposed that she was lucky to be paid anything.

He had finished with her for now, 'Go to the kitchen. You will find food there, make lunch for twelve people, served in the dining room at one. Dinner, also for twelve, ready at seven. Go'.

Eloise turned obediently towards the door but as she took her first step, Brauer said quietly, 'Verstehst du Deutsch, Madame?' German had been one of the languages that Eloise had taught, and she knew exactly what he was saying, he was asking her if she understood German. For some unknown reason, it was suddenly vital to her that he didn't know, so she did not hesitate but kept walking, and he did not call her back.

The remainder of the day was spent in seemingly endless labour, preparing food, serving it, clearing it away, washing everything then starting again. She was a good cook, it was true, taught by her mother, but she was having to work at top speed, and although she managed to put enough good French food on the table for twelve hungry men, twice, it was utterly exhausting process, and she feared that she would never stand the pace, with breakfasts to do as well.

One of the orderlies, a middle-aged man named Hans, had taken pity on her, and scrubbed out pans for her after lunch, while she started on the preparations for dinner. He chattered away in German while he worked, and part of her wanted to respond, but she had to maintain the fiction of only being able to communicate in French, so the only thanks she could give him were a few words in that language, and a smile or two. He had helped her after dinner too, and as she left, he had pressed a package of left-over chicken into her hands, 'Für die kinder, Madame'.

She wept a little on the way home, mostly from exhaustion but also because the orderly had treated her like a person, and had thought of her children. Perhaps he had children of his own, and was thinking about them, so far from home.

Monsieur Hervé and Madame Le Roux, Gilbert and Clarisse, had been beside themselves with worry when she had not returned in the afternoon, but what could they do? It had taken the efforts of both of them to look after the children for so long, and eventually they had put them to bed and hoped that Eloise would return. It was far too late for their mother to wake the children, in order to take them home, and Clarisse made a suggestion.

'Eloise, the Boche are going to work you until you drop, if you manage six hours sleep, you will be very lucky. My house is large, even with this old fool', gesturing towards Gilbert, 'squatting here. I would like you and the children to live with us, until these Germans are sent home'.

Eloise began to interrupt, but Clarisse held the floor, 'It will mean less work for you, and the children will not be moved around, night and morning. We have enough money between us', gesturing again at Gilbert, 'and if the Boche pay you something, even if it is in cold chicken, like tonight, we will manage. What do you say?'

Eloise was overcome. It was as if all the grief and pain of the last year poured out of her, as Clarisse held her, and Gilbert fussed around, offering her wine or a little brandy. By the time her tears ran dry, the three of them were exhausted. Yes, she was very grateful for the offer, and she knew that the children would benefit, and be happy with the arrangement.

Bed followed soon after, but before Eloise took herself off, she spoke quietly with Monsieur Hervé, while Clarisse was in the kitchen, 'Gilbert, you were right. That oaf of an unteroffizier threatened my babies, he told me that if I was even suspected of contact with the Résistance, I would never see them again. You must promise me that there is no question of them coming here, like they did to the chateau'.

Gilbert still looked chastened, 'Of course, my dear, I promise. Your children are the future of France, and we will cherish them, never fear'.

Somehow, the next day was not as frightening to Eloise as the first had been. Perhaps it was because she knew what was expected of her, and that she had not been harassed or continually watched over while doing her work. It seemed that, as long as enough tasty food arrived promptly, she was as good as invisible to the officers and NCOs stationed in the house. When she entered the dining room to serve the meal, they continued to talk as if she was not there, and she was careful to keep her face expressionless, and to leave them as quickly as she could.

Hans continued to help her, when his own duties allowed, and she found herself looking forward to seeing his cheerful face and hearing his constant chatter, which she continued to feign not to understand. He treated her in a way that allowed her a little dignity, and her instinctive trust in him was proven when she overheard a conversation between him and Brauer.

Brauer had been passing through the kitchen when he had noticed Hans, who was peeling potatoes at the kitchen sink.

'What are you doing here, Schmidt?' the Unteroffizier had asked, 'don't you have enough of your own work to do, or are you looking for her to warm your bed?'

Hans had looked and sounded affronted, 'Mein herr, there is too much work for one person to do, that is, if you want a good dinner and on time. I help only when my own work is done, but if the Unteroffizier would like me to stop…..'

'No, no', answered Brauer hurriedly, for Eloise's cooking had impressed everyone already, and if she needed a little help, so be it, 'just don't do too much for her, that's all, and', grinning, 'you never know, she might find a way to pay you back'.

It took all of Eloise's resolve not to shrink away at such a remark, but Hans dealt with it himself, 'No, mein herr, she deserves my respect, as does my own wife'.

Brauer had grunted, then walked on, Hans staring at his back as he left the kitchen. 'What a fucking degenerate that man is', Hans had muttered to himself, then had turned to Eloise, a smile appearing on his face for her benefit, 'What would Madame like me to do next, after the potatoes?' She had, as usual, pretended not to understand him, and it was only when he acted out the action of chopping vegetables that she caught on, thanking him, 'Oui, oui, Monsieur Hans, merci, merci'.

She was ordered to serve dinner one hour earlier than usual, at six o'clock, and what a rush it was to prepare it on time. Dinner was two large joints of pork, stuffed with apricots, and Brauer had ordered her to carve the joints at a side-table in the dining room, while the soldiers sat and chatted while they waited.

'What time do you want my men tonight, sir?' asked Brauer of a young-looking Oberleutnant.

There was a silence, then Brauer's voice again, 'No, she has no German, sir, she cooks like an angel but has shit for brains, you can say whatever you like. Even if she had a few words, she knows that I will take her children if she misbehaves'.

Yet again, it took all of her self-possession to keep working and not look up, for she was sure that they would all be looking at her.

'Alright, I will take your word for it, Brauer, she does look rather stupid!' and a titter went around the group, 'Be there at 2200, it is the house next to the auberge, I want five men at the back, the same at the front. Break the door in, and we'll see who we find'.

'Do you want prisoners, sir?' Brauer again.

'Yes', answered the Oberleutnant, 'I want information, not bodies, at least, not yet', and another laugh circulated around the table.

At this point, Eloise placed the carved joints on the table, and the soldiers tucked in, forgetting their conversation while they ate. She forced herself to walk steadily out of the dining room, while every nerve in her body was telling her to run. What had she overheard?

It sounded as if there was going to be a military operation tonight. She knew the house next to the auberge, if it was Lilia that they were talking about. It was owned by Monsieur Hamon, a widower, who lived there with his grown-up son. She did not know much about him, he was a lawyer, she thought, as was his son, and they worked from an office in Brest. Henri had travelled into work with them, on occasion, she remembered, when the car would not start.

What could she do? Perhaps, with dinner being an hour early, she might leave for home at an earlier hour? That would give her time to call at the Hamon house, to warn them. But what if it was watched? She would be condemning her own children, and Gilbert and Clarisse, and of course, herself.

She could telephone the house. No, the call would have to be put through at the exchange, in German hands like everywhere else, and she would be found out.

She could not come to a decision, every option seemed equally impossible but any hope of leaving early disappeared when Brauer came into the kitchen as she was scrubbing pans.

'Madame', he said, in his awful French, 'make a cold supper for twelve before you go home, and leave it on the table in here. My men will be calling in to eat later'.

'Sir', she advanced nervously, 'I was hoping to leave a little early this evening, my children......'

He interrupted her, savagely, 'Do not hope for anything, woman! You work for the Reich now, and you do what I tell you, understand?' He terrified her, and she covered her face in fear, 'Yes, sir'.

'Get on with it', he ordered brusquely and, turning on his heel, left the kitchen.

Hans had witnessed this incident from the corridor, and Brauer spoke to him as he headed for the guardroom door. He gave Eloise a moment to collect herself, then walked into the kitchen.

'I will help you this evening, Madame', he announced, 'I know that you don't understand one word in a hundred that I say, but never mind. I heard what that old bastard said to you, I will be your pot-boy, and clean everything up, and you make the supper. May I suggest', walking into the larder, then coming out with his arms full, 'your wonderful French cheese, with this bread. There are apples too. Not fare for officers, perhaps, but the soldiers will love it'.

For once, Eloise could not respond to his smiles and encouragement, and they worked through the remainder of the evening in silence. It was obvious to Hans that she was troubled, but what more could he do?

It was after nine thirty when she was able to leave, and she rushed home, desperate to see that her children were safe, there was no reason that they would not be but the events of the day, and her inability to do anything with the information that she had learned, had upset everything once again.

It was almost ten o'clock as Eloise opened the door to the Le Roux house, and as she did, she heard a crackle of rifle and machine gun fire, from the direction of the village. Gilbert heard the firing too, but it was short-lived, and he pulled her inside, shutting the door behind them.

'What's going on', he asked, 'that sounds like it's in the village', never imagining that Eloise knew exactly what was happening, and she wasted no time in telling him. He sat down on the stairs with a thump, head in his hands, and looked up as Clarisse joined them.

'Paul Hamon is a member of the Résistance in Brittany, as is his son, someone must have betrayed them. Did the Germans say how they found out about him?'

'Enough!' exclaimed Clarisse, the anger plain in her face, 'she will not become your spy, Gilbert! I know all about your stupid games with the Résistance! Think of the children! Would you see them without their mother? If you wish to make more trouble with your friends, go ahead, but you will not live in my house for a minute longer!'

Hervé quailed at her fury, saying that of course he would not risk anyone's safety, least of all the children, it was just that he knew Hamon, and liked him, a true Breton and a good Frenchman.

'I know that', she answered, 'he is my lawyer, for God's sake, but I cannot help him and neither can you'. Then, turning to Eloise, she took a softer tone, 'You will hear secret things in that place, my dear, but for your children's sake, you can do nothing. You must close your ears, do your work and come home to your children. You are all that they have'.

Madame Le Roux was correct, she knew that, for she loved her babies more than anything in the world, but what if she learned something so terrible, so vile, that keeping it to herself destroyed her own worth. Could she live with that? She would have to.

Chapter 5

HMS 'Milfoil', a 'Flower' class corvette had first met the little convoy as it laboured through choppy seas, making its triumphant return to Lagos from Fernando Po. Their meeting was no accident, having been pre-arranged but the world would be told that 'Milfoil' had happened to spy strange ships on the horizon, and had intercepted them, only to find that they belonged to the enemy, so could legally be seized on the open ocean. No one would believe them, of course, but the message would be understood, there was no safe haven for enemy ships.

The operation itself had gone more smoothly than anyone could have anticipated, and almost a month later, as 'Milfoil' made her way into the chops of the English Channel, heading for Portsmouth, Tom went over the action in his mind. If only they were always this simple!

The 'Matron' had reached Lagos on time, just, and they had been transferred to the little tug 'Rugby', while the party who would cut out the German tug moved to 'Hercules', a similar vessel. There had been no time for a run on shore, for it was late evening and it would take forty-eight hours to reach the island, intending to be in position at 2330.

Of the eleven men that would board the 'Duchessa', five men would be detailed to locate the anchor chains, and prepare to destroy them with explosives. Five sounded excessive for probably two chains, but as Pearson explained, they might also need to defend themselves, and would have to take up the tow from 'Rugby'. The remaining six men would divide into three groups of two; Geraint and Phil would locate and take the wireless cabin, and would deal with anyone on the bridge, while Pearson and George would go below on the port side, and Tom and Bud would do the same from starboard, locating and confining any members of the crew that they could find. Violent resistance was thought to be unlikely, as it was a cargo ship with a civilian crew, but no one could be sure.

'Rugby' had crept into the harbour at low speed, with hardly a bow-wave showing, while 'Hercules' did the same on the other side of the harbour, where the German tug was moored. The eleven men whispered 'Good luck', 'Break a leg' and similar to each other, as soldiers do, and prepared to board on the port side of the 'Duchessa', where there would be an accommodation ladder, or so they had been informed. There had been no message to abort from the SOE agent on shore, in the port of Santa Isabel, so all was primed and ready to go. They were armed, but not as heavily as most of them were used to. Pearson and Tom carried heavy Webley pistols, as did two of the men responsible for cutting the anchor chains, but the remainder carried either a naval truncheon or a cosh, George describing his as his 'Persuader'.

As the little tug came around the stern of the 'Duchessa', the boarding party all gathered in the bows, two small lights suddenly shone down onto them from the ship. Everyone froze, but there was no challenge, just a few words exchanged between the two men holding the torches, then nothing more. Clearly, they were not expecting an attack!

'Rugby' kissed gently against the accommodation ladder, and the anchor party raced up first and separated, two to the bows and three to the stern.

Phil and Geraint followed next, heading for the bridge, for surely the wireless office would be close. One ladder and one companionway later, they found themselves on the deserted bridge, no one in sight at all, and started looking for the wireless cabin. Sure enough, it was on the same level, connecting to the bridge via two doors and a short passageway, and Geraint took possession. There was still no one in sight, although they could hear shouting, briefly, at the bow. Phil moved back to the bridge, but it remained deserted.

Tom and Bud had been next to board, racing across the deck to the starboard side, where Bud quickly located a likely looking door. Sure enough, it opened onto a long passageway, with doors opening off it to the right. Most of the doors were closed, but one was open, furthest away from them, and bright light was spilling out into the passage, along with a loud hum of conversation and bursts of laughter, perhaps it was the seamen's mess. As they moved closer to the door, Bud signalled that he would find a way through to the other side, and that Tom should make his move in one minute. There was no time to fully explain to Tom, but Bud's sea-time told him that there would almost certainly be another door leading out of the room, opposite to the one that was open, and that if they entered together through one, the sailors might leave through the other!

Tom counted down a single minute then, with the big revolver cocked and ready to fire, he moved to the doorway, stepping over the coaming and into the light. For a second or two, the hubbub continued unchanged, then suddenly stopped as the men inside, perhaps a dozen of them, noticed this tall, grim figure, face blackened, pointing a barrel that must have looked like a small cannon to the men nearest to him. Hands instinctively shot upwards, as they calculated the odds of escaping past this frightening figure, and sensibly decided that surrender was the best option. Two men, more enterprising perhaps, ran to the open door on the other side of the room and went to step through it, but reversed their course when Bud's truncheon came whistling down, twice, on their bare forearms.

To Tom's surprise, Bud shouted something at the men, in Italian, Tom guessed, and men started to sit down again, a couple even going back to their drinks. He then called across to Tom, 'Go outside and shut the door and latch it. I've told them that we have more men outside, and that they'll be shot if they try to come out'. Tom did as he was instructed, for Bud obviously knew what he was doing.

Pearson and George, last off the tug-boat, ran along the port-side of the ship towards the stern, and wrenching open the door of a companionway, saw a ladder leading downwards into the belly of the ship. There were bulkhead lights, so it was easy enough to climb quietly down to a steel platform, from which another ladder descended. This was the engine space, and the racket of a generator, supplying power while the ship's engines were still, clattered around them.

Pearson led again, but just as his feet touched the steel grating at the foot of the ladder, two powerful hands seized the back of his shirt and crashed him, sideways, into a steel bulkhead. The side of his head made painful contact a split second after his shoulder, and he dropped senseless to the floor.

George, several steps above Pearson on the ladder, and looking down at the commotion, let go of the rungs and dropped down onto the head and shoulders of the attacker, knocking him onto his knees. This time, George's lack of bulk acted against him for, instead of his assailant being flattened, he merely shrugged the Welshman off and stood up, ready to attack again. He loomed over him, looking at least as tall as Phil, but with an extra stone or two around the middle, and George knew that if this giant cornered him, he would have very little chance of escape.

As the colossus lurched forward to grab him, George moved to dodge behind the ladder, where a narrow passageway continued between two banks of machinery. He avoided being crushed between the enormous bulk of the man and the steel rungs but one big hand, with fingers the size of bananas, shot between the rungs, seized him by the shirt-front and pulled him forward. He was far too strong for George to resist, and he realised that, if the monster managed to get both hands on him, he was finished. So, turning a little sideways, as far as he could, so that his left shoulder smashed into the steel rungs first, he pulled his Persuader from his belt with his right hand and smashed it down with all the power that he could muster, onto the wrist that was holding him.

The big man let out a howl of agony and, letting go of George's shirt, staggered backwards from the ladder, clutching his wrist in agony. I hope I've broken the bloody thing, and if you've got any bloody sense, you'll surrender, thought George, and stepped out from behind the ladder, keeping the Persuader raised in front of him.

It was as well he did, for the giant seaman quickly straightened up and swung an enormous punch, with his undamaged left hand, towards George's head. It would have mowed him down, if it had connected, but the wily soldier had been expecting it, and simply ducked. The big hand soared over his head, and with an audible crunch, hammered into the side of the steel ladder. This time, George decided to take no chances, and as his opponent crouched, roaring with the additional pain of his now fractured, crooked fingers, George took a swing with his bludgeon and crashed it into the man's temple. His eyes rolled up immediately, and down he went, like a tree in a hurricane.

Pearson was unconscious but breathing strongly, and as George turned him onto his side, he began to stir. Are you there sir, are you with me?' he asked, as Pearson's eyelids fluttered and slowly opened, 'you'll have a headache, Captain, but nothing compared to this big bugger', giving the insensible Italian a gentle kick.

He pulled Pearson into a sitting position, the Captain was clutching his head, 'What happened, Corporal? I can remember starting down that ladder and then, nothing'.

'You was clobbered, sir, by this here Goliath, he got you from behind, I think your head might have dented the bulkhead, sir'.

'Very funny, Corporal, I'm sure. How did you stop him?'

'Bit of luck, sir, broke both of his hands first, then put him to sleep'.

'Have you killed him?'

George checked, 'No, sir, he's sleeping like a baby, but how we'll get him back up that ladder, I haven't a bloody clue, sir'.

'The sod can wait. Here, give me a hand'.

Up on deck, everything was in hand. 'Rugby' was fastened on at the bow, and would be ready to tow, as soon as the anchor chains were blown. There were no casualties, other than Pearson and the Italian giant, and they waited for 'Hercules' and the German tug to make the first move.

Then, crack crack, two small explosions from the deck of the captured tug as the anchor chains were severed, and Pearson immediately made the same order. With a crash, the chains that held 'Duchessa' to her anchors parted, and the 'Rugby' took the strain. Within seconds, they could detect a little way on her as she moved, oh so slowly, towards the harbour entrance.

This was a dangerous moment, for their intelligence was that there were 150 mm guns in a position onshore, for the protection of the harbour, which would be more than enough to stop them. The surprise, though, must have been total, for although a searchlight eventually caught them, not a shot was fired, and they quickly disappeared into the darkness.

HMS 'Milfoil' had found them, on course but behind schedule, late the next morning, and it was just as well, for both 'Rugby' and 'Hercules' were flagging, out in the open sea. She sent off a message to Lagos for relief, and stood by them as they staggered onwards.

The huge Italian, who was in fact a boilerman named Alfredo, was eventually strapped to a stretcher and winched up from the engine room. As the only real casualty, he had the sickbay to himself, and once he had been made as comfortable as possible, pending proper medical treatment in Lagos, George was often found in the sickbay with him, both of them chattering happily away in their own language, as George gave him drinks, food and a daily shave. Alfredo had been worried when George had first produced his cut-throat razor, but must have thought better of it and had allowed himself to be shaved. There were other, more personal tasks that he helped him with too, and by the end of two days, when the extra tugs from Lagos were in view, they had become friends. After all, both had been merely doing their jobs.

Lagos had sent out a small tanker from which 'Milfoil' re-fuelled, and the assault parties transferred to her for the voyage home. The skipper of the corvette passed on a message from the Admiralty, that their Lordships were delighted with the success of the raid, and especially that their act of modern piracy was still officially deniable. Pearson was convinced that the action would have done both the SSRF and the SOE no harm at all, for Churchill was known to appreciate a little flair and daring, and they had shown both.

Captain Pearson also took Tom to one side, 'Sergeant, you and your men performed admirably, Smith said that you were a skilled bunch, and he was right, you are'.

'Thank you, sir', replied Tom, wondering if this was leading somewhere, for in his experience, captains were usually sparing with praise.

'Did Smith explain why you were returning home, Sergeant?'

'Not really, sir. He mentioned training for an operation, that's all'.

'I'm authorised to tell you a little more, Sergeant. The operation, or operations, we're not sure yet, is in France, and it's with us, you're being taken onto the strength of the SSRF. SOE will still have a call on you, but your talents are reckoned to be more in the, ah, offensive type of operation, rather than undercover'.

Tom could not disagree, 'That sounds about right, sir, that's what we're best at'.

'What do you think about Private Wilson, Sergeant, our American friend?'

Tom didn't hesitate, 'Good man, sir. Athletic, strong, and confident with it. He sized up the best way to bottle-up the sailors in their mess, and had the nerve to run with it, sir'.

'You didn't mind?'

'Not a bit, sir. He's a sailor, he was in his element. Of course, if it had gone wrong, I wouldn't be so happy but it didn't. Corporal Parry has got to know him best, sir, and he rates him, so that's good enough for me'.

'Pleased to hear it, Sergeant, because I want him to join your group. I've got great hopes for him but he's inexperienced, I think he'll learn a lot from you'.

'Sir', was the only answer Tom could give but he had no issue with Bud Wilson, he had behaved well and was a good fit.

It was a popular decision, and Phil was one of the first to shake Wilson's hand. He had a question for him though, 'Why did your Mum and Dad call you 'Bud'? It's a nice short name, easy to remember but I never read it in the Bible or anything, you look more like a 'William' to me'.

Bud had fielded this question many times since joining up, 'It's a nickname, I was baptised Bernard, after my American grand-daddy but everyone calls me Bud, always have'.

'Then Bud it is, mind you, if you was English, we'd have to call you 'Tug', being as you're a sailor'.

'Why Tug?' asked Bud.

'Because you're a Wilson. Every Wilson gets called Tug, like every Watson gets called 'Soapy'. Now young Geraint there', pointing at the young German, grinning in the background, for he had gone through this confusing education from Phil in the recent past, 'young Geraint, he's a matelot too, we got a choice with him. He could be 'Sparks' 'cause he's a wireless operator, or 'Bungey' 'cause he's a Williams or 'Taff' 'cause he's Welsh, except he isn't really, so we just call him Geraint, it's less confusing'.

'And what do you call Tom?'

'Ah, we call him Sergeant!'

The 'Milfoil' tagged onto a slow convoy, heading from the Cape to Liverpool, and stayed with it until, with Ushant just over the horizon, they could part company and enter the Channel. This leg of the journey, mostly trundling along at eight knots, the speed of the slowest steamer, took nearly four weeks, and Captain Pearson had decided to start their training.

He was convinced that a basic understanding of the French language would be a useful skill for everyone, given that, with any luck, they would soon be operating on the mainland of France. He was fluent, and was cheered to discover that Geraint, previously a language student in University, already had a good grasp and could share some of the teaching with him. Of the others, Tom had learned conversational Greek, prior to their raid into Crete, and had discovered, to his delight, a previously unknown affinity for absorbing language. He made quick progress, as did Phil, much to his own surprise.

Phil had always acted, unwittingly, as the archetypal Englishman abroad, convinced of the power and superiority of the British Empire, as exemplified by the Royal Navy, which had been his home since teenage. His world had shifted enormously after joining up with Tom and the resistance fighters of Crete, rapidly understanding that poor, uneducated peasants, 'without two ha'pennies to rub together', were as capable of nobility and courage and fidelity as anyone else, and that if he opened his eyes, he could learn so much. None of the men applied themselves to the language lessons as wholly as he did, and by the time the Isle of Wight came into view, looming through the fog of a bitterly cold, winter's morning, he had more than the essentials of a second language within his grasp.

Chapter 6

The following morning was cold, wet and even darker than usual, or so it seemed, when Eloise arrived at the chateau. All seemed quiet, and she immediately set on with breakfast. For this first hour, the building was usually quiet, with the NCOs moving around but the officers still in their beds. The first pot of coffee was almost brewed when Brauer strode into the kitchen.

'Madame', he stated, 'last night, on your way home, you will have heard gunshots'.

There was no point in denying it, 'Yes, sir, I did'.

'Do you know where the firing was coming from?' She had to be on her guard!

'From the direction of the village, sir? I could not really say'.

'Do you know a Monsieur Hamon, Madame?'

'I know the name, sir, he is a lawyer, I believe. My late husband knew him'.

He moved closer, and loomed over her, demanding, in his harsh voice, 'What more do you know, anything? Tell me if you do, for if you lie, I will know!'

'I know nothing more, sir!' She was terrified now, 'I was never introduced to him, perhaps I saw him in church, I don't know!'

Brauer stepped back a pace, for her fear was genuine and he believed her, or appeared to.

'Last night's shooting was at Hamon's house, he is, or was, one of your terrorists. That fool and his son tried to defend themselves, they shot two of my men! Hamon is dead but we have the son, and he will wish that he was dead once the Gestapo have him'.

She had heard of the Gestapo, the Nazi's secret police. They had a terrible reputation already in France, as an organisation that would stop at nothing to gain information. Rumour had it that torture and murder were nothing to them, and she shuddered.

'Ah, you know of their reputation, Madame', gloated Brauer, 'I am telling you this because I know that you will speak to your neighbours and your friends, you will tell them that anyone who helps these terrorists will be shot, all of their family, their neighbours too, every one, no one will be spared! Make sure that the news gets around', and, turning on his heel, he left the kitchen.

Eloise felt the blood draining from her face, it was horrific. The whole village, the whole neighbourhood, would pay if the Résistance tried to organise locally. As far as she knew, there had been no attacks or sabotage in this part of Brittany, so Hamon had been detected before he had even done anything. How did the Germans know about him? He must surely have been betrayed by someone that he knew.

For the rest of morning, and through lunch, she was in a daze, thinking of Hamon and his son, of her own children and their safety, and how precarious life was now. Hans came through to help her, but such was her preoccupation that she barely even tried to be polite. Usually she would nod and smile as he chattered away, pretending not to understand what he was saying, but today, her distraction did not allow her to manage even that. He eventually gave up and worked away in silence, for he was a sensitive man and had an idea of what might be upsetting her.

About an hour after lunch, staring through the kitchen window as she worked, she saw a pair of black cars pulling up in the yard at the rear of the chateau. Hans was standing next to her, and frowned as two men in civilian clothing climbed out of the first car, wearing long overcoats against the cold, and with homburgs pulled down, partially concealing their faces. Two more men climbed out of the second car, but they looked more military, with greatcoats covering an occasional glimpse of a grey uniform underneath. 'Gestapo, Madame', explained Hans.

Brauer appeared, from around the side of the chateau, and joined the first two men in conversation for a moment, then led them into the first of the stables. It had been impossible for Eloise to hear any of the conversation, with the doors and windows shut, but it was not difficult to imagine whom they were visiting in the stable, Monsieur Hamon's son, and she pitied him.

Beside her, Hans stirred and turned her away from the window, wagging his finger in a motion to discourage her, 'Do not look, Madame, the Gestapo are not for the likes of you or I, they are savage and without pity, keep out of their way'. It took an effort for Eloise to keep the uncomprehending look upon her face, but Hans's expression was clear enough. He was frightened of the Gestapo, and so should she be.

Hans helped her for a further hour, then left her alone to continue with the preparation for dinner. She could not get the Hamon boy out of her mind, and felt wretched at the thought of what might be happening to him inside the stable, but she knew that there was nothing that she could do.

She was at the kitchen window again when she saw the stable door opening, and the two civilians, with Brauer behind them, walking out to the first car. There were no smiles, just words exchanged and their 'Heil Hitler' salute.

As they stepped into the car, Brauer watching them respectfully, the remaining two men came out of the stable, but this time with a burden. They had linked arms with a slumped figure between them, and they were hauling him to the car, his head down and his feet dragging along through the mud of the stable yard. They brought him around to the side of the car that was facing the house, and she saw, with horror, that blood was dripping from his face and hands and onto the ground.

As he was bundled into the back of the car, his head lifted up for a second, and she caught a glimpse of his face, and behind the mask of blood and the discolouration of fresh bruising, there was a depth of despair and terror and hopelessness that shocked her to her core. She had known tragedy and loss herself, losing both parents in the past five years, and then her husband, but she knew that she had never plumbed the depths that the Hamon boy was at now.

She felt pity and disgust and revulsion but also a fierce anger, a terrible resentment that her neighbours could be dealt with in such a foul way by these invaders. She knew, from that second onwards, that she would find a way to fight back. It would take time and planning, and she would not risk her children's lives, but she could not sit back and do nothing.

The cars drew away, and Brauer stamped back into the chateau. As he passed back through the kitchen, he glanced across and saw her standing, still staring out of the window. Stopping, he called across the room, 'Ah, you saw, Madame. Good, now you know what happens to traitors. Tomorrow morning, he will be shot but by then, the Gestapo will have every secret that he possesses. Tell your neighbours, tell your friends, the Résistance will never live in Brittany!' Laughing he left the room, leaving a cold and bitter Eloise to continue with her work.

Hans returned, after dinner was served and cleared away, to help her in the kitchen, and immediately noticed the difference in her demeanour. She seemed colder, more distant and contained than previously, and it did not take a genius to understand why. He already had a feeling that there was more to Eloise than she chose to reveal, something behind those eyes that would surprise people. He was convinced that she understood more of his prattle than she let on, he wasn't sure why, it was just a feeling but he would put money on it. She took everything in, that was it! She missed nothing and seemed to store it all away inside.

He decided to take a chance, for the house was quiet, and grasping her hand, he turned her towards him, looking at her directly, 'Madame, listen well. Do not try anything stupid for France. These bastards here will kill you, and everyone you love, without a second thought. Continue with your work, see and hear nothing, and you will survive this war. I will help you when I can, but if they suspect you of treachery, you are dead. Do you understand me?'

As he spoke, he watched her eyes closely, and his instinct told him that there was some understanding there, so perhaps she spoke German after all? Maybe. Her answer was, 'Désolé, Monsieur, je ne comprends pas', but his gut told him something different.

Eloise watched Hans as he left the room. He was a good man, a decent man, but he was an enemy too. She would take his words as a warning, not to shut her eyes and ears, but to conceal her real feelings even further inside herself, where no one could see them. She would have to be patient, for what could she achieve as one woman on her own?

There was plenty that she could do. She would watch, listen, and try to understand how the Germans were organised, and where their information was coming from. There must be informers, for how else could Hamon and his son have been discovered? It would be a slow process, spying on these Nazis without placing herself in obvious danger, but she would accumulate more and more knowledge about their activities, until the day arrived when she could use it to help bring them down. They may have killed Hamon but in time, he would be replaced. There would be many more Frenchmen and women, outraged at this occupation of their homeland, and the pitiless way in which it was enforced, and surely, they would emerge and start to fight back.

The weeks passed, and Hans could not but notice her increased reserve, for although she had not spoken much before the Résistance boy was captured, she was even quieter now. Before, he might have heard her, off-guard, singing a French song softly to herself, but now, there were just pursed lips and virtual silence. She would speak if Brauer spoke to her, but would keep her eyes downcast, as if she dared not look at him directly. She remained polite with Hans, thanking him for his help in the kitchen but it was as if she had strengthened and reinforced the wall that would always be there between them, separating conqueror and conquered.

This was not a bad thing, Hans concluded, if it meant that she had taken his advice, and would show no curiosity in what was going on around her. She reminded him a little of his own wife, Hilda, at home in Koblenz, not in looks but in the impression of good sense and competence that she displayed, and if he could help her live, then perhaps Hilda might survive too. In his head, Hans knew that this was foolish superstition, for how could there be a connection between two women, hundreds of miles apart, there was none, but his heart told him something different.

The connection, for indeed there was one, did exist. It was him, Hans Schmidt, but for now, he did not see it. It would become clearer, as time passed.

As an orderly, Hans had no involvement in the counterterrorism and military activities conducted from the chateau. However, rather like Eloise but even more so, he was 'part of the furniture', almost invisible to the fighting men because he was always there. He would walk in on private meetings, serving coffee or delivering documents, and not a head would look his way, nor acknowledge his presence at all. This did not concern him, for their business was not his and he had no wish to be thanked for his labours on their behalf, for he was no Nazi and believed that, in time, the war would be lost. All Hitler had to do, for God's sake, was to read the history books and he would soon learn that illegitimate conquests of sovereign nations nearly always ended in failure. It might take time, but they always failed because conquered people don't lie down indefinitely, they fight back until they are free.

No one could have detected these treasonous thoughts, for Hans was an expert in concealing them, and wished to outlast the war, so he continued to be party to the most secret information. He was not a traitor however, even though he disapproved of, and was revolted by, much of what he heard. He was careful to betray nothing of his opinions to Eloise, for it was even less of her business than it was of his.

Eloise did not push herself forward, but inevitably, there were times when she found herself accidentally eavesdropping on private discussions when performing her duties. Occasionally, someone would look up and see her and the conversation would pause until she left, but more often than not, it would continue. In this way, she learned a list of names of Gestapo officers and where they were based, of the numbers of troops that could be used at any one time and the arms that they could deploy, and most interestingly, where they were garrisoned.

The most tantalising piece of information came to her in a different way. Early in March, she had been told to prepare a more elaborate dinner, to celebrate Heroes' Memorial Day, the day when those who had been killed in the defence of the Third Reich were remembered. It seemed to her that it was simply an excuse for an elaborate dinner and too much to drink, but she was careful to follow Brauer's instructions with care, producing a delicious, almost lavish, spread. Both she and Hans were involved in serving and clearing away the five courses, and by the time that they had washed the mountain of dishes and tidied the kitchen for the next morning, it was an hour after her usual finishing time.

Eloise was in a rush to get home, but as she collected her bicycle from the stable, she realised that she had forgotten to pick up a few slices of beef that Hans had put to one side for her in the kitchen, enough to feed everyone at home the next day. She cursed to herself, for going back inside would make her even later getting home, but the others needed the food and it would only take a moment. So, wheeling her bicycle to the rear door of the house, that lead directly into the now dark kitchen, she grasped the door handle, only to be dazzled as the electric light in the kitchen was switched on. Instinctively, she shrank back into the shadows as Brauer and another man in civilian clothes moved to the kitchen table and sat down.

Brauer was facing the window, and every feature in his hard, familiar face was visible. The other man, unfortunately, was turned away from her, so she could only see the back of his balding, grey head and his right ear. He wore no spectacles, as far as she could tell, and at this angle, there was the merest hint of a grey moustache. He appeared to be wearing tweed, but she could only see his shoulders so it could have been a coat or a jacket. He could have been anyone but surely Brauer would not entertain Gestapo in the kitchen?

They were conversing, and Eloise fixed on his profile as he spoke to Brauer, for if he was local, he might be someone that she knew. Both men stood up to leave, still talking, and as quickly as she could, Eloise pushed her bicycle to the front of the house, saying goodnight to the sentry at the main gate as she left.

As she pedalled through the darkness, Eloise thought about what she had seen. Someone in civilian clothing, not important enough to be entertained or interviewed in the main part of the house but someone whom Brauer would listen to. Someone of middle age onwards, with a bald patch and greying hair. It could be someone with a genuine reason to be there, talking to Brauer, but at ten-thirty at night? If the civilian clothes were not Gestapo-issue, could they belong to a Frenchman, and could this be her first pointer to the informant?

Eloise was almost at the Le Roux villa, when she heard a car driving up the road behind her, with a sharp bend in the road to negotiate before it was on her tail. The road was narrow here, and the use of headlights was illegal, so it was her usual practice to jump off her bicycle and squeeze herself up against the tall hedge, to let them pass safely, and that is what she did.

The car was travelling slowly in the gloom, but as it passed her, the faint light from the instrument panel illuminated the driver. It was only momentary, and once again, only the side of the head was visible but she was positive that it was the same man that she had seen in the kitchen, a few minutes beforehand.

The driver had not appeared to spot her in the darkness and the car carried on in the direction of the village.

Brauer cornered her the following morning, 'Madame, did you go straight home after the dinner last night, I know that you worked later than usual'.

'Yes, sir. Herr Schmidt helped me to finish everything and then I left, sir'.

'What do you do when you leave, Madame?

'Sir?' She did not understand.

'What is your routine when you leave, tell me!'

'Sir, I check that everything is put away, switch off the kitchen lights, collect my bicycle and leave, sir'.

'And were the kitchen lights on when you left?' Ah, now he was getting to the point! He was checking if she had seen anything.

'No, sir, the yard was in darkness'.

'The sentry said that you were late leaving'.

'Sir, there was so much to do, crockery for five courses, three glasses for each guest, so many pans....'

'Yes, yes', he interrupted her, 'and did any cars pass you on the road?'

'No, sir, not one'.

He seemed satisfied, 'Alright, carry on, but remember, if I catch you loitering around the chateau when you should be at home, I will have some very serious questions to ask of you'.

The fool, thought Eloise to herself as he left the kitchen, he has just told me that his visitor last night must be kept secret. There must be a reason for that, and I will discover it!

Chapter 7

Leave had been granted when they landed at Portsmouth, just seven days, with orders to gather on their return at Anderson Manor, the new base for the SSRF in Dorset. George disappeared immediately, for it had been nearly eighteen months since he had seen his family, and he was desperate not to waste a single minute, and Tom accompanied him, for his parents' farm was only over the hill from Welshpool, and they could share a train together as far as Shrewsbury. Bud left for Seaford and Newhaven, where he had great hopes that Mary would be waiting for him, which left Phil and Geraint.

For Geraint, this was his first visit to the country that he must call home, at least for the remainder of the war, and he had no idea where he should go or what he should do. He had money, having been paid when they disembarked, but what to do with it?

Phil was his saviour. He had not had leave in England for over two years, but he had no family and nowhere particular to stay either, so he suggested to Geraint that they stick together, but where might they go? As it was Geraint's first visit, they settled on London, and within a couple of hours, they were on a train to Waterloo.

When Phil had first met Geraint, in the midst of his dramatic rescue as the sole survivor from a sunken German patrol boat, he had seen him as just another blond-haired Fritz, but as the story emerged, of his Jewish heritage and of his missing relatives, he had taken shape as a person. He had fought as hard as anyone in Crete, and the more Phil came to know him, the more impressed he was. There was his ability with languages, for example, even though he had been conscripted out of his university course before he had finished his studies. This skill had opened doors for him, for a second language made a third and fourth easier to learn, and if he was honest, this is what had inspired Phil to follow his example.

So, on the train, they spoke in French, much to the bemusement of the other passengers, who were even more confused when Phil occasionally broke out in his own Devonian burr! When they arrived in London, neither of them wanted to stay in a hostel, after having lived cheek by jowl with other men for months on end, so they searched for, and found, a small hotel off the Charing Cross Road where Phil had stayed once before. There was hot water and clean sheets to spare, and it seemed like Heaven!

They spent the week walking around the City and the West End, seeing the sights but also aghast at the destruction from the Blitz and in Geraint's case, feeling some guilt at the damage that his countrymen had caused. London was as lively as ever, full of soldiers and sailors and airmen from most countries of the Empire, and all looking for entertainment. They filled the pubs to bursting point in the evenings, and although there was occasionally trouble as the alcohol took charge, Phil's bulk was enough to dissuade people from including them in their brawls. Their most visited pub was the 'York Minster' in Soho, the favourite destination for French servicemen, and there they were able to practice their French, almost as if they were in France. Phil found the sheer speed of conversation difficult to follow, but not impossible, and his efforts, although stumbling, were applauded.

At the end of their leave, they managed to hitch a lift to Anderson Manor from the railway station at Hamworthy, and found that their comrades had returned before them, albeit only a few hours ahead. After describing their week, Phil asked Tom about his stay in Shropshire.

'Not so good, mate', he replied. His father had been gassed in the trenches during the Great War, and although he had been fit enough to return to farming on a small scale, his health had remained fragile. When Tom had unexpectedly arrived, it was to find his father confined to his bed, his lungs bubbling with pneumonia. His mother was trying to work the farm on her own, but had confided to Tom that she was trying to persuade his father to sell the farm and retire. Her own health was not robust but so far, the old boy would not countenance it, saying that he had worked too long and too hard just to give it away. Tom knew better than to argue with him, and had spent the week labouring around the farm. At the very least, it had given his mother a short break but he had been loath to leave them.

He had already broken the news of his marriage, but he did not have even a photograph to show them of his bride, and it had felt a little unreal when he tried to describe Elena to them. His mother and father had tried to be pleased for him, but he could see that it was difficult for them. Of course it was, he realised, his life now was as far from a quiet hill-farm in Shropshire as you might imagine, and there was no going back. He had left at the end of the week, feeling worried for them, guilty that there was not more that he could do to help but also secretly relieved that he was returning to the life where he now belonged.

George's week had been simpler. Rachel, his wife, well-used to his long, military absences, had welcomed him back into her mother's home as if he had only been away for a few weeks. She had learned, over the years, to keep a place in the family routine for him, and he was able to fit back in with minimum fuss. Bethan and Jenny, his two daughters, were the lights of his life, and Rachel had listened in pride and contentment as they had chattered with their father, late into the night. There were tears when it was time for him to return to duty, but there was always the prospect of more leave in the future, now that he was stationed in England.

Bud had found his Mary in Newhaven, and although he had discovered, via an interfering acquaintance, that she had found replacement male company in his absence, they had picked up where they had left off months previously. As he had explained to Phil, 'I don't see no wedding bells in the plan anyway, and one of these days, I might not come back, so good luck to her'. It seemed that she was joining the WAAFs, and could be posted anywhere, so maybe things would fizzle out naturally.

While they were away, Japan had attacked the United States at Pearl Harbour, and Germany had declared war four days later, so, as Captain Pearson had explained, Bud was free to return home to fight for the country of his birth. To everyone's surprise, he had declined, 'Thank you, sir, but no. I'd be fighting the same folks, and I'd have to go through another packet of training. Guess I'll stay, if it's all the same to you'.

Training started the following morning, and Captain Pearson was a hard taskmaster. Weeks onboard the 'Queen', followed by more weeks on a cramped corvette, had softened them up, and Pearson needed to bring them back to fighting condition as soon as possible. They started off with a five-mile run, unburdened with kit to begin with, but with the promise that, as the days passed, they would be running longer distances and faster, and with increasing weights upon their backs.

There was training in man to man combat, covering use of a combat knife, use of the garotte and knuckle-dusters among other things, and methods of incapacitating an opponent without the use of weapons. George had assumed that, in his more than twenty years' service, that he had picked up most of what there was to learn about unarmed combat, but even he was in for a shock. He knew how to use his forehead and fists, but now he was using the sides of his hands, his elbows and knees, his boots in ways other than a kick to the crotch, and most importantly of all, his use of balance and weight and movement. He found that, as long as he moved quickly and decisively, his small stature was no handicap, and the sight of him repeatedly dumping Phil onto the ground, with a minimum of visible effort, always raised a smile. If he didn't move quickly enough though, Phil would return the compliment, usually by lifting him above his head with one strong arm!

Weapons training was more familiar, and Geraint was useful in demonstrating some of the tricks involved in the field management of German weaponry. They practiced shooting with handguns, not the heavy Webley, but with the Colt 1911 semi-automatic pistol. Bud showed the most aptitude for that weapon, but when they moved on to rifles, Phil's sniper skills, as learned in Palestine and practiced in Crete, came to the fore.

Boat-handling was going to be crucial for successful landings in France, so bitterly cold days were spent in practicing how to handle the dory, the lightweight, flat-bottomed boat that the SSRF liked to use. They would be delivered across the Channel by motor torpedo-boat but the last miles would involve a quiet approach by dory. They became adept at lowering the little boat into the sea from the MTB, in all conditions, and then reversing the process, hauling it back up on to the deck. Phil and Geraint, with their backgrounds in the Royal Navy and Kriegsmarine respectively, had enough skill to manage the boat in motion, even though Phil had been principally a gunner and Geraint, a wireless operator. Bud, as an experienced deck-hand, and having crossed the Atlantic, no less, was equally skilled, and knew how to fettle a struggling engine.

George had mastered the basics of explosive demolition in Palestine, and leapt at the opportunity of learning more. Bud was chosen as his deputy, and together, they spent many happy hours, demolishing walls and old machinery.

Finally, there was French conversation, and Pearson was pleasantly surprised at the progress that they had made. None of them would be able to pass as a native, but they would all, at the very least, be able to give and receive basic information, while Geraint and Phil would be capable of more.

Spring arrived, still damp and cold, but without the numbing chill of winter, and Pearson decided that they were ready for their first operation. They were assembled in a training room one afternoon, and with a flourish, he uncovered a wall map and gestured to them all to gather around it.

'Some of you may recognise the coast of Finistère, that's north-west Brittany, south-west of here, more or less. There's a large German garrison at Brest, and others at Lorient and St-Malo', pointing them out on the map, 'but you will be pleased to hear that they don't interest us, not yet'. He had their close attention, for here was what they been training for.

'Just about one mile off the coast, here', placing his forefinger over a small island, 'is the Île Vierge, the Island of the Virgin, and on it, the biggest lighthouse you've ever seen, 270 feet from the ground to the light. It's not operational, of course, our information is that the Germans use it as a wireless transmitting station for their U-boats. Our job is to destroy the transmitter, take whatever prisoners we can and snaffle any codebooks and anything else on paper that we can lay our hands on'.

There was an immediate buzz around the table, it sounded like a fairly straightforward business, but much would depend upon the details.

'There'll be a guard sir, do we know how many?' asked Tom.

'Our information is that there's no more than ten people altogether, so perhaps half of those will be the guard'.

'Perhaps, sir?'

'Yes, Sergeant, perhaps. Unfortunately, our source in Lilia, that's the nearest village on the mainland, he's gone quiet in the past month. He was clear about a maximum of ten, but we've not been able to raise him on the wireless since, so it could be he's been caught, got cold feet or the wireless has packed up'.

'Now', he continued, 'we think that the German transmitter and the generator are on the ground floor of the lighthouse, together with the operators, but the guards are housed in the old, original lighthouse, just twenty yards away, we think that's a dormitory and a kitchen there too. We'll need to clear both buildings before we let George smash everything to pieces'.

The purpose of the meeting was not simply for Pearson to pass on information, it was to work up the detail of the raid, and the remainder of the afternoon and the evening, punctuated by a hurried meal, was spent in devising the quickest way to subdue the German personnel and thoroughly destroy the machinery. Pearson was clear that it was not a committee, for the final decision would be his, but these men had experience and expertise, and he would be a fool not to make use of it.

George had a suggestion, 'Sir, we could demolish the lighthouse, stop them using it again?' He caught Bud's eye, and winked.

'It's certainly possible, Corporal, but I think not, and I'll tell you why. First of all, the priorities are the transmitter and the personnel, that's where we use our time on the island. Secondly, that lighthouse was built to face Atlantic storms and it would take quite an effort to guarantee knocking it down. I'm sure you could do it, Corporal, but we would need to carry more explosives and it would slow us down. Thirdly, and this is the clincher, the brass want it left intact. They would be more than happy if Jerry guards it with twenty or thirty men after we've been, because that means twenty or thirty men less to guard somewhere else, and perhaps they'll increase the guards on all the transmitting stations. No, your job, with Bud, is to smash that generator and transmitter and if they replace it, we'll blow it up again!'

There was one further meeting between Pearson and Tom, and the plan was complete. The Captain needed approval 'from above' before they proceeded, but as far as he could tell, that should be forthcoming. Combined Operations wanted things to move quickly, and Pearson would oblige.

'Sergeant, do any parts of the operation bother you more than others?' Pearson enquired.

'A few, sir', answered Tom, 'weather, of course, it will be a difficult landing if the weather isn't right, and if they get any notion we're on the way, but you could say that about any raid'. Pearson nodded, it was a risky enterprise, and that had to be accepted.

Tom continued, 'My only real worry is if we can't keep the Germans at ground level. A man with a rifle or, God help us, a machine gun at the top of the light could make a withdrawal impossible. At that height, we'd be in his range for quite a distance'.

Tom was right, realised Pearson. They would be lucky to get back to the dory, and would be an easy target until they disappeared into the darkness, if they even got that far. 'What do you suggest, Sergeant?'

'The first man in heads for the stairs, sir, as soon as he can, stops anyone getting up them. The Germans are well organised, sir, and they'll have thought of it already. One of them will be detailed to get to the top platform, to snipe and probably to signal the mainland'.

'PO Watson is detailed as first man in isn't he?'

'Yes, sir, and he'd do very well. First in will have to fight to the stairs and Phil takes a lot of stopping'.

'Please speak to him then, Sergeant, make sure he understands that's his priority'.

Phil would understand alright, thought Tom. His Petty Officer rank was equivalent to Tom's, and he was more than capable of stepping into Tom's shoes, if the need ever arose. Irregular warfare suited him. Up until now, he had deferred to Tom on land, but in time, he was an obvious candidate to lead.

Navigation was difficult around Île Vierge, for it was one rocky island, surrounded by numerous others and there were countless reefs, just below the surface of the water. The raid would have to take place on or near the full moon, both for the illumination and for the spring tide that, with luck, would carry them over any rocky obstructions.

'Provisional date then, Sergeant, is the fourth of April, that leaves us with a week to iron out any details. Let the chaps know. No one leaves base until after the raid, not even to the pub'.

Chapter 8

Despite her increased vigilance, Eloise saw no more strangers at the chateau, so either Brauer's visitor was calling later in the evening, or he was meeting him elsewhere. Under different circumstances, if the man was local, she might have spotted him in the locality but as it was, she was at the chateau for so many hours every day that there was no opportunity to go further afield. It was as much as she could do to keep up with the work, and sometimes, it seemed as if her children were becoming strangers to her, she saw so little of them.

March was almost stepping into April when, one evening, as she pedalled up to the villa after another long day's work, she could not fail to see a car pulled up outside the house. A visitor, she thought, and put her bicycle away as usual, before letting herself in through the front door. Walking along the hall to the kitchen, she could hear voices as she passed the closed door to the lounge and hoped that she would be able to get to bed without troubling to socialise with whoever the visitor might be.

As ever, Clarisse was sewing in the warm light of an oil lamp that was perched on the kitchen table. Their routine was to share a mug of warm milk together, then Eloise would relax quietly for ten minutes alone, then look in at the sleeping children before taking herself off to bed. Tonight was to be different, however.

'Gilbert has a visitor, chérie', explained Clarisse, 'an old friend whom he would like you to meet. You go through, dear, and I'll bring your milk through. I've told them, no more than ten minutes because you need your sleep'.

Eloise was not happy, these few minutes before bed was the only time that she could call her own, it was precious to her but what could she do? She quickly decided that it would be churlish to refuse, so, after hanging up her coat, she walked through the connecting door into the lounge.

Gilbert, sitting in a wing-backed chair at one side of the fire, smiled as she entered, and stood up, 'Eloise, my dear, I would like you to meet an old friend of mine, Louis Quiniou'. He gestured to a figure sitting in the other chair across from him. Whoever it was, they were facing away from Eloise, but as she moved further into the room and the person started to rise to greet her, she caught a glimpse of his profile in the second or two before he faced her, and what she saw caused her to catch her breath.

She had seen that profile before, she was sure of it, sitting in the kitchen at the chateau, across the table from Brauer.

The man standing in front of her was of a similar age to Gilbert, neatly dressed in a brown suit, ancient-looking but of good quality, covering an old-fashioned waistcoat and a shirt with a winged collar. He was gaunt, particularly in his face, sunken even, and a sparse, grey moustache matched the cropped, thin hair upon his head. He was smiling at her, holding out his hand to be shaken, but the smile seemed to be plastered on, rather than coming from within. 'Madame', he said, and Eloise replied politely, 'Monsieur Quiniou'. What did he want? She would not make this easy for him.

'Louis and I were at school together', explained Gilbert, 'his parents moved away to Paris when he was, oh, fourteen, Louis?' 'Yes, fourteen', confirmed Quiniou. 'He worked all his life in Paris', continued Gilbert, 'but with the Boche filling up the city, he thought he would retire back to the old village, isn't that right, Louis?'

Quiniou spoke carefully and precisely, 'Quite correct, Gilbert. I came back three months ago, Madame, but only now have I found the time to look up my old friend. I went to the chateau and found it full of Germans, but it was not difficult to find Gilbert, I knew he would not move far away from Lilia'.

Eloise smiled politely, sipping the milk that Clarisse had brought in for her, and waited for the point of the conversation, for it was all nonsense. Why would it have taken him three months to find his old friend? Everyone knew that the chateau was in German hands, he didn't need to go there to find it out. Why had he come back, really? Paris might be full of German soldiers, but it was a big city, they could not be everywhere! They were just as visible, if not more so, in Brittany.

'Gilbert tells me that you work in the chateau, Madame'. Ah, here we go!

'Yes, sir, I am the cook'.

'I expect you see and hear all sorts of things up there, don't you? Conversations in meetings, papers, visiting officers, many useful things for a patriot to hear'.

She would put a stop to this, and quickly, 'Useful to whom? Sir, I am a cook. I take no notice of what might be happening around me, none, and I speak no German anyway! I think that your next words will be to ask me to spy for you, and I will not, never!'

'Cherie', started Gilbert, but she cut him off, 'I am surprised at you, Monsieur Hervé, inviting this man into Madame Le Roux's home. For all you know, he is trying to suck you and me into the Résistance, and then where would we be? Where would my babies be?'

Clarisse was angry too, and coldly told Monsieur Quiniou that she thought that he should leave. Quiniou said nothing, just bowed slightly as Hervé handed him his tweed overcoat and left, his expression impenetrable.

As his car disappeared down the lane, both women turned on the quailing Hervé, 'Before you damn me to hell, ladies, I did not know that he was going to ask from information from you, Eloise, I truly did not. I have not seen him for more than fifty years, so it was a great surprise to me when he turned up on the doorstep. I could not turn him away but we were not really good friends when we were boys, he was a bully and no one liked him, his father was a crook, never paid his bills, that's why they moved to Paris, why he should come.......'

He would have rambled on for minutes longer but Eloise interrupted him, 'Gilbert, I believe you, but I don't trust Monsieur Quiniou', and she sat them down and told them about having seen Quiniou at the chateau with Brauer.

'He was trying to entrap me', explained Eloise, 'and you. He works for the Germans now. He must have heard that I was working at the chateau, or perhaps Brauer sent him to try to trick me. The question is, what do we do now? I wouldn't be surprised if it was him that betrayed Monsieur Hamon and his son'.

Hervé sat up straighter, 'He asked me, what did I think about Hamon being shot, and his son arrested'.

'What did you say?'

'I said it was very sad'.

'Is that all?'

'Yes, I told you, I hadn't seen him since 1885 or something, I wasn't going to open my heart to him, was I? Do you think I am stupid?'

Clarisse laughed, 'Don't ask, Gilbert, don't ask!' They went to bed, and Eloise was about to sit down for her precious few minutes of solitude, when she had an idea. She pulled down her coat from the hook, and moving quietly, went back out through the front door.

Quiniou had driven off in the direction of the chateau. Perhaps he was going home, or perhaps not. She would cycle back down towards the chateau and see if Gilbert's old friend was who she thought he was. The moon was still a few days from full, so there would perhaps be enough darkness to hide in, and she would be able to conceal herself in the spinney opposite the chateau.

At this hour, the road, never busy, was deserted and she made the journey in a few minutes. Two minutes' walk before reaching the chateau, she stashed her bicycle behind a tree, then continued on foot. It was a still night, and although her heart was beating fast in trepidation, she was confident that she would hear anyone coming before they were close enough to see her and could hide until they were past.

Moving as quietly as she could, Eloise stepped into the spinney on her right, and tracked the road until she could see the lights of the chateau opposite her. There was a dim light in the sentry's hut by the gate, and another at the front door, and by the illumination of that second light, she could just see the shape of a small car on the gravel drive. It was approaching midnight now, so hardly the time for visitors, and she settled down to wait, for surely whoever was there would be leaving soon.

She was not disappointed. She had only been waiting for ten minutes or so when the door opened, and out stepped Quiniou. She was only thirty metres away from him, and there could be no mistake, it was definitely him. Brauer was behind him, and as they turned to face each other, both of them gave the Nazi salute. There could be no innocent explanation for that, she thought, it was definite. Quiniou had visited the villa to entrap her if he could, and now he was reporting back to his master. He was a traitor, bought and paid for.

Work the following day was an ordeal for Eloise. She had only managed four hours in bed and felt exhausted. Hans had taken pity on her, and had helped her for longer than usual, seeing that she was struggling to work with her normal efficiency. She had mimed nursing the baby, as an explanation for her fatigue, and he had laughed sympathetically, thinking back to the days when his children were young.

Brauer showed his face later that morning, smirking at her as he walked through the kitchen, so he must have been satisfied with his spy's report. He made no effort to speak to her and eventually, the work was done and she could go home. She knew that she would not have managed without Hans's help and she thanked him profusely as she left. How sad that such a kind man should be an enemy, and one of her own, Quiniou, a born and bred Breton, should be a traitor. Life could be so contrary.

Gilbert and Clarisse had still been asleep when she had left home that morning, and they were both shocked when she arrived home as she described her bicycle ride back to the chateau on the previous night, and what she had seen. They all agreed, there was no doubt now where Quiniou's loyalties lay but the question was, what could they do about it, if anything? There was no time for discussion, for Eloise needed sleep more than talk.

April arrived, and along with an improvement in the weather, everything seemed to quieten down. Quiniou had not shown his face again, neither at the villa nor at the chateau, and Brauer had not crossed her path. There were no more late dinners to prepare, so Eloise was able to return home at a reasonable hour, to catch up with her sleep, and even to hope that she had convinced Quiniou of her disinterest in anything to do with the Résistance. Perhaps he would leave them all alone now.

She came home one evening to find Hervé waiting for her at the gate, and he beckoned her silently to move out of the view from the door. 'Clarisse must not know that I have spoken to you about this', he whispered. Eloise was intrigued, what could it be?

'I called in at the estaminet this morning for my café and cognac before lunch, and Pierre Galou was there'. The name meant nothing to Eloise, and her ignorance must have shown in her face for he continued, 'He has taken over from Hamon, it was Pierre who used to hide his guns in the stable but don't worry, don't worry, he knows that I cannot help him now'. She was well aware that under different circumstances, he would still have been supporting the Résistance but he had given his word not to, for the sake of the children, and she trusted him.

He lowered his voice even further, 'Pierre has known me for all of his life, he is the road mender, and he tells me things when probably, he should not. He told me this morning that Quiniou keeps asking him and others if they know anyone in the Résistance because he wants to help, he catches them in the estaminet or stops them on the street'.

Eloise made to interrupt but he spoke over her, 'Of course, no one has said anything, for they do not trust Quiniou yet but they want to, the local group is short of volunteers, especially since Hamon and his son were killed, and Quiniou is known to have money, which they need'.

'What did you tell him?' Eloise asked urgently, for if Galou knew that she had incriminating information about Quiniou, then it would be spread throughout the group, and if anyone was caught by the Germans and interrogated, her name would be divulged, that was certain.

'I told him to say nothing, I said that Quiniou was a liar as a child and that there was no reason to think that he would have changed. I could see that he thought I was being hard on Quiniou without evidence, but I could not tell him that you had seen him with the Germans. What shall we do, Eloise? If he betrays fellow Frenchmen to the Germans when I could have stopped him, I will never forgive myself'.

'We can do nothing tonight, Gilbert', answered Eloise firmly, 'but tomorrow you must speak to Galou again and tell him that Quiniou had come to you also, asking similar questions but you knew nothing and asked him to leave. If he respects your judgement, he will send Quiniou away'.

'And if not?'

'If not, Quiniou will betray him, and everyone else in the group, and when they are interrogated and tortured, Gilbert, your name will be mentioned and that will be the end for all of us'.

Hervé looked aghast but knew that she was right. At the hands of the Gestapo, no one could keep secrets.

'I will speak to Galou tomorrow', he promised, 'and tell him that if he only ever takes one piece of advice from me, it must be this, do not speak to Quiniou, on any account, for it will end badly'.

'And if he takes no notice?'

Neither put it into words, there and then, but Quiniou would have to die, for if he did not, then many others would, because of him.

Clarisse called from the door, 'Gilbert, are you there? Is there any sign of Eloise? Danielle is awake and only her Mama will do!'

'I am here, Clarisse, I will come in now', and she did, and was soon pacifying her youngest child. How precious she was, as was her older brother, reminding Eloise, as if she needed reminding, that she would do anything to keep them safe.

Eloise was tired herself, and before she realised it, she had fallen asleep on the little bed, next to her daughter. She might have laid there all night, but an hour or so later, she woke suddenly and sat up. Outside, there was noise, a crack-crack-crack, repeated over and over again, what was it?

Gradually her head cleared and she ran to the window, just as Gilbert stepped into the room. He beckoned her to him, and they moved into his bedroom where they could look out of the window without disturbing the children, and Clarisse joined them.

The noise was coming from out to sea, in the direction of the lighthouse, and strings of coloured lights were flying across the bay, towards the Île Vierge.

'It is a raid', explained Gilbert, 'the Tommies are attacking the lighthouse, what else can it be, but the Germans are fighting back, and they've got a message to shore, judging from the firing'.

'Why would they attack a lighthouse?' asked Clarisse, mystified, 'there are no soldiers there'.

'Ah, there are, my dear. I have seen them in their boat, heading for the Île, many times'.

'But what are they doing there? The light has been disused since the war started'.

'Village gossip is that it's some sort of observation post or radio station, that sort of thing'. He knew perfectly well what it was but understood that it was best to say as little as possible.

The shooting continued for a few more minutes, then suddenly stopped. They continued watching for another half an hour, and a few vehicles, German, roared past but it seemed that the raid really was over. Eloise wondered how on earth she would sleep now, after all this excitement, and with the loathsome Quiniou lurking at the edge of her mind, but she did.

Almost before she knew it, it was morning, and after a cold-water wash, she quietly left the house, careful not to disturb the children or her hosts. The chateau would be in an uproar, she knew, and no doubt Brauer would be questioning her before the day was much older.

Her bicycle was leaning up against the house wall, where she had left it, but as she turned to push it down the path, a voice called out to her, the loudest whisper that she had ever heard, from inside Madame Le Roux's wood store.

'Hey, Madame, êtes-vous française?'

Chapter 9

The weather forecast for the fourth of April was close to ideal. The wind from the south-west was predicted at ten miles per hour with gusts to fifteen, nothing that the dory couldn't handle for a few miles, and they would slip in just before the tide reached its peak, then motor out at slack water. Even if they were delayed and the operation took longer than the estimated half an hour, they would be returning to the MTB with the tide and the wind in their favour.

The Channel crossing in the MTB was easy and uneventful. German E-boats were a potential threat, with a six-knot speed advantage and a much heavier armament, but on the night of the fourth, they must have been hunting elsewhere. They would definitely be out though, given the almost balmy weather and the full moon.

At a distance of three miles from the shore, the transfer was made to the dory. Everyone was armed, but mostly for close quarter, short range combat. Each man carried a pistol and two Mills bombs, with three Thompsons shared between Pearson, Tom and Bud. Somehow, Phil had persuaded the captain that one long rifle was an absolute necessity, and he carried his Lee-Enfield slung tightly across his body. George carried, in addition to his Colt pistol, a sledge hammer to destroy the transmitter and anything else that was breakable but also a small amount of Explosive 808, the green plastic explosive, 'just in case'. Bud was similarly equipped, but carried detonators, time-pencils, instead of explosives.

The plan, moving in from the open sea, was not to head straight for the island, for that would increase the chances of being seen by a lookout. They would aim to make the coast one mile to the west of the island, then slowly motor in, hidden among the loom of the mainland behind them. Phil took the tiller, while Bud sat in the bows, watching for the tell-tale turbulence of any just-submerged obstructions.

The inboard engine, with just enough revolutions on her to move the dory quietly through the water, thumped away gently, and within minutes, the island with its towering lighthouse was in sight. No one spoke but the tension built as they moved closer and closer to their target. The island was equipped with a small jetty and slipway and tonight their luck was in, for it was not lit. They would be able to quietly moor up, and it would make their withdrawal easier too.

Phil slowed the engine even further as the little boat came within the shelter of the island, and almost drifted her in to the jetty, turning her 180 degrees so she was directly facing the sea for when the time came to leave. They disembarked silently, separating into two parties, with every man concentrating on his particular task.

Pearson, Geraint and Bud made for the old lighthouse where, according to their information, a kitchen and living quarters occupied the square building at the foot of the tower. The remainder of the team, Tom, George and Phil, sprinted for the newer tower, only twenty yards away across the grass and waited for Pearson to give the 'all-ready' signal, in this instance a simple shout of 'Go!'.

Pearson bellowed the signal and turning the handle of the heavy old door in front of him, burst into the soldiers' accommodation, with Geraint and Bud at his heels.

The door opened straight into a kitchen and dining room, and two men in uniform, sitting at a scrubbed table, jumped up in alarm as the three soldiers piled into the room. One made the mistake of reaching for his rifle from where it leaned against the table and received a quick burst into his torso from the Captain's gun, throwing him backwards across the room in a welter of blood. The other German, rather more sensible, held up his arms in surrender and Pearson gestured Geraint forward to secure him with handcuffs brought for this very purpose. As the young German busied himself securing the prisoner, Bud and the Captain moved further into the building.

A door at the back of the dining led into a short corridor with doors leading off it, and they checked out four rooms, empty except for boxes of supplies, before opening a fifth door which revealed a set of steep stairs, leading to a floor above. The Captain wanted to give any further defenders the minimum time to organise and ran up the stairs, which opened out onto a broad landing, with Bud a couple of yards behind him.

The second that Pearson cleared the top of the stairs and turned to the left to continue the search, a volley of shots crashed out from in front of him, and he staggered, then was thrown backwards against the wall as heavy bullets thumped into his body, to leave him, sitting down, head slumped forward and gun useless by his side.

Bud, behind him, knew that hesitation would be fatal and as fast as thought, primed a Mills bomb and rolled it around the corner, in the direction from where he guessed that the shots had come. The deafening crash of the explosion came quickly, and as he bowled his second grenade along the wooden floor, he could just hear an agonised cry, although his ears were ringing painfully from the blast.

After the second explosion, he covered the last few steps in a rush and emptied the magazine of his Thompson in the same direction. To his surprise and relief, there was no return fire and, dropping the machine gun and un-holstering his pistol, he stepped forward into the aftermath of the brief firefight.

The remains of two soldiers lay in a doorway, their blood and flesh intermingling. His grenades had eviscerated one, while the other had lost his face and the top of his head in the blast. They had numerous other wounds, and to Bud's inexperienced eye, they looked like people no longer, just burst bags of blood and bone and shit, spread across the floor.

Gathering himself, he rapidly checked three more rooms but they were empty, and as he turned to deal with Captain Pearson, it was to find Geraint already there. He was checking the officer for a pulse but looked up and shook his head.

The stairs carried on, up into the old lighthouse proper, and Bud raced up to the top, with a fresh magazine in his Thompson. The lightroom was empty, and he descended hurriedly, to join Geraint downstairs. The plan was to drop any prisoners straight into the boat, but as they each took an arm of the prisoner to pull him outside, bullets crashed through the open doorway, hitting the stone floor and ricocheting into the ceiling and around the room. Geraint gestured to Bud, the shots were coming in at an acute angle, fired from a height, and the American nodded his understanding, someone was shooting from a perch in the new lighthouse. What had happened to Tom and the rest? They waited for a pause in the firing, then ran, prisoner in hand to the jetty, pushing him down into the boat and quickly chaining him, via his handcuffs, to a steel rail on the gunwale. As they ran back up toward the lighthouse, they were jolted in surprise as two red lights burst into the sky above it, the defenders had signalled the mainland! This had to be finished quickly.

Phil had crashed through the door and found himself in a round room, the base of the lighthouse tower. It was one single, large room, with just one door, and at the far side, a stone staircase with a metal balustrade started its long spiral up to the light. There had been a low buzz of conversation as Phil had burst in, but that changed to angry shouts as the inhabitants of the room realised that this was no ordinary interruption.

Phil was briefly aware of two figures sitting in front of an electrically lit machine and two others, sitting at a table with books and paperwork in front of them. He ignored them completely, relying upon his comrades to deal with them, and made for the stairs, hearing a brief rattle of a Thompson, then another, then silence.

He looked upwards at the spiral staircase, climbing in circles around the inside wall of the tower, up and up and into the gloom. Was anyone up there? He could not see if there was, but his question was soon answered as a bullet smashed into the white-tiled wall next to him. He turned and shouted to Tom, 'Sniper above!' then mounted the stairs, rifle in one hand, and started to ascend, keeping as close to the wall as he could.

Below him, his comrades had control of the transmitter and its operators. One of the men at the table had jumped up, as if to tackle them, but a well-placed burst past his head from Tom's Thompson had encouraged him back into his chair, and another few rounds into the transmitter had put it immediately out of action. The odd shot was still coming down from above, but as long as everyone walked around the walls of the round chamber, it seemed that the shooter, high up in the structure, could not find an angle to shoot at them directly.

George got to work with his sledgehammer, and in less than a minute, the transmitter was so much pulverised scrap. As he finished and went outside to do the same to the generator, Bud rushed in through the open door.

'All done over there?' asked Tom.

Bud nodded, 'One prisoner in the boat, three dead'.

'What about Pearson and Geraint?'

Bud shook his head, 'Geraint has started trashing the gen, Pearson, well, he screwed up, he's dead'.

Damn, the first loss! Afterwards, Tom would realise that he was not surprised, for Pearson led from the front, that was his style.

Now was not the time to ask Bud what he meant by 'screwed up', that would do for later, for he was now in command of the raid and they needed to get finished and away, but there was more news to come.

'And they got a signal off', continued Bud, 'so we can expect visitors pretty soon'.

'Prisoners to the boat', ordered Tom quickly, for they had all been handcuffed and their transport back to Poole for interrogation was one of the main aims of the raid.

'What about Phil?' asked Bud, guessing he was following the plan and was hunting the remaining defenders of the lighthouse.

'Leave him to me', rapped Tom, 'tell George, everyone to the boat, give it five minutes then leave, understand? Five minutes', and with that, he started up the steps where Phil had gone a few minutes earlier.

Phil's progress had been perilous, for he had been under fire for most of his ascent of the never-ending stairs, with bullets snapping past him and either glancing off the steps at his feet, as he climbed laboriously onwards, or shattering more of the tiles on the wall. A few rounds from his pistol might have discouraged the shooter but there were only seven rounds in the magazine and he might need them all later, so he just kept moving and climbing.

His thigh muscles were burning with the effort, and his breath was short, so short, when the steps in front of him suddenly changed. It was mostly in darkness here, at this height, but some moonlight, shining through the glazed windows that were pierced through the walls of the lighthouse every fifty feet or so, provided some illumination, enough for him to see that the steps led into a circular wooden-floored room that had been built across the whole diameter of the tower. As he stepped off the last step, spotting the light of a doorway ahead of him, a shot cracked past his ear and instinctively he dived forward, shortening the range between him and whoever had fired the shot.

The lighthouse was at its narrowest point here, and he felt himself crash into a body in front of him. Christ, how had the bugger missed him!

He felt something heavy and hard thump into the side of his head, almost taking his ear off, or so it felt, then sliding down with a terrible impact between his neck and shoulder. The arm on that side of his body went numb immediately and he dropped his rifle but his other arm was free, and Phil went to work. Pulling back his fist, he slammed it forward in the hope that it would connect with something vital, and heard a crack as it slammed into ribs, followed by a whoosh of air as the air was driven out of his opponent's lungs.

As his assailant bent forward, winded and in sudden pain, dropping his own rifle to the floor, Phil gripped him by the throat and threw him against the stone wall. The impact was immense, and as he rebounded back into the centre of the room, still on his feet but more or less insensible, Phil was just able to see enough to drop him to the floor with an easy punch to the side of his head.

The doorway led out to a masonry walkway that seemed to circle the exterior, bounded by a low wall. Although he had parachuted into Crete, Phil was no fan of great heights and besides, he had no parachute! Gingerly, he scouted around it and it was deserted, but then from above his head, he heard the crack of a rifle. Above head-height he could see the glass of the enormous light, and then found a steel ladder, fastened into the stone, that led upwards.

Enough feeling had come back into his arm so, gripping the ladder with that hand, and with his pistol clutched in the other, he moved quietly upwards. Another shot rang out, not aimed at him, as he reached the even narrower platform that encircled the light room. Phil could see through the protective glass of the massive lantern, right through to the other side, although the prisms of the light inside restricted his view, and he detected some movement there.

Although it was a calm night by Channel standards, there was still a breeze at this height, and he could feel it clutching at his body as he edged his way carefully to the other side, accompanied by the sound of further shots from the rifleman. His pistol, cocked and ready, was in his free hand, while the other clutched the guttering of the lantern room, and as he reached the position where the soldier was lying, shooting down at the team as they rushed to the boat, he did not hesitate. Two shots into his head brought his sniping to an abrupt and permanent end.

The sniper had been firing down towards the jetty, and beyond it, Phil could look out over a mile of sea to the mainland. It looked deceptively close in the moonlight, and with a jolt, he spotted a boat heading toward the island. It was still a way off and was having to steer around the reefs and shoals that littered this part of the coast, and he estimated that he and the team had more than five minutes, and less than ten, to make their escape.

He continued his airy walk around the circular lantern, until he reached the metal ladder once again, and climbed carefully down it. As he reached the walkway and turned toward the door, Tom's voice shouted out, 'Phil', and he was able to immediately reply, much to Tom's relief.

He was waiting in the little circular room, standing next to Phil's first opponent, who was still out for the count, and he continued, 'Time to go, mate, they managed to send off a signal, it could be they'll send a party to check it out'.

'They already have, Tom, there's a boat on the way'.

Phil collected his rifle but there were no more words, just a pell-mell descent of those endless stairs. Going down was quicker than going up and they were out of the door and intending to sprint down towards the jetty, but as Phil looked out towards the mainland, he stopped and cursed. From this height above the jetty, the German boat was already in sight. It had moved faster than he had anticipated.

Unshipping his rifle, he turned to Tom, 'Mate, there's no time to argue. I'll hold them off with Bessie here, but I've only got twenty rounds. You cast off, get around to sea side of the island where you'll be out of their sight and wait for me there for five minutes. If I don't show, go'.

Tom did not argue because he knew that Phil was right. He was the only one of them with a long rifle, and only he had a hope of holding off the German for a few minutes, Thompsons and Colts were useless at anything other than short range. They could not allow themselves to be pinned down against the jetty, that would mean certain annihilation, and of course, now that Pearson was dead, it was his responsibility to make the mission a success, whatever the cost.

He nodded his agreement and ran the few yards down to the jetty. As he leapt into the boat, he could see the others looking for Phil, but quickly ordered Bud to cast off and make for the far side of the little island. As they moved carefully between the sharp rocks that made navigation so difficult, they heard Phil opening a careful fire over the top of their heads.

Phil estimated that the German boat, similar in size to their own, was at about six hundred yards before he opened fire. It was difficult shooting, over open sights and in moonlight, but he had discovered a rare talent in himself over the past six months, and it was within his range. He had no doubt that they would shoot back at him but he would be an elusive target.

At his second shot, the German helmsman swerved his boat sharply to starboard, clearly hoping to maintain their distance from the island or even gradually to move away, but all he managed to do was to present the whole length of his vessel to Phil's fire, rather than just his bow. The Petty Officer took full advantage, peppering the boat from stem to stern, but someone on board kept their nerve, for a return fire from at least three automatic weapons came his way. It must have been guesswork, invisible as he was against the bulk of the little island, but bullets rained down around him, and all he could do for a few minutes was to hunker down behind a small rock and hope to survive.

By the time Phil looked up again, the boat had almost reached the jetty, and worse than that, he had a horrible feeling that his time was up. He knew that Tom would try to wait for as long as he could but the success of the raid was paramount, more important than one or two casualties, however regrettable. He would have to leave.

Keeping low to the ground, and with his rifle strapped tightly around his body once more, Phil scooted past the lighthouse and down to the other side of the tiny island. As he had suspected, the boat had gone, and he could just make out its stern, just, as it disappeared out to sea. There would be a rapid transfer to the MTB and they would be home before breakfast. Now, what was he going to do?

Aboard the dory, and despite the success of the raid, there was an air of loss and depression. The powers that be would be satisfied, without question, and medals would be awarded, but would that make up for the loss of their officer and their good friend? Of course not.

While they waited behind the island, Tom explained Phil's plan and although no one was happy with it, least of all Tom, they could understand the reasoning. He stretched out the five minutes for as long as possible, but when the firing stopped, his conclusion had to be that it was all over and time to leave. He gave the order reluctantly, and Bud turned her around and headed out to sea. None of the others envied Tom that level of responsibility.

Phil, meanwhile, had come to the conclusion that he would have to get to the French mainland, one way or another. How he would escape to Blighty after that was another matter, but first things first. One of his qualities was the possession of a very practical nature, and he thrived when he had a problem to bite on.

Stealing their boat was out of the question. He had crawled back around the rocky shore until the jetty came into view and saw that they had left three men guarding the boat while the others investigated what had been happening on Île de Vierge. He could knock out the three soldiers with his remaining bullets but the others would not be stupid enough to let him get away.

There was just one answer, he would have to swim. He had estimated the distance at one mile, well within his capabilities, even when dressed, for he had swum further in training. He would not be quick but he would make it.

Chapter 10

Eloise was a late arrival at the chateau that morning and, rushing into the kitchen, she was relieved and grateful to see Hans already at work. Coffee was brewing, he had assembled the cold food to be carried through to the dining room and the hot food, ready to be cooked, was lined up by the side of the stove. Instinctively, she gave his arm a squeeze in gratitude, murmuring, 'Danke, mein freund', as she dashed past him to put on her pinafore. He put down the knife that he was using to butter bread and looked at her, 'Ein vergnügen, meine liebe'. It was his pleasure to help her, for it reminded him of his life at home, and the fact that she had spoken German to him for the first time passed him by.

The building was in a turmoil that morning, hardly surprising after the happenings of the previous night, with NCOs and officers scurrying from room to room. The two men from the Gestapo arrived again, and she took coffee to them as they sat in an angry breakfast conference with Brauer and an officer. If anything, she felt even more invisible than previously, for she been half-expecting Brauer to take her to one side and ask her if she had heard anything unusual in the night but he had not.

Two truckloads of troops arrived immediately after breakfast and Brauer went off with one truck while the officer went with the other. Eloise hoped that Gilbert and Clarisse would have the hidden the giant Tommy somewhere away from the house for it looked as if the Germans were going to conduct a local search in case any of the Lighthouse raiders had come ashore. They returned three hours later, the officer in a foul temper and shouting at Brauer, 'I told you, they all escaped in their boat and there's no sign of a landing anywhere. Why do you waste my time, Unteroffizier Brauer, it was a small raid and nothing more!'

They ordered coffee and brandy, and when Eloise took it in, Brauer took the opportunity to question her.

'Madame, you will have heard gunfire last night, from the direction of the lighthouse?'

'Yes, sir, it woke us all up'.

'And what did you think it was?'

'I didn't know, sir. Were your soldiers practicing their fighting, sir?'

'No, they were not', he bawled, impatient at her apparent stupidity, 'the British attacked the lighthouse and killed some of my men. Did you see anything unusual when you left home to come here this morning, Madame? People you did not recognise, men who might be soldiers? Answer me, woman!'

She was saved from answering when Leutnant Schäfer butted in, 'She is a half-wit, Brauer, look at her, as dumb as a cow. She knows nothing', and dismissed her, much to Eloise's relief. She felt less relieved though when Schäfer added, as she closed the door behind her, 'Lucky for her she cooks so well or she would be in the whorehouse'. What degenerates they were, Hans was right. They had stolen the country and now they wanted to steal the people too.

Eloise had time later to ponder the events of the morning. The big man hiding in the woodstore had asked her if she was French? What did he think she was, Chinese? Her natural good sense had cut in at that point, and she had simply answered, 'Oui, Monsieur'. He looked relieved and in halting French, told her that he was a sailor from Britain and needed her help. He was soaking wet and looked exhausted, but what could she do? She wanted to keep the war at arm's length but how difficult that was becoming! She was working, unwillingly, for the German Army, that worm, Quiniou, was suspicious of her and now there was a Tommy in the woodshed!

All she had time to do, after telling the sailor to wait, was to rush back into the house and wake Monsieur Hervé, telling that there was a British sailor concealed in the woodshed, and that he must do something about it, either help him or ask him to leave. Leaving Hervé to get dressed, she told the sailor that the master of the house was coming down to assist him, that he would only be a moment and then wished him a good morning and left.

She laughed to herself, remembering that final remark. How could he possibly have a good morning? He was soaking wet, in a foreign country and would undoubtedly be shot if the Germans laid their hands on him. She hoped, with all her heart, that Hervé could help him by getting him away from the house and out of their lives, before something awful happened.

The mile to shore was about the most difficult swim that Phil had ever endured. He had tied his boots around his neck, deciding that they were essential equipment once he was on dry land, and was also loaded down with his rifle and the Colt, for the thought of landing in enemy territory unarmed was not something he could contemplate. He had ditched his webbing, including the two grenades he carried, then slipped into the water, hoping to make it to shore before the party on the island made their return.

The water was bitterly cold, and it was not long before he could feel it leeching the warmth and the energy from his muscles. Fortunately, it was still slack water when he set off, so he had made more than half of the distance before he felt the change in the tide. It called for more and more effort to keep up his powerful breast-stroke and finally, it was only his grit and stubbornness that propelled him onwards and finally dropped him onto the sand. He lay there for minutes before he roused himself and, scrambling up a low, rocky bank that bounded the beach, he crawled into the shelter of some bushes. He would never know how long he lay, it might have been an hour or longer but he knew that he had to move further inland, the Boche would be bound to run a patrol along the beach at some time and he needed to be away. There was no immediate search though, as far as he could tell, so Phil was sure that his escape had been unobserved.

He would have to make contact with the French underground, the Résistance they called them, to find a way to escape home, but first of all, he needed to avoid capture. Forcing himself to rise, he stumbled onwards in the darkness, breaking through hedges and over dry-stone walls, where there was no gate, until finally coming upon a narrow road, more like a lane. On the other side of the road, he could see the shape of a building, a house perhaps or a barn? He would have to hide up there, for he felt as if his energy was nearly gone, and that morning could not be far away. Later, he would think about his next move. It was a house, he realised, as he came closer, with a woodshed in the corner of the narrow front garden. That will do, he thought to himself, I'll be sheltered for a few hours, at least, and crawled behind a pile of chopped wood.

It had been a surprise when, not long after sunrise, he had heard a door close quietly and peeked out to see a young woman pushing a bicycle down the path to the road. Without any pause for thought or trepidation, for he had to ask for help sometime so why not now, he spoke up, or rather whispered loudly, asking her if she was French and asking for help. In recollection, it was not the most intelligent question, but it served, for after almost dropping her bicycle in shock, she told him to wait while she fetched some help. She could have been in the process of betraying him, of course, but she had an honest face, if he was any judge, and anyway, what else could he do? She had passed him again, a few minutes later, in a great hurry, telling him that the man of the house would see him in a moment, then cycled off at speed.

What could Phil do but wait, although he kept his Colt in his hand, ready to fire. He was not waiting for long before an old man, not ancient but definitely old, came quietly out of the house, calling, 'Anglais, Anglais, I am friend, amis'. Phil replied in his basic French, which brought a smile to the old man's face, and he beckoned Phil into the house.

An elderly woman was in the kitchen, and when she saw Phil, all hell broke loose.

'What are you doing, Hervé? Who is this?'

Phil found it impossible to keep up with their exchange, it was so fast and so shrill, but from their gestures and from the few words that he did catch, it was apparent that the woman did not want him in the house. He decided that he should interrupt.

'Madame', he interjected, but their furious exchange did not falter, 'MADAME', he roared, as if bellowing the length of the lower deck, and then he had their attention.

'Madame, I am sorry to put you in danger. I will leave you now. I would like to take some food with me'. His French was staccato and laboured, but at least it was intelligible, for she understood immediately.

'No, Monsieur, you cannot leave now, it is too dangerous and where would you go? I do not want you here but here you are. This old fool', she gestured at the old man, 'will speak to someone from the Résistance this morning, and they will look after you, take you somewhere safe. This house is not safe'. While she was speaking, the old man had put on some old shoes and an overcoat, preparing to leave the house. She continued, 'While we wait, you will first dry your clothes in front of the fire, go on', she gestured, 'take them off, hang them up, and I will feed you. Hervé', pointing at the old man, 'will bring someone to collect you, and then you will leave'.

She was a formidable woman, and if she was able to deliver what she was promising, then Phil had truly fallen on his feet. Could he trust them? His instinct told him that he could.

'Madame, you are most kind. I put myself in your hands'.

Hervé left the house and set out across the fields, hoping to catch Galou at home before he set out for work, and luckily for him, he did. He explained the situation and unsurprisingly, Galou made the connection with the shooting overnight.

'Yes, I was expecting a raid sometime, or rather Hamon was. I have stayed off the wireless since his capture, those damned Boche will certainly be listening out for it. Has he told you anything about himself, this Tommy?'

'Nothing, but then I came straight to you, there was not time to ask him questions'. He omitted the painful conversation with Clarisse, when she had ordered him from her house, and not to come back unless someone from the Résistance was with him!

Hervé took the chance to tell Galou that Quiniou had been asking him the same questions about the Résistance that he had asked him, that he had told him nothing, and that he, Galou, should continue to do the same, for Quiniou was not to be trusted at all. He was shocked at Galou's reply.

'Gilbert, I have decided to speak to him. I have asked questions in the village, and although people remember him and his thieving father, that was all years ago and no one can fault him now. He has given money to the church and is no lover of the Germans, that is for sure, the way he talks about them. He will be in the estaminet tomorrow morning, I will invite him here and speak privately to him'.

Gilbert realised that he would have to tell him more. 'Pierre, what I am about to tell you now must go no further. You must repeat it to no one, even in your group, for lives will depend upon your silence. Do you agree?'

Galou was mystified but readily agreed, and his face grew longer and more stern as Hervé told him what Eloise had seen, of Quiniou leaving the chateau and making the Nazi salute to Brauer.

'Could she have been mistaken?' asked Galou, but Hervé could see that he was half-convinced already. 'No, she was sure, and she is an intelligent woman, she would not make such an accusation if she was not certain. You understand why I asked you to say nothing, Pierre? If the Germans learned that she had seen Quiniou with them, her life would be worth nothing'.

They talked some more, and Galou agreed to take the Tommy into his care but he could not come until tonight, it was not safe to move him in daylight. Hervé was to tell Madame Le Roux that she must keep him out of sight, in case the Germans came calling, but that Galou guaranteed that he would take the Englishman off her hands this evening, and would continue to give Quiniou the cold shoulder.

Clarisse would not be happy, Hervé knew, but it was the best that could be done. She would give him hell because of the danger to Eloise and the babies but he would defend himself. He would remind her that he had not invited the Englishman into her garden, and he had been following Eloise's bidding. No, he couldn't say that, he would sound like a coward, putting the blame on the young mother. He was still pondering what to say when he rapped on the kitchen door, and Clarisse let him back in to her villa.

A startling sight met his eyes. The enormous English sailor, dressed only in singlet and underpants, was sitting at the kitchen table with Adrien, Eloise's little boy, perched on his knee. They were both eating toast and eggs, courtesy of the chateau kitchen, and laughing together, while Danielle, in her high chair, was solemnly watching them, occasionally turning her attention to her breakfast, then looking again at this fascinating giant who was entertaining her brother. His khaki trousers, blouse, boots and socks were drying in front of the fire, and his rifle and pistol, both partially disassembled, were there too.

Gilbert gave his message and was astonished when Clarisse accepted that the sailor would have to stay with them for the remainder of the day. At this point, Phil spoke up, 'Madame, Monsieur, you have been very kind to me but I cannot stay in your house, even for one day. If Germans come here, you will be in trouble. My clothes are dry, please tell me where I can hide until this evening'.

He was correct, of course, for it was light now, and very likely that the Germans would organise local searches after last night's attack. So, where could they hide him?

As Phil dressed, Clarisse came up with an idea, and it was simple. Buildings were to be avoided, she surmised, because they were obvious places to hide, and if the Germans searched, they would search buildings first. Her suggestion was that he should conceal himself within the steep banks of the little stream that ran down the field next to her garden. He would be hidden from the road but would be able to hear if any vehicles stopped at the villa. If that happened, then he could retreat further up and along the stream bed and he would always be out of sight, at least until he was nearly a kilometre further upstream. It sounded quick and easy, and within fifteen minutes, he was gone. Clarisse had given him more food, and he had begged a little mineral oil and a rag to try to work on his rifle and pistol, for sea water did not agree with them, and he might well need them very soon.

The morning was still cool so, with a borrowed overcoat, Phil used the first forty minutes to strip, dry and lubricate his weapons. He only had eight rounds left for the rifle and five for the pistol, enough to do some damage perhaps, but he would soon be out of ammunition once cornered. He would just have to avoid it.

He spent the next hour following the stream-bed up the slope of the hill, marking the few places where he could climb out of it unobserved and run into sparse woodland. Being realistic though, evading the enemy here would be more difficult than it had been in Crete. There were more people, more roads and no wilderness to hand that he could disappear into. He would have to rely upon the bravery and patriotism of the Resistance.

The day seemed interminable, but gradually it passed. Phil heard traffic passing the house but nothing seemed to stop, so perhaps the Germans had concluded that all of the attackers had escaped by sea. He hoped that it was the case for it would make his escape less difficult. He eked out the food given to him by Clarisse and wondered how Tom and the others would be taking his absence. For all they knew, he was dead, and would have to be replaced. Perhaps the Resistance were in communication with London, and would be able to report his presence, but would that be seen as bad security, an unnecessary risk? He didn't know. Darkness fell, and still he waited.

To her surprise, Brauer told Eloise that she must finish early that evening, she was to serve dinner but then leave Hans to finish off in the kitchen. Hans was as surprised as she was but waved her away, pleased that she would have a few more hours with her children for at least one evening. She took no persuading and was back at the villa two hours earlier than usual.

Clarisse and Monsieur Hervé were startled at Eloise's early return and soon brought her up to date regarding the English sailor and the arrangement with Galou. She heard all about the children's fascination with their visitor, and of his easy way with them. Adrien had cried after he had left and had asked repeatedly where the big man had gone. Perhaps, she thought, she had been a little abrupt with him that morning, although how could she have been otherwise, with impatient and suspicious German officers and NCOs waiting at the chateau? No, he was a danger to them all, and she would be glad when he left. She was not pleased to learn that Galou now knew all about her observation of Quiniou but realised that Hervé had had no choice but to share the information. If Galou had spoken to Quiniou and told him about the local Résistance, disaster would surely have followed close behind.

Clarisse had saved a plate of rabbit stew for the fugitive and Eloise offered to take it out to him, rather than for him come back down to the house and put everyone in danger again. It seemed hard on the poor man, leaving him in the damp and the cool of the evening, but Galou would be here soon, to take him away into shelter somewhere.

With a dish of stew in one hand, and a small pot of coffee and a mug in the other, Eloise walked out into the darkness. The moon had not yet risen, so she walked gingerly across the rough ground to the steep bank of the stream but rather than climb down into it, she walked along the top, calling out softly, 'Monsieur, are you there? Monsieur?' several times, but there was no reply. Just as she was about to admit defeat and return to the house, she was startled, almost dropping her burden, as a tall and imposing figure rose up from the ground in front of her. Stifling a squeak of terror, she staggered on the brink, close to tumbling down into the stream, but a massive hand engulfed her arm and set her back firmly on her feet.

'Madame, I did not introduce myself this morning. My name is Phil, of His Majesty's Royal Navy. Is that my dinner I can smell?

Chapter 11

Phil was famished, and the stew disappeared in a flash, washed down with the coffee. They sat down, side by side, on the bank while he ate, and she watched him, surreptitiously, as he concentrated on his food. He was a fine physical specimen, there was no doubt of that, head and shoulders above her and more. His French was a little comical, and he would never be taken for a native, but he was polite, so the least she could do was to be polite in return. Clarisse had been quite taken with him, she could tell, so perhaps there was more to this outsized Englishman than met the eye.

He finished his hurried meal and turned to her, 'Madame, I am sorry to have imposed myself upon you and your family, and I will leave as soon as the gentleman from the Résistance arrives. You will not see me again, for I would not wish to put you and your husband and children into any more danger'.

The sentiment was beautifully expressed, even if the pronunciation was less than perfect, and Eloise found herself responding in kind, 'Ah, Monsieur, it was an accident, I know, that you found your way to our door, and I am happy that you understand why you cannot stay any longer with us. As for my husband, he was killed defending France, and Clarisse and Gilbert have kindly taken us in'. Now why did I tell him that, she pondered, I could have left him believing that Henri was still alive, perhaps away working. Too late now.

'I am sorry to hear about your husband, Madame. You have two beautiful children, and he would be a very proud man. They are happy and curious, just how children should be'.

How kind this sailor was, she thought. 'He never saw his daughter, and his son does not remember him, I am afraid. The war has taken him from us, and they will never know him'. Eloise was reminded, as she spoke, of how tired she was of being brave and having to cope, and how hard her life had become.

She told him of her life at the chateau, of the brutish Brauer and the thoughtfulness of Hans, and of having to leave her children in the care of her kind-hearted friends, and sometimes not speaking to them for days because they were asleep whenever she was in the house. She did not know how it was going to end, and what sort of a life would her children have, brought up in this chaos.

Phil listened attentively, not saying a word, as the words poured out of her. After a while, Eloise remembered herself, and became conscious of the quiet man sitting comfortably next to her, apparently soaking up her distress. She felt embarrassed, revealing her pain to a stranger, but he gently brushed off her apologies, 'We all need someone to talk to, Madame, and I am happy that it was me, although if someone had told me yesterday that I would sitting on a damp hillside in Brittany tonight, talking to a French lady, I would not have believed them!' They both laughed, for it was true, war could set off the strangest chains of events.

'And you, Monsieur, your wife will worry about you when you do not return to England'.

Phil laughed, 'I have no wife, Madame, I've been too busy in the Navy to get married'.

'I thought that you sailors had a wife in every port?' she asked, mischievously.

'Not this one. One day perhaps, when the war is won'.

They sat in companionable silence for a few more minutes, broken eventually by Gilbert's voice, quietly calling for them, and they made their way back down to the house. Pierre Galou had arrived.

His plan, as he explained it, was to guide Phil back over the fields to his house. It had never been searched by the Boche, so was probably safe, at least for now. Phil could stay there for a few days, any longer than that and he would have to be moved on to another safe house. He, Pierre, would speak to London by wireless and perhaps, in a little time, his friends would come to collect him.

Phil had another idea, thought up while he was sitting out there on the hillside. He was less convinced than Galou that his presence would remain a secret for very long in this tiny community, and he wasn't happy to put other people's lives at risk in concealing or rescuing him.

'Monsieur Galou, I am a sailor, and my natural home is the sea. If you can find me a small boat tomorrow, with an engine or a sail, I don't care which, I will disappear into the Channel and find my own way back to England. You will not need to hide me for more than twenty-four hours. Can you do that?'

Galou shrugged, 'Yes, there are sail boats to spare here, either their owners are dead or they have stopped fishing because of the Germans. I could find something for you but are you sure? There are E-boats in Brest that patrol up here, not every night perhaps. If one of those saw you.....'

'I will take my chance, Monsieur. If I can get out into open water, there is a chance that my own Navy would find me first'. It was agreed, after more discussion, that Galou would find a boat for him in the morning, and that if he sailed after sunset, he could, with a kind wind, be halfway or further across the Channel by daylight.

Eloise had listened in fascination, but then in horror, as the English sailor explained his plan. It sounded threadbare to her, and so reliant upon good fortune that its chances of success were surely very small. She wanted him to leave, because his continued presence threatened their safety, but surely there was a better plan?

She said nothing, but her expression must have betrayed her thoughts, for as Phil prepared to leave with Galou, exchanging hugs and handshakes all round, he caught her eye. The other three were talking to each other and took no particular notice as they spoke to each other.

'Madame Eloise, thank you for your kindness. I hope that happier days will come to you and to your children, and who knows, we may meet again'.

Eloise did not know quite what to say but somehow, the words took over, 'Travel safely, Monsieur Phil, and come back to France soon'. With those few words, Phil was gone.

He and Galou cut across the fields towards the Frenchman's house but halfway there, he decided to make a small diversion. Soon, they were looking down and across to the chateau, at the same angle from which Eloise had spied Quiniou leaving, but further up the hill and above the trees. They were at least three times further away than she had been, but the view was less obstructed. Cars were visible outside the building, and as they settled down on the grass, Galou explained to Phil why he had brought them there. Eloise had been sent home early that evening, and the Boche would not do that from the kindness of their hearts! They might be planning something and did not want her, however harmless, on the premises. Perhaps there was someone whom they did not wish her to see. They would give it one hour, if Monsieur had no objection, and watch for who came out of the chateau.

They had been waiting for almost the full hour, and Galou was beginning to think about leaving, when abruptly, a bright light flooded the doorway of the chateau, someone was leaving! A tall, thin figure, a civilian, came out first, and Galou cursed quietly as he recognised Quiniou, even at this distance.

'There is the traitor, Monsieur Phil', he whispered, 'I did not wish to believe Eloise but she was correct. He will have to die'.

Phil glanced across at his companion, 'I could hit him from here', hefting his rifle, 'but I wouldn't give much for our chances of getting away afterwards, what do you reckon?'

Galou was tempted, but shook his head, 'No, it would cause more trouble than it is worth. I will tell my comrades to say nothing to him, but his time will come'.

They saw Quiniou climb into his car and drive away, soon followed by two more civilians, and this time, they were people that Galou did not know. They wore overcoats and hats and were treated with respect by the German officer who was seeing them off, so maybe they were Gestapo or some other plain clothes service. Something was being cooked up, that was certain, but it could be anything. At least they now knew for certain that Quiniou had changed sides.

They were back at Galou's cottage within a further ten minutes, and although it was now approaching midnight, he took a good look outside to make sure that no one was around before preparing his wireless for transmission. It was hidden in a corner of his loft, under a heap of timber, and with an aerial threaded out between the stone tiles, and out onto the roof. It did not look like the most secure hiding place to Phil, being an obvious place to hide something, in his opinion, but he said nothing, for Galou must know his business.

'Monsieur Phil, I will tell London to expect a package, that's you, in seventy-two hours. They will understand that a package can only travel by sea and we will hope that someone will be waiting for you, out in the Channel'.

Phil was aghast, 'Pierre, I cannot stay with you for seventy-two hours, it is too dangerous. We said twenty-four….'

'Yes, we did, but do you think that I would say twenty-four hours in my message? Of course not. If the Boche are listening, we don't want them on alert at this time tomorrow night, do we? London will know it is twenty-four hours but the Boche will not. Ingenious, eh?' Phil was not convinced, it all seemed rather school-boyish to him, and the Germans were not schoolboys, far from it.

'Do not be concerned, mon brave', continued Galou, 'the message will be coded, and unless the Germans break the code quickly, they will never know about you. All we need now is a boat for you, and calm weather'.

To give him his due, Galou's coding was quick and his Morse rapid, and he received an immediate acknowledgement. He hid the wireless away again, and led Phil out of the loft, and outside to an outhouse, where he could sleep. 'It is safer for you. If by some ill-chance we are raided, run straight over the hill behind us. It is two kilometres to the sea, and directly ahead of you is Beg ar Spins, just a house or two. A few boats are moored there, so….'. He shrugged, 'Far better that you get a good sleep, and I arrange a boat for you'.

Phil slept solidly, in danger or not, and was woken by Galou, who handed him a bowl of coffee and a piece of bread and cheese. 'I drink mine in the estaminet every morning, and I will be missed if I don't go there now. After that, I will find a boat. Stay out of sight until I return. If we leave here at 2200, you will be at sea in one hour, with hours of darkness in front of you'.

It sounded as much as Phil could hope for, and he settled down for the day. Galou's cottage was isolated, at the end of a muddy lane, so there were no passers-by and his day was uninterrupted. He was a lucky man, able to sleep at any hour, and the time passed quickly.

Galou returned, and alerted Phil to his presence with a cheerful Breton song. It was late afternoon, and as he prepared fresh fish and potatoes for their dinner, he told Phil about his day.

'Quiniou worked on me again at the café, asking me to put him in touch with the Résistance, saying if I could not help him, who could? This time, now I know where his true allegiance lies, I told him that I know nothing of the Résistance, and that he should think of his own safety. I asked him, what would the Germans think if they heard that he was asking these questions? He was putting himself in danger! The stupid bastard, he was so angry, his face was purple! I told him not to ask me again and left. I hope that's the end of it but who knows?'

He continued, 'There's a little boat for you at Beg ar Spins, very small, just four metres but she doesn't leak too much and the sail has another season in it. I've put water on board'.

The chateau was a hive of activity already, when Eloise arrived for her work that morning, and as she was putting her coat away, the two Gestapo drove up, and this time they were accompanied by four more of their kind. She and Hans were ordered by Brauer to produce more breakfast than usual, and to keep coffee coming until they were told to stop.

The dining room, immediately after breakfast, had been turned into a meeting room for the day, and as Eloise trailed in and out all morning with trays of cakes and coffee, apparently invisible to the participants, she could not help but overhear some of their discussion, and to glance at a map that they had pinned to a wall.

The map was straightforward; it covered their part of Brittany, with Brest in the south-west corner and Morlaix in the north-east. Her eyes automatically located Lilia and she noticed a blue circle drawn further down the coast, perhaps three kilometres. What did that mean? She could not look any closer, not in a room with six Gestapo and eight Wehrmacht soldiers, but it intrigued her. She knew where the circle was, in relation to Madame Le Roux's house, and would ask her later. She overheard conversation also and picked out something about U-Boot-Besatzung. It didn't mean anything to her, it sounded technical, but she would remember the phrase.

It became clearer at the end of the evening, when Brauer stopped her, just as she was leaving to go home. 'Madame, your work is changing. Ten days from today, you will spend three days in every seven at Manoir du Vaugalain. Do you know where that is?'

She guessed that it was something to do with the blue circle on the map but shook her head, it was better to continue to be ignorant.

'The Manoir will be used by select groups of servants of the Reich for three days together. They are the bravest of our warriors, and your job will be to cook for them. You will be provided with food of the highest quality and you will put your very best dishes on the dining table. You have been selected for this honour because you are the most skilled cook in the district, but remember', and his voice hardened, 'if you do not do your job well, or if there are complaints, I will hold you responsible. Think of your family'.

Eloise summoned up enough courage to ask a question, 'How many people will there be, sir? If I am to cook alone'.

'Forty-five at most, Madame, but do not be concerned, Hans will accompany you, and I will find two more orderlies who will do most of the fetching and carrying. There will be no excuses'.

So this what the meetings had been about. Whoever these warriors were, the army and the Gestapo together were guaranteeing their safety. Had this been why Quiniou had been trying to infiltrate the Résistance, and why the raid on the Île de Vierge lighthouse had caused less chaos than she had expected?

Eloise nodded goodnight to Hans and en route to the villa, on an impulse, steered her bicycle up the lane where Galou lived. The Résistance should hear of this! Everything was dark at the cottage, so perhaps Galou was out but she hammered on the door anyway and called out, 'Galou, Galou, are you there?'

A voice from behind the door called out, 'Who is it at this hour? Go away'.

'Galou, it is Eloise Beauchêne, now open the damned door, I don't have much time'.

A shamefaced Galou opened the door to Eloise, and motioned her in, 'I am sorry, my dear, but I must be careful, our English friend is just about to leave'. Across the room, dimly lit by an oil lamp, stood Phil, pistol in hand.

'I hope that you are not going to shoot me, Monsieur Phil?' she asked, with a smile.

'Certainly not, Madame', he replied, grinning back at her and tucking the pistol back in his belt.

She was about to say something else to the Englishman but Galou was conscious that time was short for Phil to leave. 'What is it, Eloise? It must be something important, be quick, we must go'.

Eloise recalled her intention, and dragged her eyes back to Galou, 'I am sorry, Pierre, I was surprised to see Monsieur Phil here', and went on to describe the meetings at the chateau and Brauer's orders. Both men's interests were engaged, especially when she repeated the German phrase that was such a mystery to her.

'Madame', explained Phil, 'U-Boot-Besatzung means submarine crew. It sounds like the Boche are planning to bring their sub crews to this manoir for rest and recuperation between voyages'.

'Oh la la', exclaimed Galou, 'what a target they would make! What a blow we could strike!'

Phil agreed, but there was no more time to discuss it. Eloise had to get home to her children, and Phil had a boat to sail, so while Galou made up a little package of food for Phil to take with him, they said their goodbyes.

They both started to speak at the same instant and laughed together in their brief embarrassment.

'Madame Eloise', started Phil, 'I had not expected to see you again so soon'.

'Nor I you, Monsieur. I pray that you will travel safely back to England tonight'.

Phil grinned, 'I have webbed feet, Madame, I am sure that I will'. He took a breath, then jumped in with his boots on, as Geraint might say, for he might never have the opportunity again, 'Eloise, I hope very much that we will meet again, it has been a great pleasure for me to spend a little time with you and your children'.

There was a pause, and Phil was beginning to think to himself, Watson, you've planted your size twelves just where they're not wanted again, then Eloise smiled in return, 'Beautifully said, Phil, your French is improving and yes, I hope too that this war will allow you to visit us again. My son was most upset that you had left him', and with that, she pecked his cheek and let herself out.

At the closing of the door, Galou came back in from the kitchen. 'Ah', he said, 'Eloise has gone. She is a real daughter of France, that one. Do you not agree, Phil?' 'I do, Pierre, I do'. Phil had always been described, sometimes to his face, as a rough diamond, but it seemed to him that he was losing some of his sharp edges.

Neither Eloise nor Phil were aware of it yet, but they would meet again and sooner than either of them might have imagined.

Chapter 12

It was a subdued group that arrived back in Poole Harbour as daylight was breaking. The raid had achieved its objectives, and while casualties of one dead and one missing would be regarded by the hierarchy as both moderate and acceptable, given the success of the operation, Tom and the rest took it personally.

They were met at the harbour by Major Barton, who shook everyone's hands as they climbed up from the MTB and directed them to a lorry that would take them back to Anderson Manor. The prisoners were handed over to some unnamed soldiers who took them off for interrogation, along with the code books and signals logs that had accompanied them.

Half an hour later, Tom led his men into the converted ballroom where the first debrief would take place. All they wanted to do was to eat and sleep but Major Barton needed to hear the essentials of what had happened. There would be opportunities later to dissect the detail, and to look at how things might have been done differently, but for now, the CO needed an outline.

Tom took the lead, bringing in the others individually when they were better placed to describe a part of the action. He wanted to know what Bud had meant when had commented that Pearson had 'screwed up' but decided that he would ask him privately later, he had no wish to put him in an awkward position in front of the major.

He did not have to wait for long, because Bud followed him into breakfast and brought his food to the same table, for there was no separate Sergeants' Mess. 'Sergeant', he started, 'I got to tell you why I said that Captain Pearson screwed up'. The others quietened down and listened, curious to hear his explanation.

He blushed, not wanting the attention of the experienced soldiers around him, but he knew that he had to justify his comment, even if it was made in the heat of the moment.

'He should not have been killed, Sergeant, leastways, not how it happened. I was a yard behind him going up those stairs, and when he hit the landing at the top, he was dead before he took a shot'.

'What's your point, Bud?' asked George, 'what do you think he should have done?'

'I guess he should have used his head and taken a peek from the top of the stairs, to see what he was up against, rolled a grenade into them first, then finished them off. He didn't think, Sergeant, he screwed up and got himself killed, and now we're short of a captain'.

There was a short silence as everyone considered what Bud had said. Pearson had been a brave, resourceful soldier, Tom silently agreed, but Bud was right, aggression on its own was not enough. It needed to be tempered with some cool thinking. There were times when an all-out rush was the only way but it had to be planned, not instinctual.

'Out of the mouth of babes', commented George, 'you might well be right, but if I was you, young Bud, I would be careful who I said it to. I have a feeling that the Major wouldn't be so keen to hear it, what with Pearson just dead and such, he might take it the wrong way'.

'What about Phil?' Tom broached the question that no one wanted to face. Phil had done his job and more, for delaying the Germans in their boat, thus giving the others time to escape, was the right decision but for all they knew, Phil was dead on that piddling little island.

Geraint shook his head decisively, and everyone looked at him. 'Phil is alive. I cannot explain how I know. All I can say is that I would know if he was dead, and his time has not yet come'. It was a strong feeling, and he had no idea himself where it came from but it was there. Phil was not dead, he just knew it. He seemed so certain, and everyone there hoped that he was right, so no one argued.

Sleep was welcome, followed by a full debrief in the evening. Major Barton wanted more detail this time, and to everyone's surprise, he picked up himself on the way that Pearson had died.

'Any comments on the bust into the old lighthouse? If I understand it correctly, Captain Pearson ran headlong into heavy fire without any knowledge of what he might be facing, warning having been given to any defenders upstairs by the firing from downstairs. Am I correct?'

'Sir'.

'Captain Pearson will be honoured for his gallantry, of course, but in my opinion, he might have achieved his objective of taking the building and possibly survived if he had considered his position rather more carefully. Does anyone disagree?'

No one spoke. 'Private Wilson?'

'Yes, sir?'

'You acted correctly and quite possibly saved the operation. If those two upstairs had put you out of action too, we could be talking about much higher casualties. There will be a Mention in Dispatches for you, congratulations. Now, what about PO Watson? The decision to leave him to hold off the approaching enemy was correct, Sergeant Lane, and you have my full support. He was the only member of the team with a weapon accurate over long range, and that is something that we need to look at in future planning. Now, from what you've told me, he could be either dead or wounded, a prisoner or on the run, there's no way of telling. He'll be posted as Missing in Action and we'll see if any information filters back. I would be surprised if his actions in taking out the enemy at the top of the lighthouse and holding off the boat were not recognised as deserving of a gong, and I hope that he will be able to collect it in person one day'.

The room was silent. They were pleased for Bud but Phil's loss had hit them hard. Everyone knew that losing comrades was part of the business, especially in close-contact, high risk operations of the type that the SSRF and SOE were involved in. It was something that they had to face and accept, but it was nothing that they would ever become used to. Working in small teams brought people even closer together, and that made losses more painful.

'Thank you for your efforts, gentlemen', concluded Barton, 'the raid was a success, despite the casualties, and I congratulate you. You're excused from duties for the next two days but travel no further than Poole, in case I need you in a hurry. Dismissed'.

As the men filed out of the room, Major Barton beckoned Tom over, 'Sergeant, I will be replacing Captain Pearson as soon as possible, more likely a lieutenant than a captain, not enough captains to go around, you see. It might take a week or more but I can't think that there will be another raid for some time, so there will be plenty of opportunity for more training'.

The next day, a truck took them to Poole, for no one wanted to sit about in the Manor, it made more sense to go to town and forget about the war for a few hours. That was the intention but no one could clear it from their minds, whatever they did.

George and Tom went to the cinema, to watch a new film from America called 'Citizen Kane', while Geraint and Bud settled for a walk around the harbour, followed by a few pints of Palmer's bitter beer in the King Charles Inn. They were just into their second pint when George and Tom walked in to join them, George complaining, 'This bugger wouldn't settle for the film, wriggling about like his pants were on fire, that's a shilling wasted', and Tom retorting, 'You weren't much better, you old devil'. They were both too preoccupied with what might have happened to Phil to pay any attention to a film, or a movie as Bud called it, and had decided that drowning their sorrows was a better idea.

They had scarcely taken a sip when their driver came bustling into the pub, 'There you are, I knew you'd be in a boozer somewhere'. He was not due to collect them for another three hours, so something must be up. 'Major Barton wants you back at the Manor, briefing at 1500'. He did not say why, and no one asked, for Barton would not have told him, but it must be important to bring them back early.

Barton was waiting for them in the dining room, 'Sorry to bugger up your day off but something's come in and you won't want to miss it'. He had their attention, and the room was utterly still and silent.

'SOE had a wireless message last night from an agent in Brittany, just on the mainland from that lighthouse. It was short, telling them to 'expect your package' in twenty-four hours. What does it mean? Well, a package always means a person, usually an agent or a refugee, and the only way to send it, noting that he did not ask for air transport, would be by sea. He wrote 'your package' which means that the person is known to SOE. This is the interesting part'. He paused.

'The only recent action by SOE in Brittany was your raid the night before last, so there is a chance, but no more than that, that someone connected with the raid is coming over the water'. The silence in the room grew even more profound.

'It could be an agent from another part of France who has travelled to Brittany for a quiet run home, but it could also mean that SOE's local man has been captured or turned, and it's a trap. It could even be our PO Watson'. Not a word was spoken, for it was as if everyone was holding their breath.

'Plymouth is a shorter, more direct route but I have taken it upon myself to volunteer you for the job of locating this 'package' and bringing him or her back to England'.

Tom spoke for everyone, 'Thank you, sir. When do we leave?'

'2100, from Poole, same MTB, same skipper. Draw your weapons from the armoury, and this time, take a Bren and rifles. Plenty of machine guns on the boat but another one wouldn't hurt. What else? You'll be taking the dory with you, in case you need to go inshore, but let's hope not, eh'.

He continued, 'Look out for fishing boats, anything else small that might float, this 'package' might be a passenger or on their own, we don't know. It's on the cards that there might be E-boats about, from Brest or St-Malo, but you will just have to keep a good watch. They'll out-gun you for certain. Any questions?'

'How long will we have, sir?' asked Geraint.

'Skipper has orders to head for home at 0400 at the very latest, whether you find anyone or not. Any more questions? No? There will be a meal served for you in an hour, you'll leave here at 1930. Dismissed'.

They had four hours, long enough to draw and prepare their arms, and to sight them in at the range behind the old house. George was allocated the Bren, his favourite tool of war, and by the time he had finished with it, he was confident that he would hit anything that he aimed at, as long as it wasn't too far over the 600-yard range of the weapon. Everyone else took Lee-Enfield rifles and pistols, for it was possible that they would have to go ashore or board another vessel.

'What do you reckon, mate?' asked George, as the MTB motored away from its mooring in Poole Harbour, 'do you think there's a chance it might be Phil we're after?'

'Your guess is as good as mine, George', Tom replied, 'but if anyone could do it, it's him. Geraint thinks he's alive and by God, I hope he's right'.

Although waning, there was still considerable moonlight reflecting from a calm sea, and their vessel made good time across the Channel, with no sightings of the enemy, in the air or on the water. They were buzzed, then circled, by a twin-engined aircraft at midnight, but the intention was friendly, with a message flashed down to the boat with a signalling lamp, before climbing off to the south-west, in the direction of the Bay of Biscay. Tom was in the wheelhouse with the skipper, a lieutenant, and not being familiar with Morse, asked him what the message had been. 'Just a comedian from Coastal Command, Sergeant, the full message was 'Does your mother know you're out this late?' Cheeky bastard'.

By 0200, they were four nautical miles off the Breton coast, with look-outs scouring the horizon and the sky at every point of the compass. The skipper, slowing to reduce noise and wake, gradually closed the coast, and the imposing Phare de l'Île Vierge, the towering lighthouse, slowly hove into view. No one had thought that they would see it again so soon, but even unlit, it acted as an unmissable signpost.

For more than ninety minutes, the skipper patrolled a three-mile line, south-west to north-east then return, up and down, up and down but with no result, for the sea remained empty. He turned to Tom, 'Sergeant, the wind is from the south-west and it's strengthening, so it's possible a small vessel could have been blown further to the north-east than I've allowed. I'm proposing extending the line a further five miles in that direction, but if we don't spot anyone, well, that's it, I'm afraid'. It would be after 0400 by then, and time to be gone. Tom couldn't argue, they had been within touching distance of the enemy coast for more than two hours, and with a long journey back to port.

They were reaching the final mile of their extended search when the look-out in the bows shouted, 'Broad on the port bow! Sail, 600 yards'. Everyone looked in that direction, and those with binoculars could just see the faint white patch of what could be a sail in the distance. The lieutenant opened the throttle and within seconds, even the naked eye could make out a small sailing vessel. It hove to as the MTB closed up on it, and a figure could be seen, sitting at the tiller in the stern.

'Quel bateau? Quel bateau?' shouted the skipper, over the rumble of the engines, only to be stunned into silence as the helmsman replied, 'Well it's not the Good Ship fucking Lollipop, I'll tell you that much!' The lieutenant shone a big torch down into the boat and Tom almost cheered! There was the familiar figure of PO Phil Watson, sitting in the stern with his rifle across his lap.

It was a few seconds work for the crew to throw a line to Phil to make fast in the little crab-boat, then pull the tiny vessel alongside. The relief was enormous, on every side, but just as Phil was explaining how his craft had looked big enough when it was tied to the pier, but had seemed to shrink the further out to sea that he had sailed, another lookout, sharp-eyed and alert, roared out.

'Bow-wave, forward of the starboard beam, closing fast', then a second later, 'Two bow-waves, two bow waves!' It could only be pursuit. The Lieutenant opened up the taps and the MTB surged forward, her bows gradually lifting from the water as her speed increased. He ordered all but his deck-crew below and the pursuit began.

The moon was going down but still shed some light, and the pursuing vessels were soon identified as E-boats, the German equivalent of the British MTB, except that they were bigger, faster and more heavily armed. The first indication of this was a shell-burst to port followed by another to starboard. The skipper judged that the next one would be a hit, so turned hard to port, decks awash as she dipped into the waves. Sure enough, the third shell dropped where she would have been, had she not made the turn, but the skipper knew that every turn lost him distance, and that the range would soon be point-blank.

The MTB had twin Vickers machine guns in her stern, and the Lieutenant gave the order to open fire. Every fifth round was a tracer, and the first volley could be seen hitting the sea, short of the pursuing German vessel. The E-boat was closing though, and by the third burst, rounds could be seen bouncing off the hull of the leading chaser. Their pursuers were not idle though, and a heavy machine gun opened up from the German. It was either a lucky shot, or a fantastic one, but this first burst smashed into the machine gun mounting and ricocheted, leaving the gunners prone and bleeding upon the deck, and their now silent machinegun pointing harmlessly up into the air.

Tom and others, below deck, felt the impact of the hits and the subsequent silence of the defence. Without a word or an order, they climbed out onto the afterdeck and set to.

Tom took the twin Vickers, with Geraint and Bud as his loaders, and quickly started returning fire. The racket from the two guns was deafening, with the enormous recoil absorbed by the mount but it was not long before Tom had his range and was registering hits.

George had his beloved Bren, and quickly set it up on the transom. He had used steadier gun platforms, and he was at the mercy of the motion of the boat, but every time the closest E-boat passed through his sights, it received a short burst. There was no revealing tracer for George but such was his experience that he was sure of his accuracy. Phil had his rifle but decided that he would be of more use as George's loader, so between them, the three machine guns returned a heavy fire.

Shells were still coming in their direction, but at a reduced rate, for it seemed that the German gunners were perhaps discouraged by what was coming their way. It would only take another hit though to tip the odds in their favour.

No one could say why it happened, perhaps George had put a shot through the German helmsman's shutter, or maybe Tom's concentrated fire had hit a control, but without warning, the first E-boat swung hard to port, exposing the length of its starboard flank. Tom and George, never ones to miss an opportunity, fired sustained bursts into the hull and the superstructure, and left their pursuer wallowing in the water.

That was only half the battle, and the other E-boat, previously partially hidden behind its comrade, began to overhaul the British vessel. Whoever commanded the German boat was no fool, for after shortening the range to a half-mile, he hung back and commenced firing his cannon, out of effective range of George and Tom with their rifle-calibre weapons.

The skipper had opened up the engines as far as he could and the MTB was flying, but it could only be a matter of time before one of the incoming shells damaged an engine, and then she would be dead in the water, or close to it. This was clear in his mind, but the only tactic he had left was to come about as fast as possible, hope to find himself on the beam of his pursuer and then bring the forward machine guns into play, along with those in the stern. It would almost certainly fail, given the disparity in armour and firepower but the alternative, of just ploughing on until the end inevitably came, was not the Navy way. Just as he was about to roar the order for the most rapid 'Hard a'port' that he had ever given, he was deafened by the thunderous roar of aero engines passing over his head.

Looking up, the aircraft was a dark shadow in the sky, and it was impossible to tell if it was friend or foe, but he saw it bank steeply ahead of them, then return, diving over their heads, heading straight for the E-boat that was still pursuing them. Even above the roar of their own engines, and the clamour of the plane's twin engines, everyone heard the thud-thud-thud of cannon fire and saw the sudden bursts of flame and debris leaping from the German vessel. The plane carved around in another tight circle, and this time, attacked from the beam, piercing the hull at will. As it turned for the third time, the men on the MTB could see that the E-boat was awash and sinking, shattered by the tremendous firepower of the attacker.

The plane circled again, and this time, the skipper's signaller flashed up a brief message, 'Thank you, the drinks are on us', and was answered, 'I will tell mother you are coming home'. The plane passed over them once more, dipping its wings, then headed north, climbing steadily.

'Coastal Command again, probably the same Beaufighter that checked us on the way down. They go out after subs in Biscay, flying low, and it was just our luck that they thought they would investigate all this shooting on the way home. I wouldn't have given us another ten minutes'.

'What about survivors?' asked Tom. The lieutenant looked at Tom, amused. 'What about them? The other fella is still around somewhere, he can pick 'em up, we've got to get back before another pair of those buggers get after us'.

The original gunners from the twin Vickers had been carried below, where Geraint and Phil worked on their wounds. One had been shot through the cheek, losing teeth as the bullet clipped his bottom jaw before exiting through his mouth, and all they were able to do was to fasten a dressing over the wound and help him to spit out the blood that was filling his mouth. The other man had a round through his upper arm, shattering the bone but somehow missing the artery. His pain was excruciating but after numbing him with morphine, they were able to bandage and then immobilise his arm.

First aid completed, they sat back and looked at each other as the MTB hammered northwards.

'Mate', started Phil, 'it don't feel right that these chaps got shot looking for me, just one fella'.

Geraint grinned back at him, 'Don't you worry about that, my friend. No one knew that it was you, all we knew was that a package was coming, it could have been a glamorous spy or a case of champagne!' but Phil was not amused.

Geraint picked up his mood, and continued more soberly, 'Phil, these two boys got shot but there's one, maybe two E-boats that won't be fighting anyone. It's war, you know that, and we have to kill Nazis when we can. Tonight would have been worthwhile, even if we'd missed you, my friend'.

Chapter 13

Work continued unabated at the chateau for the next week. The Gestapo would call in on most days, usually just before lunch, provoking Hans to remark, 'They think it's their bloody canteen, the scrounging bastards', and Eloise struggled not to laugh. On one particular day, they were joined by four officers in elegant, dark blue uniforms, their jackets trimmed with gold rings around the arms, and caps with gold braid at the peak. They seemed very grand, making everyone else look rather shabby, and were treated, at least to their faces, with great respect by Brauer and the others. He came through to the kitchen and told her, in his bad French, that they were Kriegsmarine officers, here to inspect both the Manoir du Vaugalain and her cooking, so she must make sure that everything is perfect. She did her best, and as there were no complaints, she guessed that her efforts had been judged acceptable.

At the end of that week, she was transported, with Hans, to the Manoir, and shown around the impressive building. The kitchen was more spacious and better equipped than in the chateau and there were two dining rooms, one for officers and one for NCOs and ratings. There was a large wine cellar, already stocked with the best of French wines, and in a cold store, sides of beef and venison were hanging up, ready to be jointed and cooked.

Even the furnishings were of a quality not often seen in this part of France and Eloise was reminded of the luxury hotel in Paris that she and Henri had stayed in for one night on their honeymoon. There were beautiful carpets and acres of polished wood, made elegant with Louis XIV furniture and beautiful tapestries decorating the walls.

Brauer took Eloise to one side, 'You have the rest of the day to find out what else you need. Crockery, cutlery, linen, anything that you need, you must tell me before the end of the day and I will find it for you. Madame, you will need to organise a menu for up to forty-five men for three days and nights. Bread, cheeses, vegetables, coffee, dairy, they will all be delivered daily, and you will receive fresh fish, seafood and oysters for day three of their stay. You will work the same hours as you do at the chateau but you will have two more men, with Hans, to help you, preparing food and with service, serving drinks, washing dishes, all of that work'.

He paused for effect, 'This duty is an honour for all of us, Madame, and make sure that you do not fail me. The men that you will be looking after are the heroes of the Reich, and there will be no mistakes'.

Eloise quickly understood that Brauer had much riding upon the success or failure of this venture, and that for it to succeed, he must be able to guarantee her contribution. She would test him.

She looked him in the face, 'Sir, you had promised to pay me 800 francs every week for my work at the chateau but you have not'. His face started to colour with rage, and she hurriedly continued, 'I know that you have been very busy, sir, and perhaps you have forgotten but now with this vital work, do you think that you might remember that promise, sir, for this work will take all of my skill'.

'I promised you nothing, woman!' he snapped back, 'and do not push me, I am warning you'. This was his normal, arrogant self and Eloise stepped back, thinking that she had pushed him too far, but she had not, for a false smile appeared on his face, and he continued, 'If your work here goes well, you will receive 800 francs at the end of the third day, for every week that you are here. I know that you take food home, with the connivance of Hans, and that can continue but I warn you, any failure on your part will be punished severely. Do you understand?'

Now was the time to look meek, and she did so, staring down at her feet and answering, 'Yes, sir', in a tone that she hoped sounded obedient enough. There was her proof, for by his standards, he had been almost conciliatory. He needed her, and she would use that knowledge to her own advantage.

The remainder of the day was frantic, inventing menus and listing the items and quantities of food that she needed to fulfil them, while simultaneously conducting, with Hans, an inventory of what had already been supplied. It was a long list that she gave to Brauer later that evening, but he scarcely looked at it, telling her that everything would be delivered to the Manoir by tomorrow evening.

She left the chateau at the usual hour, and on impulse, cycled up the lane towards Pierre Galou's cottage. She saw a curtain twitch as she knocked on the door, and Galou quickly let her in. 'What is it, Eloise, I thought that you did not want anything to do with the Résistance'.

It was true, she had always said that, citing the safety of her children, but it seemed to her now that she was allowing herself to become involved. Was it circumstance, because she happened to work for the Germans and could not help but learn of their plans? Or was she deliberately setting out to do what she could to sabotage and cause them difficulties? Talking to Galou felt like the latter, and she reminded herself that she must keep some distance between herself and any action that the Résistance might take.

'Do you know if Monsieur Phil reached England safely?'

'Ah, our English Hercules, I thought that I detected a little frisson between you!'

He was joking, but Eloise bristled at his impertinence, and he stepped back, holding up his arms in mock surrender, 'Just a little humour, Madame, nothing more! And in answer to your question, I had a message from London the following night, 'package delivered', so I think we can say that he is safely back with his friends'. He did not mention that London had also asked for more details about the submariners.

A feeling of relief swept through Eloise, which surprised her, and she quickly changed the subject. 'Pierre, I start work at the Manoir du Vaugalain on the day after tomorrow, for four days, one day in preparation, then three days feeding up to forty-five men. There will be myself and three German orderlies looking after them'.

'What about guards?' he asked, 'they will post guards to look after their heroes'.

She had not thought of that, 'I don't know, I have not heard'. Damn! Of course, they would be guarded, especially if the Reich thought so much of them.

'Then observe carefully when you are there', he instructed, 'count them and learn where they are stationed. If you can get an idea of how they are armed, so much the better, and dates, I must know the dates that these submariners are coming. Will the dates be fixed, or will they vary, depending upon crews returning to base?'

He was asking her to be a spy, something that she had bawled out Monsieur Hervé for trying to do but perhaps something had changed inside her, for she had not been in close contact with the German soldiers then and had not yet witnessed the treatment that they had meted out to the Hamon boy.

Nevertheless, 'Pierre, I must think of my babies, I cannot be identified with you or the Résistance, for they have no one but me'.

Galou smiled sympathetically, 'I understand, Madame. You will only speak to me, and no one else will know that we are in contact. Only return here when you have the information for me. Say nothing to Hervé or Madame Le Roux, then they cannot betray you'.

Eloise started to say that they would never dream of betraying her, but he interrupted, 'Don't be naïve, Madame. The Gestapo can make anyone talk, they are experts'.

'Then how do I know that you will not betray me, Pierre?'

He answered, 'Because, Madame, they will not take me alive. I will destroy myself first', then, 'Don't look shocked, they would kill me anyway, whatever I told them, so I would just be, ah, hurrying things along. Now, you must leave me and get home, or Hervé will be out looking for you. Come back if you have information, otherwise you must stay away. Your submariners would be a juicy target but there are others'.

She nodded and left, leaving Galou to ponder. She could certainly be of great help to the patriotic cause but could he keep her so far in the background that no one would suspect her? He doubted it. If the submariners were attacked, she would be an obvious suspect and would be interrogated to her death.

Eloise worked for one more day at the chateau, spending much of it instructing the orderlies who would take her place in the kitchen while she was at the Manoir. Many were the smiles that she hid as she instructed, for Brauer and his officer friends were in for a shock, having become used to good French cuisine since Eloise had cooked for them. They would be eating plain food, bereft of the subtle sauces and particular combinations which made Breton food so good. The submariners would not be popular with their Wehrmacht comrades!

She and Hans spent the first morning at the Manoir in organising and storing the lavish supplies that Brauer had supplied. There were items here that she had not seen for years, Pâté de Foie Gras, truffles, both black and white, that must have been brought up from further south, and three enormous Bayonne hams. This was food for kings, she thought to herself, probably looted from the farmers who had produced it, or perhaps bought at a grossly reduced rate. She knew that many of the local fisherman had stopped fishing because they had been forced to sell their catch to the occupiers for a ridiculous price but their little victory had been short-lived, for many of them had then been sent to work as slave labour in the Fatherland. Meanwhile their families starved, unable to buy enough food for their needs.

The afternoon and evening were spent producing food that could sit in the cool larder for a day or two and not spoil, and she kept Hans and the other two orderlies busy, chopping and peeling vegetables, then jointing meat and poultry, while she assembled and cooked dishes, in large quantities, fit for the highest in the land.

Before she finished for the evening, Brauer came to inspect her handiwork, and despite himself, he was impressed. Securing a cook, no, a chef, with the talent that Eloise possessed was a coup, for they were hard to find in this country, and if this provision of rest and first-class food for the submariners was successful, then perhaps a promotion for himself might be close behind. Even if it was not, a soft posting in France was surely better than fighting it out against the Untermensch in Russia.

'Madam, be here at six tomorrow. Your guests will arrive mid-morning, they will want coffee and cakes. Give them lunch and dinner at whatever time they desire. You may leave at the usual time but Hans and the others will be sleeping here and can deal with any of their needs after you have left. Do you have everything that you require?'

'Yes, sir'.

'Then you may leave now. I will call in every day. If you need anything, tell Hans and he will call me.'

The following three days were among the most hectic and most pressured that Eloise had ever endured. Forty-four men, the entire crew of U-256, arrived two hours before lunch and, until they left, after breakfast on the fourth day, she and her team never stopped. Their first request to Brauer was for more hands, and Eloise soon had another two men working, for even he could see that their guess of Eloise plus three was not enough.

The difficulty, which no one had foreseen, was that the submariners, after weeks at sea, were not going to confine themselves to a strict timetable. They ate and drank heartily but when they felt the urge, not at any particular hour. Thus, lunch and dinner ran together into two buffets that the men dipped in and out of when they felt hungry. Breakfast was replaced, for at least half of the men, by a supper in the middle of the night, causing Hans to observe, quite correctly, that food and drink was being consumed over every one of the twenty-four hours.

Brauer, unhappy that his ordered plans had been sabotaged, complained to the Kapitän, and came away fuming but defeated, having been told that, 'My men have been stuck in a fucking snuff-box for nearly three months and they deserve some freedom, Unteroffizier Brauer, so fuck off, there's a good chap, and don't bother me again'.

Another problem arose, and this one was more predictable. Forty-five men, far away from home, had been confined in a submarine for eleven weeks, without female company, and Eloise was the first woman that they had been in close proximity to since coming ashore. Some of them started to loiter around the kitchen, trying to talk to her and getting in the way, hindering her work. Hans tried to encourage them to leave but no one took much notice of a mere orderly. Eventually, Eloise decided to deal with it herself.

After lunch on the second day of their stay, as she started to help Hans to clear the dining table, she deliberately caught the Kapitän's eye.

'That beef was a work of art, Madame', he commented, in good French, 'now, do you have something to say to me?'

'Thank you, sir. Sir, some of your men are following me around, trying to talk to me, stopping me from working, even trying to kiss me! If this continues, sir, I cannot work here. I am a respectable woman, sir', holding up her hand with its wedding ring, 'but I am frightened, scared that....'

He held up his hand, interrupting her, 'You must understand, Madame, that my men have been without a woman for weeks, and you are here, and they think that one thing follows on from the other, it is nature'. Eloise started to protest but he held up his hand again, 'I have not finished. You have your job to do, and you do it very well'. Turning to the officer sitting next to him, he ordered, in French for Eloise's benefit, 'This woman is strictly out of bounds. Pass the word, any infraction will be punished severely, and remind them, there are plenty of mademoiselles who will take their money in Brest'.

It was a crude demonstration of his authority, reminding his men that there would be hungry women waiting to oblige them back in port, but it was effective, for she was not bothered again.

Hans made sure that she always had food to take home for the children, and even escorted her through the guards around the house and past the ones at the gate, when it was time to leave. Eloise found that it was impossible to hate him as an enemy, for he was a genuinely kind and thoughtful man. He worked hard and, as they took a short break on the first night, to catch their breath and to drink some coffee, he showed her a photograph of round-cheeked woman, in a flowery dress, smiling at the camera. 'Meine frau', he explained, 'ma femme', as he smiled down at the image. She felt for him, so far away from his wife, but at the same time, reminded herself that his comrades had deprived her children of their father forever, and that could never be forgiven. She said nothing but he may have detected some of her emotion, for he quickly put the photograph away, muttering, 'Pardon, Madame, pardon'.

By lunchtime on the fourth day, the submariners had left, leaving the Manoir in a turmoil, and the wine cellars and larders almost empty. Brauer drafted in two more orderlies to help with the clearing up and cleaning but it was still evening before the work was all done. It would be empty now for two days, although Eloise, with Hans and another helper, would have to return on the second day to prepare food in advance.

Brauer had been congratulated by the Kapitän, who had been impressed by the comfort of the accommodation but almost overwhelmed by the quality of the food. 'Treat her well, Unteroffizier', he had advised Brauer, 'for without her artistry, this is just another comfortable hotel'. As Eloise left on that last evening, Brauer took her to one side and handed to her a small wad of notes, 'You worked well, Madame, and here is your 800 francs. You work at the chateau tomorrow but report back here with Hans on the following morning'.

Most of the guards had been withdrawn immediately the submariners had left but by then, Eloise had already learned and memorised their numbers and placement, and instead of cycling straight back to the villa, she diverted once again to Galou's cottage. He quickly let her in and listened intently as she listed everything that she had observed. She described the layout of the house in some detail then moved on to the personnel.

'There are always six men on duty, day and night, with a further six in the stable, which is their quarters. They work four hour shifts in the day, starting at six in the morning, but from six in the evening until the following morning, they change at six hours. There is no telephone or radio in the stable. What else? They eat in the stable, an orderly takes their food to them. I heard the orderlies talking, they were saying that through the night, the duty soldiers take turns at sleeping, two at a time, so for most of the night, there are only four soldiers patrolling'.

'What about arms, what do they have?' asked Galou.

'Either a rifle or small machinegun, one that they carry. I have not seen a larger machinegun but there could be one, in the stable'.

'The submariners? Are they armed?'

'The officers have pistols. I didn't see any rifles or anything like that'.

'What about a vehicle, how do the guards travel around?'

'Oh, they are brought in a truck, it drops them off before the submariners arrive on the first morning, then collects them after they have left. Two guards were left there today, that's all'.

'Do they receive any visitors, the submariners?'

'Two naval officers called and stayed for lunch on the third day, and two Gestapo with them, but they were gone by the middle of the afternoon'. She searched her memory and it was difficult, for most of the time, she had been hard at work in the kitchen.

'Brauer. He visited every evening, sometimes before dinner, sometimes after. It is his project, or he thinks it is, so he keeps an eye on everything'. She shuddered, for although she was in favour with Brauer for now, she knew that it would only last for as long as he considered her useful.

'You have done well, Eloise', commented Galou, 'and I will speak to London. Take note of anything else that you see but do not come here again, for someone is bound to notice. I will contact you'.

Chapter 14

On this occasion, the journey back to Anderson Manor was rather more light-hearted, verging upon joyful. Phil's escape and subsequent rescue had lifted everyone, and Geraint was privately congratulated by more than one of his comrades for not having given up hope for his mate's survival. Phil was delighted too, to be back among friends, but his pleasure was tempered a little by the knowledge of the risks that Eloise and Galou and the others had taken on his behalf. Humility was not a feeling that he was very familiar with, but he certainly felt it now. Tom had noticed Phil's uncharacteristic constraint and had asked him if anything was wrong.

'I must be going soft, Tom, and it was the same in Crete, come to think of it. We're the professionals, but these civilians risk everything to help us. They've got damn-all because the Jerries take everything for themselves, yet what little they have, they share it with us, then they help us to escape, even though there's no escape for them! Don't get me wrong, I'm happy to be back but it doesn't seem right somehow'.

Tom smiled at his friend's passion, 'Nor is it right, mate, but it's the way that war is. It brings out the best in some and the worst in others. If you was to ask them, would they help you again, they would say yes. If you asked them, would they have preferred you had gone to someone else for help, they would say yes again. They are as stuck with this war as we are, and the sooner it's over, the better'.

'There was a lass that helped me, Tom'.

'Of course there was. Pretty, was she?'

'Yes', Phil answered, 'but that's not what I was going to tell you'.

'Sorry, mate, fire away'.

Phil repeated Eloise's account of the 'rest and recuperation' plan for the submarine crews, and Tom knew immediately that a raid with them as the target would fit the brief of the SSRF perfectly. 'Speak to the Major, Phil, bring it up in the first briefing or speak to him privately, it doesn't matter.

They are always looking for fresh targets and this sounds like a good one, especially if the Resistance is already involved'.

Phil hesitated, 'The thing is, Tom, this Eloise, she cooks for these sailors, and I wouldn't want her caught up in any firefight, it wouldn't be right'.

Tom was the ideal person to raise this with, for his attachment to Elena, in Crete, had formed 'in the heat of battle' and he understood exactly how real these attachments could become. 'Then if it comes off, we'll have to find a way to keep her out of it, won't we?'

The first briefing with Major Barton was confined to a bald account of the rescue and Phil was roundly congratulated, both for his efforts in holding off the attackers at the Île de Vierge and for his initiative and enterprise in making so swift an escape himself. 'I had a lot of help from the locals, sir', he explained, but as the Major commented, 'I realise that, PO, and you would not be here without it, fair enough. Nevertheless, you had the gumption to approach the right people and then to put yourself in a position where you could be picked up. Put all that together and you have an excellent piece of soldiering', then added with a smile, 'or sailoring, in your case. I'll be making recommendations'.

Phil and Tom waited for the others to leave the meeting, then spoke to Barton about Eloise and the information that she had shared. Barton's eyes lit up, for if they were able to translate this information into a full-scale raid, not only would they cause more troops to be drafted into Brittany, hopefully creating shortages elsewhere, but the elimination, or even partial elimination of an entire U-boat crew would be a heavy blow to the Reich.

'Leave it with me, gentlemen. I'll get back on to London today, and we'll see what they can find out from their chap on the ground. If we did take it on, it would have to be a larger enterprise than knocking off that lighthouse'.

Breakfast and sleep came next, followed by the full debrief. The only criticism of note was the weight of fire that they had been able to direct at the pursuing E-boats. The twin Vickers, at the stern of the MTB, fired the same calibre bullets as their rifles, .303, and while it was a reliable, rapid-firing weapon, it was up against 22 and 37mm cannons on the

German vessels. They couldn't rely upon a rescuing Beaufighter on every raid! Major Barton agreed that they could not, but surprised them when he revealed that Coastal Command had been briefed in advance about the operation, and that it had been no surprise to the pilot when he had sighted the MTB. The second sighting, however, on his return from hunting surfaced U-boats in the Bay of Biscay, had been fortuitous, his co-pilot having spotted the flashes of tracer. Thanks had already been sent to the CO at RAF Portreath, the Beaufighter squadron's base, and there was a recognition that this inter-service support made sense and could be repeated.

Major Barton excused them all from duties for five days, and while he gave permission for them to proceed on leave if they so wished, no one took up his offer. The last few nights had been exhausting and there was serious sleep to catch up with.

George, in his fatherly way, had taken Bud under his wing, and used some of their free time to learn a little more about him. Bud's father, he had revealed to George, represented Queens, a district of New York, in the House of Representatives in Washington DC. This meant nothing to his new Welsh friend, but when it was explained to him that Mr Wilson Senior was the equivalent of a Member of Parliament in Westminster, his eyes widened.

'Then why are you slumming it with us, old mate?' George asked him, 'I know you told me all about crewing boats up and down the coast but surely to goodness, your Dad would have wanted you to do better than that'.

'You're right, George, he did. He wanted me to join the family firm, that his dad, my granddaddy, had started'.

'And quite right too, every father wants the best for his kids, that's one of the rules of life, that is. So why didn't you join it? You wouldn't be sitting here nattering with me in the rain if you had'.

'Because I have no interest in ladies' undergarments, none at all'.

'And I'm very pleased to hear it, Bud, very pleased, but what's that got to do with it?' He was being deliberately obtuse and Bud knew it but he played along.

'Dad's company makes girdles, George, and brassieres, camisoles, you name it, he makes it. It's a good business, there's plenty of dames around who want expensive underwear, right?'

George supposed that there was, knowing for a fact that his mother in law was very attached to her corset, him having laced her into it on numerous occasions when Rachel had been busy elsewhere.

'Dad's a dollar millionaire, George, and he wants to hand the business, and the money, on to me. I don't have no brother nor sister. But you know, it's different strokes for different folks, I want to find my own way in the world, you understand that, pal?'

'Course I do, Bud, course I do, and that's very worthy of you, I'm sure, but we have a saying over here, you don't look a gift horse in the mouth! You could be a millionaire, old son, and that's not to be sniffed at. I don't suppose Dad's very happy with you, is he?'

'No. He told me I got rocks in my head, and we haven't spoken since'.

'How long?'

'Two years'.

'What about your mother?'

'Yeah, she understands better. She reckons I'll grow out of it in time and anyways, it's her folks in Seaford so she don't worry too much'.

'Your Dad would have paid your fare back over to America, wouldn't he?'

'Sure, but I never asked him, too proud, I guess'.

George, probably of an age with Bud's father, decided that a little advice would do no harm.

'You don't mind if I speak my mind do you, young Bud?'

'No, but I guess you would anyway..'

'Too true. Write to Dad, tell him that you are sorry that you parted brass rags'.

Bud looked blank. 'On bad terms, you're sorry that you parted on bad terms', George continued, 'explain again that you want to find your own road, and that you will see him when the war is over, and you can talk about the future then'.

'But why would I want to say that?'

Give me fucking strength, thought George, and continued, 'Because you might get blown to shreds next week or the week after, probably will, and if you haven't made your peace with your father, he'll spend the rest of his days blaming himself, and maybe your mother will blame him too, and that wouldn't be right, would it? He just wanted the best for you, didn't he? Use your head, this isn't all about you'.

He left a more pensive, quieter Bud to think it over and smiled to himself later as he watched his young friend scribbling on some scrounged notepaper in a corner. God, I'm getting old, he thought to himself.

Geraint and Phil picked up their friendship where they had left off, and even conversed with each other in French, just to keep in practice. Phil told his friend all about his short stay in France, his gruelling swim to the beach and his desperation to find someone to help him. Mostly he spoke about Eloise and her children, and the risky situation that he had put them in, and it was obvious to Geraint that Phil felt a link to Eloise and to whatever happened to her next.

'Soapy, my friend', he commented to Phil, 'perhaps Major Barton will not send us back to these U-Boot-Besatzung, there might be other, easier targets for us'.

Phil considered, but finally shook his head, 'Possible but where will they find such a prize as this one? A valuable crew, usually at sea or in their base, where we can't touch them? Stuffing their faces for three days in a country house? A beach about a mile away at most? No, Barton will go for it, and in his position, so would I. Casualties? Not so important when the target is worth so much'.

His logic was impeccable, and Geraint could not disagree. He had huge respect for his mate, who had befriended him, despite his German background, and who looked out for him whenever he could. He was like an enormous big brother to him, certainly family, and Geraint felt that he owed him a lot.

'Phil, I will help you'. His big friend looked at him, surprised. 'You and I will make sure that your Eloise and her kinder are safe if this raid happens. I do not know how but we will'.

Phil was touched by his young friend's sentiment but if the raid happened, how could they help Eloise and the children, and perhaps the old people too? He had no idea.

The prospect of five days of inactivity soon palled, and by the morning of Day Four, they were ready to apply themselves to some work. Bud led them out on an hour's run before breakfast, and they followed that up with weapons maintenance, practice for when they were in the field with no armourer to hand, and a long session on the firing range. Phil, universally accepted as the best hand with the Lee-Enfield, took the rifle practice and George, the Bren, and by the end of the day, everyone could claim to have improved their initial scores with both weapons.

Day Five was similar, but this time the firearms work was replaced with all-in fighting, use of the knife and weapons improvisation, led by a new instructor. All-in fighting, brought to Britain by an ex-policeman from the Shanghai force, was a no holds barred, dirty but brutally effective method of using everything to hand that might disable an opponent, a version of street fighting with the single aim of winning the fight with nothing held back. George, with experience of hand to hand combat in India and the Sudan, quickly learned a few fresh techniques, while those with fewer years under arms took a little longer to jettison any remaining ideas of fair play and 'fighting clean'. It was an 'in the gutter' style, so different from the military drills that they had learned through constant repetition, but still requiring discipline and quick thinking.

It was a tired and bruised group of men who took themselves off to bed that last night, ready for duty the next morning.

Immediately after breakfast, Major Barton took Tom to one side. 'I have news for you, Sergeant. Firstly, Second Lieutenant Cullen will be arriving today, to replace Lieutenant Pearson. He's young, not much experience, and he will need your support and guidance'. Tom went to speak but the Major silenced him, 'I know, I know, this unit is hardly the place for a green lieutenant but he's all I could get, and it's up to you to help him shape up'. Both men knew that the unit could not carry any passengers, so the new man would have to learn quickly.

'Second piece of news, and for your ears only for now, is that your agent in Brittany was back on the wireless last night. Those submariners we heard about have completed their first rest-cure in the countryside and I have information about numbers, guards, weaponry and communications. I have already spoke to the Chief of Combined Operations staff and they think that Mountbatten will be interested in an operation to wipe-out one of these crews, ah, while they're at rest, so to speak'.

It sounded distasteful to Tom initially, the thought of massacring as many of these young men as possible, in the midst of their rest and recuperation, but this was war, and one submarine crew less would mean less fatalities at sea, and less interruption to Britain's war effort. It was distasteful, but it was also a necessity.

Barton continued, 'I want you in on the planning, Sergeant, along with your officer, and I want PO Watson involved too, he's the one with experience on the ground and he's met your agent over there, knows the personalities. If it comes off, it'll be a larger scale operation, larger than your raid on that lighthouse, so you'll be combining with No 12 Commando, under Captain Ryan. Meet your officer this afternoon when he arrives, and we'll have the first full meet-up tomorrow morning, here, after breakfast. You won't be needed for every meeting and nor will your men, but your first-hand knowledge will be invaluable'.

Second Lieutenant Cullen arrived after lunch, driving up, with a splash of gravel, in a battered MG TA convertible. He visited the Major first, was shown the Officer's Mess and his room, met some fellow officers and was then conducted to the wing of Anderson Manor where Tom and the others resided.

He was short, no taller than George, with a turned-up nose, freckles, and a mop of blond hair. To the older men, he looked fourteen, or fifteen at most, but solidly built, of the body type that would be ideal in a rugby scrum-half, with broader shoulders than one would expect to see in someone of his height. His most remarkable features were his eyes, sharp and green, which moved carefully from face to face as Tom introduced his men. A few words were customary when a new officer was introduced to his men, and Cullen did not disappoint, although he did surprise.

'Men, I am pleased to be here and to have you under my command. Major Barton has already briefed me regarding your past accomplishments, very impressive, very impressive indeed. However, (and at this point Tom groaned inwardly, for 'however' was just a posh way of saying 'but') it is what we achieve together in the future that counts, and to that end, I will work you very hard indeed, starting tomorrow'. Turning to Tom, he continued, 'Run at 0500 tomorrow, Sergeant, and we'll see how you all do, and if any of you don't measure up, well, I'm sure that your old units would have you back. Good evening, gentlemen, dismissed', and with that, he swept out of the room.

There was no immediate reaction, for all of them had worked under the direction of bumptious young officers in the past, and there were ways of dealing with them, in order to show them how the world really worked, but on the other hand, they were part of a disciplined service and if Cullen was to grow into being a decent officer, then he would have to be helped along, whether he thought he needed to be or not.

Chapter 15

Eloise heard Galou close the door behind her, and she walked the few yards to where her bicycle was leaned up against the wall. She would be home in fifteen minutes, and although the children would be asleep in bed, she would have her few minutes of peace before sleep claimed her. The preceding few days had been more exhausting than usual, producing all that gourmet food for the Germans to eat, and almost against her will, she had found herself taking a degree of professional pride in creating such wonderful food from the best ingredients. Was it traitorous to think like that, or was she simply making the best of a very difficult situation? After all, she was not there of her own free will, she was forced labour.

These thoughts were churning away in her mind, taking so much of her attention that she did not hear the quick footsteps approaching her, and her first intimation that something was wrong was when an arm circled around her neck, while something hard was pressed into her back.

'Do not scream, Madame Beauchêne, or I will shoot you where you stand!' The voice was speaking in French, a native speaker, and there was something familiar about it but she could not place it… 'Why are visiting Galou at this hour?' The owner of the voice was mocking her now, 'He is not your lover so perhaps you are plotting together, the Résistance perhaps? He would not speak to me but we will see what Brauer makes of it'.

It was Quiniou! It all fell together now, he had been pestering Galou about the Résistance and had got nothing, so he must have spied on him instead and caught her visiting. He would not have overheard anything but just the fact of her calling in late in the evening would be suspicion enough.

'Monsieur Quiniou, is it you? Monsieur, you are making a mistake, Galou is an old friend of the family and nothing to do with the Résistance as far as I know. I was just calling in to see that he was well, he lives alone, you see'.

Quiniou was pushing her down the stony track as she spoke, and he answered dismissively, 'Liar! I know that he is Résistance, I know it. Hamon's son would not confess but they were good friends, so how would he not be? I will take you to Brauer and his colleagues in the Gestapo, they will wring the truth out of you and when you name Galou, he will give up their whole network and my job will be done. Now keep walking!'

Eloise tried again, 'For pity's sake, Monsieur Quiniou, think of my children! I have done nothing wrong, please let me go home'. 'Keep walking and shut your mouth', was his only response and it was suddenly crystal clear to Eloise what she must do.

She stopped without warning, confident that he would not shoot her, having spoken about delivering her to Brauer, and as she felt the gun barrel push into the area of her right kidney, she spun violently into him, grabbing his gun-hand with her left hand, while slamming her right forearm and elbow into his throat and jaw. Quiniou was old, no match for a strong young woman and down he went, onto the stony ground, clutching his throat in one hand, while Eloise snatched the revolver from the other.

As he lay at her feet, gasping for breath, she noticed that he had not even cocked the revolver, so she did it now, and the loud, obvious click brought him to his senses. 'Eloise, Madame, I was not going to harm you, it was a misunderstanding, I would have taken you home...'

Eloise had seen gangster movies before the war, just like everyone else, but this was not a movie. There would be no begging for mercy or struggling for the gun or last-minute confessions. Leaning down, she pressed the barrel hard against his chest and pulled the heavy trigger. The report seemed deafening close up, but it was muffled somewhat by his clothing. Quiniou jerked once, then lay still.

Back up at the house, the door opened and Galou stood in the doorway, 'What is it, who is there?' he bawled, to be answered calmly, 'Pierre, it is Eloise, come quickly and bring some light'. Within a minute, he was there and they looked down at Quiniou's corpse, his pale face looking even more sunken in death in the dim illumination of a flashlight.

Eloise recounted what had happened, Galou shaking his head in disgust as he heard confirmation of Galou's treachery. 'Poor Hamon and his boy, they must have believed that he wanted to help the Résistance, and he betrayed them to the Boche'.

Eloise knew that they had to move quickly, 'Galou, we must move the body, then find his car and move that too. Where can they be hidden?'

'That is no problem, Madame, his is not the first body I have had to dispose of. First, I will bring a handcart and with your help, we will push him up the hill. There is a shaft of an old lead mine there, we will drop him down it and that will be the nearest that he gets to a Christian burial, God rot him! You must go home then, while I drive his car back to his house and leave it there. He is like me, no nearby neighbours, so no one will see me. He will disappear from the face of the earth and no one will be any the wiser'.

It was a hard half an hour, pushing the loaded cart up to the abandoned lead mine, then tipping Quiniou's body down the shaft. It was as if Eloise's mind had frozen since killing Quiniou, but as she cycled home, Galou having said that he would deliver the car to Quiniou's house and then clear up any blood stains, it was as if those temporary barriers came crashing down.

As the realisation hit her, that she had executed an old man, without a scintilla of hesitation or doubt, she had to throw her bicycle down into the road and rush to vomit into the ditch. Was she a murderer now? She thought that she was, yet what choice had there been? If she had meekly gone along with Quiniou, more deaths would have followed, her own first, followed by Galou, if he was not able to kill himself first then more would follow. No, Quiniou's killing had been necessary, she just wished that it had fallen to someone else to perform.

The acid test was, if the same situation occurred in the future, would she kill again? The answer was an unequivocal yes, of course she would, and somehow that left her feeling, if not better, then at least justified. She was at war, as was the whole of France, and people had to choose where to stand.

Hervé and Madame Le Roux were waiting anxiously at the villa, fearful for what might have happened to her. She was almost three hours later than her usual time, but the relief they felt when they heard her bicycle on the path turned to horror when saw that her jacket and dress were soaked in blood.

'Ah, my God, what have they done? Are you wounded?' shrieked Clarisse and pulled her into the house.

'No, I am not and please, don't wake the children', Eloise coolly replied, 'sit down and I will tell you all about it'.

She related the tale of Quiniou's treachery, to expressions of dismay and anger from both Gilbert and Clarisse, but when she described how she had disarmed him and then killed him with his own revolver, Clarisse could not conceal her shock and horror. 'How could you do such a thing?' exclaimed Clarisse, 'and may God forgive you', crossing herself furiously.

Hervé had been astounded to hear of her actions but he had already concluded that Quiniou's death was required, before he did any more damage, so he took a more pragmatic view.

'You should thank God, my dove, that Eloise had the presence of mind to put that rat out of his misery. He would have betrayed all of us, like he did Hamon and his boy, and then where would we be? No, if anyone deserved to die, it was him'. Clarisse went to speak but he closed her down, 'No, we will talk in the morning, after some rest and thought'. Then turning to Eloise, 'Now, young woman, I will turn my back while you take off those clothes and Clarisse will put them straight onto the fire. Underwear too, if the blood has soaked through, and shoes, everything. Then you must wash any blood from your body and go to bed, for you must work in four hours!'

Clarisse did as she was told and left for the bathroom, smiling as she overheard Clarisse say to Gilbert, 'I am not your dove, you old goat, whatever gave you that idea?'

It felt as if she had hardly gone to bed at all before it was time to get up again. To her great surprise, Clarisse was already up and about, and handed her a bowl of coffee as she walked wearily into the kitchen, following it with an affectionate hug, 'I am sorry, my dear, I was just tired and frightened for you. You did what you had to, I understand now. Gilbert and I talked about it in bed'. She blushed, for as far as the world knew, she and Gilbert had separate bedrooms but clearly, things had moved on. Eloise said nothing but returned the hug and left for the chateau.

The building was quiet that morning, but there was plenty of work for Eloise and Hans to do. The orderlies who had taken their places, while they were at the Manoir, had left a disorganised mess in the kitchen and larders, to the extent that they were twenty minutes late in serving breakfast. She expected to be reprimanded but it seemed that the NCOs and officers were so relieved to be eating good French food again, even if it was only for one day, that other than a few disgruntled rumbles, nothing was said.

The morning passed quickly, with food to prepare for the remainder of that day but also to begin to prepare some dishes for the next, that the orderlies could finish and serve. Eloise had concluded that her best plan for survival in this place would be to make herself indispensable, 'part of the furniture' and therefore invisible.

In the middle of the afternoon, when lunch had been served, consumed and cleared away, Brauer came striding into the kitchen. 'Madame', he started, it is good to have you back here, even for one day. My comrades have been pining for your cuisine'.

He was being uncharacteristically polite, perhaps softening her up for something and sure it enough, it came in a sudden question, 'Madame, tell me, do you know a Monsieur Louis Quiniou?'

Eloise had guessed that, one day soon, this question would be posed, so she had her answer ready. 'Yes, sir, I do'.

'And when did you last see Monsieur Quiniou?'

She had guessed that Quiniou would have told Brauer of his visit to Madame Leroux's villa so, 'Sir, he visited Monsieur Hervé, perhaps three weeks ago. I had not met him before'.

'And what did you talk about with him?'

Yes, he was taking the direction that she thought he would. 'Sir, he was asking about the Résistance and of course, he was asked to leave. Neither Monsieur Hervé nor Madame Le Roux know anything about the Résistance, and it was a stupid thing to ask'.

Brauer did not look surprised, for he must already have had this account of the conversation with Quiniou. He was just checking to see if she would lie. 'And you, Madame', he asked, 'what do you know of the Résistance?'

'I know nothing, sir, I think of my children, that is all. He even asked me about what I might see and hear when I am working here! I told him that he wanted me to be a spy and I said that I never would be, then he was asked to leave'. Her anger was not simulated, for she was still outraged that Quiniou had sought to entrap them all, but Brauer was not to know that.

Brauer remained expressionless and Eloise took a chance, 'Sir, that was weeks ago, has he been telling lies about me? I have told you only the truth!'

'No, Madame, he has not. He is missing from his home. If you hear anything of him, you must tell me'. He turned away and was gone. Eloise felt shaken but safe enough, for she had related exactly what had happened and it must have fitted accurately with what Quiniou had reported back to his paymaster.

Galou, meanwhile, in his working guise as road mender, had taken himself off in the direction of the Manoir du Vaugalain. The road that ran past the old house was pot-holed and needed repair, so it was convincing cover. He worked his way slowly past the house, breaking and tamping down stones into the holes but always taking the time to build up a picture of the Manoir and its surroundings in his mind.

On the other side of the road to the old house, small fields separated by dry-stone walls ran down to the sea, ending in a shallow-angled cliff of about ten metres. This dropped down to the beach, and as long as any boat with a draft of one metre or less came in from a north-north-west direction, anything from 340 to 345 degrees, they would avoid the reefs that guarded the little bay. Perhaps a light, shining from the beach, would be needed, he did not know, he would leave that to the sailors.

To the west of the Manoir, trees had been planted as a barrier from the prevailing wind. The trees had been planted in staggered rows, about eight or ten deep, and although they were no taller than the house, and kept small by the regular Atlantic gales that blew in off the sea, they did the job that they were designed for. They would also, realised Galou, form a discreet staging-point before any attack.

The ground directly behind the Manoir was open, gently rising up to a rocky bank that ran for miles above this part of the Breton coast. It made poor cover and it was to be hoped that no one would retreat in that direction, for it would take them further and further away from the sea. The remaining side of the house, facing east, bordered on a rocky stream that ran down into the sea. It would certainly make a concealed approach to the house and could serve as a line of retreat but as far as he could see, it was littered with boulders and encroaching vegetation, so it would probably not be the speediest route to take.

The Manoir itself was larger than he had remembered, it looked to be shaped like a capital E, but with the middle bar removed. Eloise had told him that the entire top-floor was sleeping accommodation for the visitors, with the officers in the western wing, and the remainder of the floor occupied by NCOs and ratings.

Downstairs, the kitchen and larder area was housed in the west wing, directly under the officers bedrooms. The long front of the Manoir, from west to east, comprised a large dining room, with a sitting-room beyond, which in turn led into a large hall with a grand staircase to the upper floors. On the far side of the hall, a short corridor led to another sitting-room, with another dining room leading off it. There were boot-rooms and cloakrooms too, with several bathrooms between the two floors.

The more he looked at the house and imagined the layout inside it as Eloise had described, the more it seemed like an impossibly complex target. For example, it would only take a few determined men at the head of the stairs to hold off a party attempting to storm up to the bedrooms. Were there servants' stairs somewhere? Could they be used? He would have to ask Eloise.

There were stables behind the main building, single-storied, that were used for dining and resting by the guards. He guessed that they would use the nearest stable to the house but Eloise would need to check that also. The main entrance, onto the drive that swept up in front of the house, was blocked with a rise and fall pole, operated from outside a wooden guard hut that looked large enough to accommodate only two men. That meant, if Eloise was correct, that another four guards would be on patrol around the house at any one time, although she had said that they had arranged for an extra two to get some illicit sleep at night.

Night would be the obvious time to attack for many reasons, not least the run across La Manche, the Channel, to the beach and the eventual retreat. That would be for the Rosbifs to decide. All he had to do now was to transmit as much information to London as he could, it would be several messages over a few nights, and hope that the Germans didn't have their direction-finder vans out.

Chapter 16

The MTB, nicknamed 'Flying Flea' for her impressive turn of speed, nosed quietly in on her auxiliary engine to within a mile of the cliffs, and the dory was carefully lowered into the water. Eleven men, comprising Tom's party except for Phil, given the night off, Second Lieutenant Cullen, Captain Ryan and five tough-looking soldiers from No 12 Commando, squeezed onto it and within minutes, were jumping out into the shallows and pulling the little boat more firmly onto the beach.

The operation to attack the submariners in Brittany had been approved in principle and detailed planning could theoretically begin. However, the first meeting was postponed until there was agreement from other services about their possible involvement, which would take time to string together, so in the meantime, this raid, Operation 'Alderman', had been organised. Much simpler in nature, the intention was to raid a coastal signalling station near Auderville, on the coast of Normandy, west of Cherbourg, and to capture signals staff for interrogation. Major Barton saw it as a dry-run for future operations involving SOE and Commandos, and therefore, much was riding on it.

The previous two weeks had been an education for Second Lieutenant Cullen. His early morning run, devised with the intention of starting a weeding-out process, had simply proven that the men were fitter than he was himself. Not knowing the locality, he had ordered a half-hour run along the lanes, then an about-turn and return to the Manor. George, built like a whippet, had set a moderate pace so that the man with the most muscle to carry, Phil, would be able to maintain it but in the event, he had to moderate it further because Cullen started to fall behind. For his own amusement, he had wound the pace up again for the final twenty minutes and by the time Cullen had stumbled back into the manor grounds, five minutes behind everyone else, Tom and his men were lined up 'at ease', waiting for his appearance.

Not a word was said, other than 'Dismiss', and they met with Cullen again after breakfast, at the firing range. He put them through their paces with Lee-Enfield rifle, Bren gun, Thompson and Colt pistol, and Tom had to concede that he knew his firearms. He could strip, then re-assemble all four weapons with his eyes closed and shoot them all accurately too. Rather foolishly, in Tom's opinion, Cullen set them all shooting competitively against each other and included himself in the competition. The end result was no surprise to Tom but Second Lieutenant looked as if he had 'lost a bob and found a tanner'. He had shot well, by his own standards, but was mortified when his cumulative score was found to be the lowest of the group.

They had taken a break, and Tom, doing his Sergeant's duty, had taken the opportunity to have a quiet word with him. Tom had never fully appreciated it himself but his experience and all-round competence gave him a natural authority and Cullen, although chastened and embarrassed, listened without interruption.

'Begging your pardon, sir, but I must talk to you very frankly. You don't need to set yourself up in competition with the men. They have years and years of service between them and they are all, without exception, very good at what they do. In point of fact, sir, I would be surprised if you could find a better bunch anywhere. They understand command, sir, and if you lead them, they will follow but you do not need to show that you can do their jobs better than they can. You can't, sir, but they can't do your job either! Get to know them, sir, good and bad points, and I am sure that your command will be a success'.

Tom had stuck his neck out, so to speak, and if Cullen decided to turn it into a matter of discipline, then they would be in front of Major Barton, and Tom knew that Barton would feel obliged to back his officer. On the other hand, would Barton risk the break-up of a successful group to save face for a junior officer? Perhaps he would soon find out.

Cullen said very little, no more than, 'Thank you, Sergeant', but from that moment onwards, Tom noticed an alteration, an adjustment in how he approached the men. He did not try to be their friend, which would have been just as disastrous, but neither did he threaten anyone again with 'return to unit'. He would ask Tom for his opinion, and although he did not always act upon it, at least he asked. His personal fitness improved, as the morning runs totted up, and a little humour crept into his exchanges with the men.

He had even shown some curiosity in their backgrounds but still had a lot to learn, and this was evident when he approached Tom for a word about Geraint.

'Sergeant, is this correct? Private Williams is a German Jew, used to be in their Navy?'

'Yes, sir, Corporal Parry and I pulled him out of the Mediterranean after his patrol-boat was sunk, sir'.

'And is he trustworthy, Sergeant?'

'How do you mean, sir?'

'Well, he's German, and he's Jewish.'

Tom was not going to make it easy for him. 'Sorry, sir, I'm still not with you'.

'For God's sake, Sergeant, the Germans are the enemy, and the Jews, well...'

'Begging your pardon, sir, being a German Jew gives him every reason to fight and be a good soldier', and he gave Cullen a potted history of Geraint's background and how his family had been incarcerated, and almost certainly murdered, by the Nazis, finishing, 'And bye the bye, sir, Private Williams has stood by me in action after action, and never given me a moment's worry, I wish that we had more like him'. Cullen had not been in action yet, and Tom knew it, and it did no harm in reminding him that the people around him, including Geraint, were vastly more experienced and battle-hardened. The young officer had blushed a little, at the implied rebuke, but carried on.

'And what about our Yankee friend, Sergeant, can I trust him too? It's like the bloody League of Nations!'

Cullen, Tom decided, was a decent enough boy underneath it all but he must have led a very sheltered life, judging by the depth of his ignorance. Tom had learned, early on in his career, that you judge a comrade by his actions, not by where he came from or his accent, and Cullen was not there yet.

'Sir, Private Wilson is a volunteer, and being an American, he could ask to be discharged back to his own armed forces whenever he wanted. In my opinion, sir, the fact that he has decided to stay with us speaks volumes and as for being trustworthy, well, I have been under fire with him on two occasions and he never turned a hair, sir. That's why he was mentioned in dispatches'.

Cullen, despite himself, was impressed and the questioning ceased. Tom noticed, however, that he watched the men closely during exercises, and he hoped that the young lieutenant was learning things that would preserve his own life and make him a better officer.

Captain Ryan sent his sergeant up the easy cliff for a quick reconnaissance and within a couple of minutes, was taking his report. There was barbed wire at the top edge of the slope, and behind it, it looked as if there might be a minefield. Beyond the minefield was a small pillbox, and fifty yards beyond that, the signalling station, just as their intelligence had indicated.

Bud Wilson and one of the commandos were designated mine clearers, and once the wire was cut, they started to clear the mines. Their technique, primitive but effective, was to use their bayonets as probes and to lift any mines they discovered and place them to one side, making two safe lanes through to the pillbox. This took twenty minutes of quiet but feverish activity but it was done without interruption.

The lack of vigilance from any defenders was explained when it was found that the pillbox was unoccupied. Perhaps two quiet years had led the little garrison to believe that it was a backwater, and that the British were either unaware of their presence or just not interested enough to attack them.

A well-worn track connected the pillbox to the signalling station, which was another concrete box, about twenty feet long by fifteen feet wide, with a height of perhaps twenty feet in two storeys and topped with a flat roof. Small unglazed apertures, hardly large enough to be described as windows, pierced the front wall and in daylight, would have provided both a limited view out to sea and a protected firing-point.

The party split into two, as planned, and silently moved into position, Captain Ryan and his commandos taking the front of the building, while Second Lieutenant Cullen and the remainder moved to the rear, where they expected to find the single entrance, a steel door. It was there, and they waited for the signal from Captain Ryan, which would be unmistakable.

Unmistakable it was, for his soldiers simultaneously posted six grenades through the little windows and they detonated almost together, seeming to rock the small building as the explosions, virtually contained within the little concrete box, wreaked their destruction. The steel door burst open and in a cloud of smoke, three figures rushed out into the air. They were armed, but before they were able to raise their rifles at the figures dimly perceived around them, they were cut down in a flurry of fire.

Yelling, 'Follow me!' Cullen ran through the door into the building, pistol in hand, with Geraint, the nearest man to him, close on his heels. The plan had been to blow the door, if necessary, and to call out any survivors in their own language, and if that failed, to complete the storming of the building. Cullen had ignored what had been agreed, and the others had no choice but to follow him in, Tom cursing at the impetuosity of the young officer.

It was a dark night, and the darkness inside the bunker was profound, made more impenetrable by the smoke from the grenades and from the fires that the explosions had set off. Tom could hear the sound of a struggle ahead of him, gunshots and the grunts and shouts of men in terrible combat, and behind that, the shrieks and whimpering of wounded men. It was hell, and how to identify and then subdue the defenders in this blackness seemed an impossible task.

Then, up ahead, Geraint, shouting in his native German, 'Hände hoch! Lass deine Waffen fallen!
Du wirst nicht geschädigt werden!' He repeated the phrases again and again, and after a tense few seconds, they were rewarded by the clatter of firearms being dropped onto the concrete floor of the room. George had a torch, and flicked it into life, to reveal a chaotic scene.

There were four bodies on the floor, three of them German, and the fourth was Cullen, pale-faced as he clutched at a wound in his thigh that was pulsing blood through his fingers. Two other enemy soldiers were standing, pressed up against the front wall, with rifles dropped at their feet. Another torch was found and Geraint started to work on the casualties, covered by Bud with his Thompson. Tom and George stepped gingerly through a narrow doorway that led into the other ground-floor room, which proved to be empty but there was a flight of concrete steps in the corner that led up to the upper floor.

George was using a Thompson for this raid, being more practical than a Bren for close quarters work, and at a nod from Tom, fired a short burst up the stairs then followed it up, firing again as he neared the top, hearing his bullets ricocheting around the room above. There was no reply, and when Tom joined him, illuminating the room with the torch, they could see that it was filled with electrical equipment, all cabinets and illuminated dials, together with desks, a telephone and a filing cabinet. There were technical manuals and what looked like codebooks on the desk, which they quickly gathered up and finally, George emptied a full magazine into the electrical boxes. They clattered down the stairs, Tom shouting, 'Friends, friends!', in case anyone was inclined to shoot them.

The room below had been cleared, and the only inhabitants now were two dead German soldiers and one other, wounded but with a dressing tied tightly around the top of his head. George stopped briefly to light him a cigarette and then they were outside, joining the others as they prepared to retrace their steps back down to the beach, along with their two unwounded prisoners.

Captain Ryan nodded as they arrived, then led the way back through the minefield. Geraint was bent forward, with Second Lieutenant Cullen on his back, hanging on grimly with his arms around the young German's neck. The descent to the beach was difficult, ensuring that Cullen kept his grip and that Geraint did not slip and fall but they made it.

By the time they crossed the few yards of sand and the boat was re-floated, the Lieutenant was unconscious and he was lifted unresisting onto the deck. In the shielded light of one of the torches, blood could be seen leaking through the dressing that Geraint had applied and he immediately got to work, tightening the original dressing and tying another on top of it, and another two at the back of the Lieutenant's thigh where the bullet had exited.

Captain Ryan spoke to Tom as the little boat re-floated and they slowly moved away from the beach, 'Your Private Wilson told me what happened, Sergeant, although I had to order him to, he didn't want to drop this young fool in the shit', gesturing down at the stricken officer, then addressing Geraint, 'Will he live, Private?' 'God willing, sir, God willing, the bullet missed the artery so he was lucky. There's a big hole where the bullet exited though, I've packed it and I'm about to bandage the whole thigh. As long as we can get him to a hospital quickly, sir, he has a chance'.

Ryan switched his attention back to Tom, 'Well done, Sergeant, you and your men saved the day, and I'll make sure that the Major gets the whole story, but how we can expect the men to follow orders if the bloody officers won't, I'll never know'.

Cullen's wounding had been predictable, given his need to keep proving himself, but he had not been a bad lad, underneath, and Tom's reflex was to defend him, 'Sir, permission to speak freely?' Ryan nodded, he had broken protocol himself, talking about a fellow officer to an NCO so openly and critically, so in good conscience, he could hardly refuse Tom.

'Sir, he's a young 'un, willing to learn but the penny hasn't quite dropped yet, he hasn't realised how little he knows, and how much more there is to know. I think we would have got him there, sir, given time, but now...'

'He's finished, Sergeant. He will never make the grade after a wound like that, he'll be returned to unit if he survives'.

He was right, and Tom felt sorry for the young man lying at his feet, for he had probably reached the end of his fighting career before it had properly started. Ironically, his disabling wound would probably save him from a serious reprimand, for not only had he put himself in danger but also the whole of the section who had followed him in.

Tom turned to Geraint, 'What did you shout in that bunker, mate? It did the trick, whatever it was'.

Geraint grinned back at him, 'Hands up, drop your weapons, you will not be hurt. I am glad that they believed me, Sergeant'.

'So am I'.

The MTB was waiting at the rendezvous, and as they moved alongside, ready to move Cullen gently onboard, George murmured in Tom's ear, 'We don't seem to have much luck with officers, do we, Sergeant?'

It was true. From the battle of France, to Crete, and back to France, they had gone through a whole list of lieutenants and captains, to the point where it was difficult to put a face to every name. They had lost plenty of pals too, it wasn't just officers, but George was right, they did not seem to stay for too long.

'They aren't in it for long enough, George, they get clobbered before they've learnt the ropes. It'll be an office job for this poor bastard'.

Chapter 17

The return across the Channel to Poole was uneventful, and an ambulance was waiting on the quay as they pulled alongside. Cullen remained unconscious and pale from loss of blood, but Geraint had reported that his heart was still strong, and that they had stemmed the bleeding, so the odds for his survival were improving. Everyone else felt exhausted, for the adrenaline-high of combat was always followed with a drop into deep fatigue. Major Barton knew this, so the first debrief was kept to a minimum, and they were sent to eat and sleep without undue delay.

Tom was up and about again by 1500 hours and was called into the Major's office, where he found him in conference with Captain Ryan. He was motioned to a chair and Major Barton recited the account of the raid that the captain had just given to him.

'Does that square with your recollection, Sergeant? Anything you disagree with?'

'Nothing to disagree with, sir. I would only add that Private Williams showed great presence of mind in ordering the defenders to disarm, sir, that alone saved a number of lives, then of course, his treatment of Second Lieutenant Cullen, sir…'

'Very commendable, Sergeant, very commendable. He showed great presence of mind and I think it's time that he should put up a stripe, don't you? I'll see him later'.

Tom was pleased for the young man, he had earned the recognition and would make a good lance-corporal.

'Second Lieutenant Cullen will not be returning. He's in hospital in Bournemouth, he'll live but he'll not be fit for active service again, too much damage to that leg and besides, his judgement showed a lot to be desired. I should not have risked your men with an inexperienced officer, Sergeant, and for that reason, I am not replacing him for the next raid. You will report direct to Captain Ryan as his second in command'.

He continued, 'We're calling it 'Operation Nightjar', and it's the raid on resting sub crews. The powers that be like the sound of it and they have agreed cooperation from the RAF. It will need to be twice the size of last night's raid, we are being given another MTB and another dory, so there will be quite a lot of training to undertake. Once again, we need a high tide and enough moonlight, so you have three weeks, give or take a couple of days, depending on when the submariners are in residence'. This was cutting it fine, given that a further dozen soldiers would need to practiced in the slick boat-handling that was so necessary, and the attack itself would have to planned in fine detail.

'First planning meeting tomorrow, gentlemen, no cancellation this time. Bring PO Watson with you, Sergeant, he's got the best idea of the ground. Both skippers are coming in, and the RAF will be sending someone. We'll use it to sketch out a broad plan, any training requirements, identify any thing you might need that you don't already have and get communication sorted. That's where these inter-service operations usually break down, communication, but it won't happen this time will it, gentlemen? The fine detail of the raid, well, that's for you two to sort out between you. I will need to sign it off, of course, but I am relying upon you to come up with something practicable, got it?'

'Yes, sir', they both replied.

'Right-oh, gentlemen, get back here at 1000 hours, ready to work'.

Ryan and Tom saluted and left the room, and outside, Ryan suggested that they take a stroll around the grounds to 'sort out a couple of matters'.

He began, 'Sergeant, I would normally expect to work with another officer and pass the decisions on down to you, but in this circumstance, I should make it clear that I am more than happy to have you as my second in command. You and your section did bloody well in Auderville, everyone knew their job and got on with it with no fuss, just the ticket'.

'Thank you, sir, they're a good bunch and we've seen a lot of action together'.

'I can see that', continued the captain, 'and the other thing I want to say is this, I expect you and Watson to contribute fully to this damned meeting tomorrow. You'll be outranked by everyone there but it's your head on the block, so if someone's talking through his backside, you speak up. I'll back you up if you need it'.

Tom had learned not to be overawed by senior officers but Ryan wasn't to know that and it was a kindly thought. 'Thank you, sir, much appreciated'.

They parted on good terms, and Tom went to find Phil, to give him some advanced warning of the meeting and to begin to pick his brains for ideas.

In fact, the next morning's meeting went smoothly. A representative from Coastal Command, a Group Captain, attended, with the message that they were prepared to commit a Beaufighter to the raid, with another in reserve. This was well-received, for their friend from RAF Portreath had made short work of the E-boat when Phil had been rescued, and just the knowledge that aerial back-up would be around made the whole thing more feasible.

A training schedule was agreed with the skippers of the MTBs, and Ryan produced a detailed sketch-map of the area, made up from information sent by the agent, then, like pulling a rabbit out of a hat, he spread out on the table, several area photographs of the Manoir, taken from different directions by three different reconnaissance Spitfires. 'Captain Ryan,

Sergeant Lane, PO Watson? These pictures confirm the intelligence from the agent, at least around the immediate environs of the house', remarked Ryan, 'you can't take copies away with you, of course, but they will remain here for you to consult. Come back with your routes from the beach as soon as you have decided upon them, at the latest by 1000 hours tomorrow. I have intelligence about guards and so on which I'll give you after this meeting, it will probably influence your approach'.

Before he left the meeting, Tom and Phil took the opportunity to personally thank the Group Captain for his pilot's intervention with the E-boat. 'Not at all, gentlemen', was the reply, 'I read the report myself, our chap was only too pleased to help. It's quite possible you might get the same chap next time too, we're happy to shoot up those damned E-boats every chance we can get!'

The three men found a quiet room in the manor, and their detailed planning began. They quickly decided, unanimously, that the Manoir would be best attacked from two sides and that therefore, the parties, although landing at the same beach, would separate and take different routes up to the old house. They agreed that it was best that the 'left-hand' party would be well-placed to take care of the guards at the gate and in the stables, while the 'right-hand' party would eliminate any guards at the other end of the building. It was decided that Tom's group, which would include six commandos, would follow the stream bed as the 'left-hand' party, and as long as they were undiscovered in their approach, they would be well-placed to knock out most of the guards. It would take longer for them to climb the stream than for the other party to follow the dry-stone walls to the road and then to conceal themselves in the windbreak, so the second party would attack only when they heard firing at the other end of the building.

Then they considered the mode of attack. It was an old building with thick, stone walls and entirely possible to defend, unless a way was found to flush out the defenders. Phil spoke up, 'Number 76 grenades. If we can get them exploding inside, the place will go up like a torch. I don't see them staying put when the place is burning down around their ears'. Getting the fragile grenades, glass bottles filled with benzene and phosphorus, across the Channel and inside the house would not be simple, but if it could be done, what a bonfire they would make! An alternative would be to bombard the house with a mortar, high-explosive rounds to break through the roof, then smoke, white phosphorus, to follow. That gave Tom another idea, involving Coastal Command, and Captain Ryan offered to raise it with the Major.

What they wanted to avoid, if at all possible, was a room by room clearance of the whole building, for it would take too long and they could sustain heavy casualties. Eventually they settled on a three- inch mortar, with high explosive and smoke rounds. They would need a crew of three to carry the mortar components, with another one or possibly two to carry the mortar bombs. Captain Ryan already had a mortar team that he could augment and they could start their practice as soon as the major approved the plan.

For this type of operation, weight of fire was vital, so automatic weapons would be the obvious choice. Brens would be fine if they were standing off but if it came down to short-range work, then Stens were available. Phil argued for at least a couple of rifles for sniping purposes, which seemed like a sensible precaution. They seemed to be getting somewhere, and the shape of the operation was gradually emerging, but then Phil complicated matters.

'Captain, there's the question of the French cook, Eloise Beauchêne, I believe her name is. Sir, most of the information about the Manoir and the submariners will have come from her and she will be in danger'.

'But we'll be attacking at night, PO. She doesn't sleep there, does she?'

God, officers were slow sometimes, thought Phil to himself.

'No, sir, she doesn't, but don't you think that the Jerries might put two and two together and decide that she was the traitor? They'll guess that someone must have told us about the submariners, sir'.

'Ah, I see what you mean, PO. I don't know what we can do though, do you, Sergeant?'

He's passing the buck, the sod, thought Tom. 'Sir, I don't think that we'll get much information in the future if we act on what informants tell us then leave them to be killed or imprisoned. My suggestion would be that, if we can find her, we give her the option of coming back to Blighty with us, sir. She might not wish to come, of course, and that would be her choice'.

Ryan was astounded, 'Sergeant, I don't think that we can ferry refugees back to England every time we do an operation, where would it end?'

'I agree with you, sir, but don't you think that a refugee or two in payment for a whole U-boat crew is a bargain really? The news will get around afterwards, sir, and who knows, we might get more intelligence, more local informants'.

Ryan pondered for a moment then, 'I see what you mean, Sergeant, I see what you mean. Alright, I'll mention it to the Major and if he's happy to go along with it, then so am I. You chaps have been working with SOE, you're more familiar with this end of the work than I am, of course you are'.

The meeting ended and Tom and Phil took a seat outside in the afternoon sunshine. 'Thanks for that, Tom, you have a better way with words than me. I don't think that I could just leave her there and hope for the best, our German friends are not that stupid!'

'Far from it, mate. They'll be onto her tracks in a wink and that goes for the old folks she's living with. The thing is, how are we going to contact them, give them the chance to leave? The raid will be in and out, as fast as possible'.

'I know', admitted Phil, 'I'll have to think of something'.

The word came through that Major Barton had approved the essentials of their plan of attack and training for the raid started the next morning. No. 12 Commando were experienced in small-boat operations but not from MTB to dory and back again. Not only did the transfers need to be done flawlessly, but they also had to be achieved in the shortest possible times. They had to get on board in the right order, with all the correct equipment, but also disembark efficiently. The order had to be decided then practiced, then practiced again. After perfection was achieved in daylight, then they would practice at night-time, until they reached the same standard. The only outstanding concern was being able to land at the correct beach. The coast was more complex than Normandy, for example, and without beacons, they could easily go wrong.

Ryan assembled his mortar team, three men plus two to carry more ammunition. Although the three-inch could, with fine-tuning, shoot at as short a range as 125 yards, the opinion of the Sergeant in charge was that a minimum of 250 yards would produce more reliable results. The flight time of each bomb would be twenty seconds, and with one in the tube every five seconds, providing that the first, ranging shot was accurate, then their planned ten rounds, six of high explosive and four of smoke, would be fired in seventy seconds. Again, the sergeant had no doubts that they could fire with the extreme accuracy that was required, providing there was sufficient ambient light for the sights and a firm enough base to stand the successive recoil of each bomb. It would have been useful to have better reconnaissance but he understood that it was not possible.

Although a room by room clearance of the Manoir would be a last resort, they practiced it nonetheless. The intelligence regarding layout was sketchy but it was all that they had, so many hours were spent attacking a pair of barns that had been mocked-up as the target. Ryan's men were designated to clear the upper floor, while Tom's would clear the ground floor and hold it, to keep their line of withdrawal open. The Sten guns, so basic that 'they look like they've been made from a bit of old water-pipe' according to George, were prone to jamming unless kept scrupulously clean and finely adjusted, another reason to be chary about a close-quarters attack.

They were twelve days into their training and were becoming polished and precise in their movements when Tom and Phil were called to a short-notice meeting with Major Barton and Captain Ryan. As they walked in through the door, greeting the MTB skippers, who were also present, they soon detected the air of anticipation that was animating everyone there.

Barton took the lead, 'In eight days, gentlemen, 'Operation Nightjar' gets underway. We've had word that there will be a crew at the Manoir, enjoying a night of gluttony and ripe to be attacked. We will talk about timings later but there are some loose ends to tie up before we go any further'. There had been a subdued muttering of satisfaction that their hard training was soon to be put into action, but they waited quietly for Barton to continue.

'We need someone on the ground in Brittany for at least twenty-four hours, perhaps longer, before our landing, and for a number of reasons. Firstly, we don't know this Resistance chappie, and although he's provided a good deal of intelligence, well, we don't know how reliable it is'. Phil took a breath to speak, for he had no doubts about Galou's integrity, but cut himself off as he felt Tom's elbow in his ribs. The time to speak would be when Major Barton had concluded his comments.

'Secondly, and as you know, there is still concern about the dories landing at the correct beach. Can we trust this Monsieur Galou to guide us in? I don't know. Thirdly, and again as you know, the mortar team is concerned about placement. They don't want to find themselves in a bog, looking for firm ground and then finding that they are too close or too far from the target'. These were the weak points of their plan and Barton was correct to point them out.

'Finally', the Major continued, 'there is the question of offering safe passage to the, ah, cook and her family because of their vulnerability after the attack. I have to say that their safety is not a priority to me but after speaking with your chaps in London', referring to SOE and nodding in Tom's direction, 'they agree with you that we should try to get them out or at least make the offer'.

No one commented, for there was more to come.

'My proposal, gentlemen, is that we put two men ashore, volunteers and French speakers preferably, forty-eight hours before the main force. Their job would be to answer the questions that I have posed and if necessary, advise to abort the operation'.

There were a few seconds of silence, then Tom took the initiative, 'Sir, I have two French speakers in my section, PO Watson here and Lance Corporal Williams. I'll leave PO Watson to speak for himself, sir'.

Phil jumped in quickly, 'Very happy to volunteer, sir. I can't speak for Williams but I have a feeling that he would jump at the chance'.

'Hold on, gentlemen', said Barton, smiling, 'let's not go off at half-cock, let's think about it first. How would you go about it, PO? Checking the intelligence, for example?'

'I have met Galou, sir, and I suppose that there is only so much that he can put in a wireless message. I would question him then check anything that seemed to need looking at again. The information about the inside of the Manoir, well, that's Madame Beauchêne, same process, sir. With regard to the landing, it should be possible, after dark, to reconnoitre a suitable position for the mortar and as for signalling the boats in, that's my stock in trade, sir'.

'Of course it is, and you would speak to Madame Beauchêne about coming back with you?'

'Yes, sir'.

Turning to the skippers, Barton asked, 'How would you suggest landing them, gentlemen, because it will be down to you? I don't suppose that you would want to take your boats too close to shore'.

'By folboat, sir', answered the younger of the two officers, 'easy to hide it when they land, we've a double stored away that they can have. Hard to spot at night, sir, ideal'.

'Alright, Lieutenant, that sounds workable'. Then turning to Tom, 'Speak to Williams, Sergeant, and if he volunteers, he can accompany PO Watson', then turning to Phil, 'You were my first choice anyway, PO, you know the land, met the people. Get the details sorted with Captain Ryan'.

Chapter 18

Word had spread among the U-boat crews at Brest and Lorient that the Manoir du Vaugalain offered the best food for many miles and there was no shortage of volunteers to fill in for wounded or sick comrades, if the opportunity arose. There was no racy nightlife there, such as a casino or a dance hall, but there was unlimited food and drink of the finest quality which, after a long patrol eating canned and dried food, with no alcohol at all, was like manna from heaven. The cook was a dish, so it was said, but she was strictly off the menu and was to be left to perform her magic in the kitchen.

Eloise would have been mortified and disgusted if she had known that she was being talked about in such a fashion but on the other hand, it might have helped her feel a little more safe. As it was, she kept her clothes plain and loose and did not dress her hair, only venturing out of the kitchen area if she was absolutely needed to help with the serving. On one occasion, she was called to the officers' dining room, arriving there in trepidation, only to find that the Captain and First Lieutenant of U-129 wished to present her with flowers and 2,000 francs, in appreciation of her hard work.

She wept a little, afterwards, as she cycled the short distance home. These German sailors were just young men, with only a few Nazis sprinkled among them, and they would have similar hopes for their lives as herself, she imagined. They would have families who worried about them and plans for the future. How sad it was that they, and she, had been sucked into this terrible war! It was difficult, sometimes, to see them as bitter enemies when they were enjoying her food and complimenting her for her cooking, just as any polite young man would do. Yet she had supplied information to the Résistance that, with good fortune, would result in the deaths of many of their comrades. What horrible things people did in wartime!

After the third crew had left the Manoir, replete and relaxed, Brauer had taken her to one side. He had been polite, even ingratiating with her, and soon revealed why, 'Madame, I want you and Hans back here tomorrow, do not go to the chateau. There will be a special delivery of food in the morning, and you will cook for four important guests in the evening. They will dine at seven and you will regard them as you would regard royalty, am I clear? If they are satisfied with your efforts, then I will reward you'.

'Yes, sir'.

The ingratiating manner disappeared, 'If, however, they are not impressed, not happy, then Madame, you will pay. Do you understand me?'

She understood, and was there to receive the special delivery of food and drink. There were crevettes and langoustine and turbot, a saddle of mutton and ribs of beef, beautiful cheeses, artichokes, asparagus and the freshest of fruit. To drink, there was Musigny and Crozes-Hermitage, Mersault and Montrachet, vintage Champagnes and the best Château de Montifaud fifty-year-old cognac. She and Hans were open-mouthed at the quality of the provisions they unpacked, it truly was food fit for royalty and of a far higher standard than was provided for the crews.

Eloise had learned that the best ingredients only required simple recipes, for the quality was already there, but the cooking had to be as close to perfection as possible. It was straightforward for her to create a beautiful menu and she and Hans rolled up their sleeves for a day of hard work. Hans had learned a lot from observing Eloise in action and, she thought, he was on the way to becoming a very useful commis-chef. Brauer had also supplied an orderly to set out the dining room, and to help with serving and odd jobs in the kitchen.

In the middle of the afternoon, a truck drew up in the yard, disgorging a dozen heavily armed guards who immediately conducted a search of the house, outbuildings and gardens. They were a fierce-looking bunch who said nothing to the two existing sentries but simply took over the security. Hans looked bemused but said nothing, he had learned that curiosity was not encouraged in the Wehrmacht.

Brauer arrived at five and seemed nervous, loitering around the kitchen and getting in the way of the workers. Eloise had learned from her mother that there could only be one cook in charge and summoning up her courage, she confronted Brauer.

'Sir, if you wish for this dinner to be perfect, you must leave the kitchen and allow me to work. I cannot cook when you are under my feet'.

There was a collective dropping of jaws at her impertinence but that was nothing to the general astonishment when Brauer simply nodded and left the kitchen! As Hans muttered to the other orderly, while trying to muffle his laughter, 'It must be royalty or Hitler himself!'

Half an hour before the first course was due to be served, there was a stirring among the guards, with a sentry placed outside the dining room, and Hans guessed that the dinner guests had arrived. Hans sent Paul, the other orderly, to serve drinks before they dined. He was back in ten minutes, his face flushed with excitement, and Eloise eavesdropped as he spoke excitedly with Hans.

'It's not royalty, mate', he grinned, 'but it's not far off, it's Dönitz, Onkel Karl, can you believe it!'

The name meant nothing to Eloise but judging from the sudden pallor of Han's face, he was familiar with it. He looked over at Eloise, 'Admiral Dönitz!' then took a deep breath, to calm himself. Dönitz was the most senior naval officer in the whole of France, in command of the Unterseeboot service, the man charged with destroying Britain's lifeline across the Atlantic Ocean.

At that second, Brauer came back into the kitchen and beckoned Eloise over. 'Madame', he explained, 'I can tell you now that your guest tonight is Admiral Dönitz, a very great man, he commands the submarines that will win the war at sea and is highly thought of by the Fuehrer. No mistakes or we are all ruined'. He was even more nervous than earlier, and Eloise merely nodded and went back to her work.

What a target he would have made, she thought to herself, if there had been warning of his coming. Killing him would have set back the whole Nazi war effort, and the British would never get this chance again. What could she do? Nothing, just give him the best meal he had ever eaten in France and get home, unharmed.

The evening flew by, for while Hans and the other orderly were serving in the dining room, Eloise was finishing off the next courses. It took all of her concentration, and she was surprised when the coffee was carried through. She felt drained but still confident that even a great Admiral would find little to complain about in the banquet that she had put in front of him. There looked to be a considerable amount of food left over, and she squirrelled some away into her bag then started to wash dishes.

She had only made a little headway when she heard footsteps and Hans was at the door to the corridor, gesturing, 'Kommen sie, Madame, kommen sie', beckoning her forward. He was smiling, so drying her hands carefully, she followed him down the corridor, towards the dining room. Brauer was hovering outside and his eyes followed her as she walked hesitantly into the smoky room. It was simply lit with candles, and around the table sat four grand-looking officers, all immaculately dressed in beautifully-cut dark blue uniforms, the deep colour broken up with lashings of gold braid around the cuffs, with more at the breast-pocket, opposite the Nazi emblem, an eagle with outstretched wings grasping a swastika, and finally set off with shiny brass buttons. The leader, sitting at the head of the table, beckoned her forward. So this was Admiral Dönitz, she thought. He was a thin-looking man, with short, grey hair and a rather severe set to his face. There was something about him though, an air of great intellectual ability and power that seemed to radiate through the room. His uniform, which might have seemed almost like a costume on a lesser man, looked entirely apt, and was set off with a black cross hanging at his throat.

'Madame', he began, and continued in excellent French, 'I called you through to praise you for the beautiful food with which you have graced this table. I have not eaten a better dinner in the two years I have been in this country'. His voice was higher than Eloise had expected, a light tenor perhaps, but very precise and modulated.

'Thank you, sir', was all that she could reply.

'Your fame reached as far as Lorient and these gentlemen', indicating the other three officers dining with him, 'persuaded me that I should, ah, sample your cuisine. I was not disappointed, Madame, not at all'. Eloise said nothing but hoped that Brauer could hear what was being said.

His next words shocked her to her core, 'I wish you to become my personal chef de cuisine, Madame, I do not see why you should be wasted on the Wehrmacht', and the other three laughed, rather sycophantically, or so Eloise thought. 'Now is not a convenient time but when my new headquarters are ready, in perhaps two weeks, I will send a car for you. Goodnight, Madame', and she was dismissed.

Eloise stumbled out of the room, her legs barely able to carry her. This Admiral, this man, was going to part her from her children, just so that he could have the pleasure of eating good food. Beautifully dressed and clever he might be but, in the end, he was just a Nazi, with the power of life or death over the people around him, and she and her children would suffer because of it.

She was in tears returning to the kitchen and Brauer was waiting for her. He must have heard the Admiral, for his first words to her were, 'You are leaving us, Madame, going on to better things with the Admiral and leaving me without a cook!' He was angry, but as Eloise could not refuse the Admiral, neither could he. 'Before you leave us, Madame, you will work, oh yes, you will work as you have never worked before and you will find me a replacement too! All the labour I have put in....' His voice was rising as his anger grew and Eloise, stepping away from him in fright, was expecting a blow, when a quiet voice cut through Brauer's fury. It was one of Dönitz's dining companions, looking gravely down his nose at Brauer, 'Unteroffizier, a message from the Admiral for you. Madame will be in perfect condition when she is collected, do you understand? You will be personally answerable if she is not'.

Brauer could do nothing but acknowledge that he did understand. He had never been this close to the Nazi hierarchy before and it was a dangerous place to be. After seeing Dönitz and his personal guards away from the Manoir, he stumped off in disgust, leaving Eloise and Hans to finish clearing up. They would be back in the morning to prepare for the next U-boat crew.

Hans had picked up the essentials of what was going to happen to Eloise but felt as helpless as she did. There was nothing that he could say, so as had become usual, he walked with her out of the house and escorted her past the two guards who lounged at the gate. He generally just walked a few yards along the road, to make sure that she was safely on her way but this time, he went a little further, murmuring, 'Es tut mir leid, Madame', I am sorry, Madame, for he had grown fond of this brave young woman, almost young enough to be his daughter, and he hated what the war was doing to her.

Eloise broke down completely when she told Gilbert and Clarisse what was going to happen. They were as distraught as she was and like her, they had no answers. Eloise could not run away, for where could she go? She could not take her babies on the run with her and even if she could, how would she live? Dönitz and the Gestapo would find her and if she fled to Vichy France, they would hand her straight back to the Germans. She would never be forgiven for fleeing and would either be imprisoned or sent off to Germany as slave labour. She was utterly helpless and perhaps she would have to follow Dönitz's orders and leave the children with Clarisse and Gilbert. At least they would be loved and cared for.

Gilbert had an idea, 'I will speak to Pierre Galou in the morning. Perhaps he will know how to make you disappear, hide you somewhere'. It was a faint hope, if that, and Eloise went to bed, her mind in a turmoil. Such was her exhaustion that sleep eventually came but it was disturbed and shallow and it was therefore no surprise when she suddenly found herself awake. Had her troubled thoughts woken her up or was it something else?

The gentle knock at her bedroom was repeated, gentle because she shared a room with the children then a voice, whispering, 'Eloise, Eloise, you must come downstairs, wake, wake'. It was Clarisse, what could she want at this hour? It must be important enough to wake her though, she realised, thoughts still sluggish with sleep, and answering, 'One minute', pushed herself slowly out of bed. Clarisse whispered again, 'Put some clothes on, quickly, quickly'. Grumbling to herself, Eloise pulled on a skirt and jumper over her nightdress, and a coat on top, then padded quietly down the stairs, leaving the infants still sleeping undisturbed.

Clarisse was waiting for her in the kitchen and tutted when she saw that Eloise was barefoot, handing her a pair of wooden-soled shoes, 'Go, go, Gilbert is waiting for you outside, I will mind the children'. Had she been more awake, Eloise would have asked, 'Go where?' but she was still a little groggy so just obeyed her friend.

The night air was cold and she gasped, but at least, she thought, it would wake her up. Hervé was indeed waiting for her and without a word, he grabbed her hand and walked her away from the house and into the darkness. 'What are you doing, where are we going?' she hissed but all she received back was a 'Ssh, ssh', and a firm tug on her hand. He would not say another word and Eloise was finding it more difficult to hide her irritation, when a stray beam of moonlight, slipping down between the moving clouds, illuminated the path ahead, and then she knew where she was. They had almost reached the far end of Madame Le Roux's garden and directly in front of them was the old pig-sty, just used these days for storing garden tools.

The old man coughed discreetly and to Eloise's surprise, he was answered, from up ahead, by the same. A figure, unidentifiable in the gloom, beckoned them forward then disappeared again behind the little stone building. It had to be Galou, she realised, for who else would be contacting them at night but why was there all this secrecy? He usually just came to the house.

Gilbert guided her around the corner of the sty and encouraged her in through the doorway. The interior was lit by a single candle and she stood there, dumbfounded, when she saw who was waiting inside. Galou was there, certainly, but next to him was a tall blond boy, looking for all the world like one of the young, fair-haired Germans she had grown so used to, and towering over him, head bent forward to avoid the low beams of the roof, was the unmistakeable form of Monsieur Phil!

Phil could see that she was bereft of words and moving a single pace forward, he gently grasped her small hand in his and nodded, 'Madame'. That broke the spell and she returned the pressure of his hand, 'Monsieur Phil, you said that you would return to France but I did not imagine that it would be so soon'.

He grinned, 'Nor I, Madame, and it is a pleasure to see you, even at this hour. Now, before I forget my manners', he turned to his blond companion, standing next to him, 'this is my friend, Geraint Williams, of the British Army'. They greeted each other politely, then all eyes turned back to Phil.

'Madame Eloise', he began, 'I will tell you why we are here', although she had already guessed.

They spent the next hour going over the description of the Manoir, both inside and out, and at the end of it, both Phil and Geraint felt confident in the accuracy of the information that they already had and had learned even more detail about the layout and the sentries. There was nothing new that would cause the raid to be cancelled or delayed.

Phil then broached what he thought would be the most problematic part of the conversation, for he knew that he had no choice but to go along with whatever Eloise decided.

Phil had been given a 'script' to memorise and began to recite it, 'Madame, our officers agree that you will be in great danger after the raid. You will be the obvious suspect for having passed information to the Allies. We think that you should be protected, so I am authorised to make this offer. You and your family, if you so wish, can be transported back to England with the raiding party. You will be safe there until the end of the war. You will be housed and work may be found for you'.

'What about Gilbert and Clarisse? I cannot leave them behind to face the Boche'.

Phil was appalled, for no one had mentioned the old couple.

'Would they want to come, Madame?' he asked, buying a little time to think.

Gilbert, who had been listening to the exchanges, realised that it was time that he said something, 'Monsieur, Clarisse and I have already decided that we will follow Eloise and the children'. Eloise turned to him, astonished. 'We spoke about it after you went to bed, my dear. I had thought that we might go somewhere warmer, perhaps in the South but never mind, England will do nicely'.

Eloise hugged him, then turned back to Phil, 'There is your answer, Monsieur. What do you say?'

What could he say? 'Then it is settled, Madame, I will provide you with precise arrangements nearer to the night of the raid. You understand that you will take nothing with you, no belongings, no treasures, just the clothes that you wear'.

It would not be easy, leaving everything behind but really, what choice did they have? She turned back to Phil and thanked him for thinking of them, asking, 'Will you visit us in England, Monsieur Phil? We will know no one, and a friendly face would mean so much to me'.

Phil blushed a little, grateful for the darkness, 'Of course I would, Madame, my pleasure, and I look forward to seeing Danielle and Adrien again very soon'.

Galou butted in, having a feeling that, left alone, these two would be exchanging pleasantries until it became light, and then they would have the devil's own job getting back to his cottage unobserved. 'Time to go, my friends, time to go, if you have everything that you need, yes?'

Yes, Phil and Geraint had heard enough and saying goodbye, they followed Galou through the doorway, but Eloise had one more question. 'When is the raid, Monsieur?'

He looked back, 'Regretfully, I cannot tell you, Madame, but very soon, very soon'.

Chapter 19

Galou led Phil and Geraint back across the fields to his cottage and they were safely ensconced in the outhouse before full daylight. Galou brought them bread and coffee then left to begin his work on the roads. Geraint was in the mood for talking, and Phil braced himself for some questions from his friend.

Geraint did not beat around the bush, 'Phil, I think that the young lady is your sweetheart, am I right? If she is not then she should be, such spirit and bravery! She thinks that you are the dog's pyjamas, my friend, I could see it in her face'.

'Mate, it's the cat's pyjamas, your mixing it up with the dog's bollocks, but you're right, she's a little spitfire! Galou told me that she disarmed a traitor and shot him with his own gun, never turned a hair. She's not my sweetheart but who knows? We all have to get home safe first'.

The intention now was to sleep and they needed it. Following a quick run across the Channel in the 'Flying Flea', they had paddled the little folboat the last two miles to the coastline and had landed on the beach at 2300, folding the canoe and hiding it in some bushes. Galou had met them, as planned, and they had made their way first to his cottage, then across the fields to Madame Le Roux's villa. They were not so much physically exhausted but the hours of high tension were utterly draining and they were soon deeply asleep. When darkness returned, they would reconnoitre the proposed landing beach, try to identify a suitable sight for the mortar and if there was time, take a little look at the Manoir, at least from the outside. If everything was satisfactory, Galou would transmit a one-word message to London and as long as the weather held, the raid would be confirmed.

As Phil understood it, the submarine crew would arrive the following morning. He would stay away from Eloise completely, to avoid spooking her with a day left to work for the Germans, but when she arrived back from the Manoir in the evening, he would be waiting for her and would conduct her, the children and the old ones down to the beach. The dories were not due to beach until 0030 but as soon as they did, he would load the would-be escapees onto one of them, and there they would have to wait until the raid was completed. There would be a guard on each boat, so they would not be alone or undefended. If all went as planned, everyone would be back on board an MTB by 0200 and on their way home but as Phil knew, battleplans only worked on paper. Unexpected things would happen and how they managed the surprises would be the key to success and survival.

Eloise dragged herself into work at the Manoir that morning. She had lost three hours of sleep from what was already a short night and was aware that, as the weeks passed, she was becoming more and more tired. The endless labour, with all the anxiety of working for a harsh, occupying power, was wearing her down, so the prospect of escape to England, something that would horrified her even weeks ago, now seemed like a timely opportunity. Consoling herself that, God willing, the end was in sight, she received the delivery of provisions for the submariners and started to work.

Hans greeted Eloise in his usual, cheery manner and unbidden, a terrible thought entered her mind; when the British attacked, and she was sure that it would be soon, what would happen to him? He stayed in the Manoir overnight when the crews were there, and surely, he would be caught up in any attack.

How could she allow that to happen? He was the only German she had met who had treated her as a person, with feelings and responsibilities of her own. He had a wife at home whom he loved, always looking at her photograph and scribbling off letters to her, and he had never once tried to take advantage of his position. How could she possibly sit back and watch him die? She couldn't, she just couldn't, but how could she protect him without risking herself and the babies and Gilbert and Clarisse? They had to take their chance and escape while they could.

This dilemma was at the forefront of her mind all day, impossible for Hans not to notice. He assumed that Eloise was upset at Dönitz and his cruel and unthinking decision to take her away from her family. In fact, it was even worse than Eloise knew, for Hans had overheard that the Admiral's new headquarters was not to be in Lorient but in Paris, another 500 kilometres distant. She would never see her children.

He felt upset for her, and when Brauer came to check on them, it was to see them silently at work, with dishes, cooked or ready to cook, mounting up. He nodded his approval and left, still resentful that Dönitz was stealing his star cook but unable to do anything about it.

At the end of the evening, Hans escorted her past the sentries at the gate and down the road, seeing her safely on her way and as usual, the two sentries made ribald comments which they both ignored. He walked with her for a few minutes but had he followed her, he would have seen her pedal past the Le Roux villa then turn down the lane that led Galou's cottage. It looked in darkness but she knew that it was an illusion, someone would be watching the lane carefully and they would know that they had a visitor.

As Eloise leaned her bicycle against the house wall, the door opened and she heard Galou's familiar voice, 'Why are you here?' he hissed, 'do you want the Boche to find us?' He was furious, and quite rightly so, she realised, as he hustled her into the house. Phil and the blond boy were standing in the kitchen doorway, a rifle and a pistol aiming in her direction but they lowered them quickly as she came into the dim light.

'Why are you here?' repeated Galou, 'it had better be something important, you are putting us all at risk!'

'It's alright, Pierre', said Phil, quietly, 'please tell us, Madame'.

Eloise explained her dilemma regarding Hans and her unwillingness to see him killed, 'He is a good man who has tried to help me and I would not want him to be slaughtered with the others, he does not deserve it'.

'Madame', answered Phil, 'most people who die in this filthy war don't deserve it. They are like you or I, doing their duty for their country. There are some who deserve to die but how you separate them out from those who deserve to live, I don't know'.

There was a quiet cough from Geraint who was still standing in the doorway, listening, 'Phil, we shouldn't forget that Tom has helped Germans before, when they needed it'. Only he and Phil, in that room, knew that he was referring to himself, when Tom and George had rescued him from drowning in the Mediterranean. They had not made any judgement then about Geraint deserving to live or die, they had seen a man in trouble who needed help and that was enough.

'Madame, all I can say is that we will help you if we can', feeling that he had to offer a little hope, if nothing more, 'but we cannot do anything that places you or the raid at more risk. There are too many other lives at stake. Now, tell me about this man's movements'.

Eloise told him all she knew, about Hans sleeping in the Manoir when there were guests and how he accompanied her along the lane for the first few yards, to make sure that she was safely on her way home.

It was little enough and all Phil could say was that he would think about it. Eloise felt disappointed but she had tried. Perhaps Phil would think about it and do nothing, but what if he tried to help Hans and was killed himself? It all seemed hopeless.

Finally, before she left for home, Phil gave her some final instructions. 'Madame, the attack is tomorrow night but do not tell the old couple, it is better that they do not know. Find a way to work for two hours longer tomorrow, that is vital, but you must be out of the Manoir by midnight, at the very latest. You will be met en-route and taken to your family'.

Suddenly, it all seemed very real to Eloise, there would be no going back.

'I know it will be difficult', he continued, 'but you must behave normally and give no reason for anyone to suspect you. Leave everything else to us, now go, you have a very long day tomorrow'.

When she had left, Phil turned to Geraint, 'Right, let's move. The beach first, then we'll find a spot for the mortar', then, to Pierre, 'My friend, we might need a spade to level the ground. Can you bring one along?'

As Galou went outside to find the spade, Geraint turned to Phil, a questioning look upon his face. 'I know, I know, I said I would think about it and I will but I'm damned if anything comes to mind', answered Phil, 'I'll think on and if you have any bright ideas, tell me'. At that moment, Pierre returned and they made final preparations for the last reconnaissance. If all went as they hoped, another twenty-four hours would see the war come to Brittany once again.

Clarisse and Gilbert were waiting anxiously for Eloise to return, and it was so difficult for her keep her promise to Phil and to say nothing about the raid. They knew it would be soon, otherwise why would Phil and Geraint be here? Clarisse was already talking about packing suitcases and although Gilbert had tried to tell her that there would be no room on the little boat for belongings, she had not wanted to believe him, so Eloise had no choice but to tell her firmly that the old man was right. She should wear plenty of clothes but nothing else could be taken on the journey, nothing.

This hit Clarisse hard for, as she tearfully explained, she had lived in the house for more than fifty years, and although, after her husband's death, she had thought about moving to something smaller, this one had so many happy memories for her that she found that she just could not. Her sadness was mostly about leaving the house, not possessions, Eloise realised, and all she could say to offer comfort was that, when the war was over, she promised that she would bring Clarisse back to the house herself. Eventually, she left the two of them comforting each other and went to bed.

Work at the Manoir the following day was an ordeal for her, although, with the submariners arriving in the late-morning, it soon became hectic and she was either cooking or preparing food or clearing up after the sailors had eaten. Like the other crews, they ate when they were hungry and this meant that she and Hans never stopped.

Although she made sure that she worked as hard and as thoroughly as ever, her mind was split between the chaos and mayhem that would happen later when the British came, and a feeling of crushing guilt regarding Hans. She watched him, dashing about the kitchen, as good-humoured and as helpful as ever, yet, unless Phil could come up with a solution, he would be at the same risk as any of the submariners but what could she do? She could not warn him, for he would feel duty-bound to tell Brauer and the others, she could do nothing.

Her mood of guilt and sadness showed on the surface but once again, Hans attributed it to the prospect of her moving away to work for Dönitz and worked even harder to make her day bearable. Brauer showed his face, as usual, grunting in satisfaction at their silent labour, and gradually, the hours passed.

Eloise had pondered how to find a reason to work the extra two hours that Phil had demanded of her, and all she could think of was to do more cooking in advance for the next day. Hans had been surprised, knowing that she was always in a hurry to return home for the children and to sleep but there was logic in it, for the more they did tonight, the less they would have to do tomorrow. He noticed though that as the time moved on, Eloise was looking paler and more tired and at a quarter to midnight, he called a halt.

'Home, Madame, or you will not be fit to work in the morning and that pig Brauer will be at our throats. Find your coat and I will see you safely on your way'.

How she wished that she could answer him back in German and thank him for his many kindnesses, telling him that his wife was so lucky in finding such a good man to be her husband, and that in peaceful times, they would have been both good friends and great cooks together. But she could say none of these things and in another hour, he might be dead, and his wife a widow, like so many others.

As usual, Hans pushed her bicycle past the two guards at the gate, but this time, when they made their crude remarks about what they would like to do with her if they had the chance, he spun on his heel, enraged.

'You fucking clowns', he grated, 'use the brains you were born with! If this was Germany, she could be your mother or your sister and how would you feel then? Eh? You're a disgrace to the uniform!'

Eloise had never seen him so angry and she pulled him away, fearful for his safety, as the taller of the two guards came out of the gatehouse, pointing his carbine in Hans's direction and threatening, 'Fuck off, Grandad and take your French piece with you, we're not in fucking Germany, are we, so we do what we want, go on, fuck off!'

Hans insisted upon walking her another hundred metres, 'well away from those goons', and then handed the bicycle to Eloise. His defence of her had made leaving him in danger even more difficult, made her feel even more guilty, but when she saw a huge black shadow move up silently behind Hans, she knew what was about to happen.

She smiled at him and said, in perfect German, 'Hans, you are a good man and I thank you for everything. Goodbye'. His mouth dropped open in surprise but that was his last conscious action, for Phil's enormous fist crashed into the side of his head and sent him sprawling, unconscious, into the ditch at the side of the road.

Without a word, Phil, face blackened, leaned over him and trussed him tightly with an old rope and finished by gagging him with a rag tied tightly around his mouth.

'Can he breathe?' asked Eloise, anxiously.

'Yes', whispered Phil, 'he's breathing through his nose and the gag just stops him talking, not breathing, he'll be fine when he wakes up'. Eloise was relieved but then Phil unslung his rifle and stood over the insensible Hans, the butt poised above his face.

'What are you doing?'

'I need to hurt him, Madame, convince his officers that he put up a fight. Turn away'.

She turned away, and cringed at the sound of two heavy, blunt impacts behind her.

'What have you done?'

'Cut his head and bust his arm, they'll probably give him a medal. Now, come on', and with that, he took her arm, not to break it but to hurry her along the road and away.

'There's one thing, Madame', he whispered as they climbed over the first wall into the field that would lead them down towards the beach.

'What is that?'

'This never happened, my officers don't need to hear about it and neither does Pierre. I met you in the road, that's all'.

'What about your blond friend, Geraint, does he know?'

Phil laughed quietly, 'It was his idea, Madame, he's the brains of the outfit. You'll see him in a few minutes with your family'.

'Now I must say one thing to you, Monsieur Phil', and pulled him to a halt, looking up at him, 'or perhaps more than one. I will never forget what you have done for us, and if you do not find us in England, I will never forgive you', hugging him tightly, 'and the other thing? We are friends so please call me Eloise'.

'Certainly, Ma…, sorry, Eloise. Call me Phil or Soapy, I don't mind. Now let's get a move on', and taking her arm again, they jogged down the hill towards the sea.

Soapy? she puzzled to herself but that thought left her mind when a challenge, in more of a hoarse whisper than the usual clear demand, sounded in front of them, 'Halt! Who goes there?' 'PO Watson and one', answered Phil, briskly but in the same loud whisper. There was the standard 'Advance and be recognised' then they were back, Eloise hugging little Adrien, while Danielle still slept in Clarisse's arms.

They were warmly dressed, in coats and hats and Gilbert had managed to bring a couple of warm blankets, so they quickly wrapped up and sat back down together. Geraint and Pierre had collected them and had been surprised to find them virtually prepared to move. 'We guessed it must be soon', explained Gilbert and they had left the villa within minutes, Clarisse shedding one final, quiet tear as she locked the door behind them. The walk in the dark had not been easy but Geraint had carried Adrien and they had met no one on their way.

Their final reconnaissance on the previous night had been successful. Pierre had located a patch of beach that he explained had a clear run-in and with space to pull the two dories onto the sand. It was in a cleft, a tiny bay, so they should be able to signal out to sea without being seen from the land. He had also found, closer to the Manoir, what he described as a charcoal-burners' hearth, a flat terrace on the hillside where generations of charcoal-burners had laid their fires. It was on the edge of a coppice now, in the field, with a clear view of the roof of the Manoir but out of sight of the windows. Phil and Geraint had a close look at it and agreed that if the mortar team were not delighted with their firing position, they could, as Geraint put it, 'sling their anchor'.

The two of them had also crept as close as they could dare to the Manoir, to get a feel of the lay-out and to double-check Pierre's intelligence. This part of the reconnaissance was less fruitful, for they had no desire to risk being detected by the guards and the darkness that night, with the Moon hidden behind clouds, was intense. Eventually, they decided that Pierre's information would have to be taken on trust and to be fair, everything that he had provided so far had been accurate. They did locate the stream-bed that ran up the left-hand side of the building and followed it up to the culvert that took it under the road and into the grounds of the Manoir. It was not dry, but neither was it a torrent, merely a dribble, so it should serve, as hoped, as a safe path to the building. The route to the right of the building was sheltered by trees, on both sides of the road, so should prove a sound, concealed approach. Commandos knew how to move quietly.

On their way back to Pierre's cottage, Geraint had floated his idea about ambushing Hans as he escorted Eloise away from the house and Phil could not think of anything better. He was not happy when Phil insisted upon undertaking it himself but someone had to help Pierre with the family, so it was reluctantly agreed. As far as Pierre was concerned though, Phil was only going to meet and escort Eloise, nothing else. They had sent off their signal to London, just the word 'Needle', the agreed code for 'Advise attack as planned'.

All that had worked through successfully and now, they just had to sit and wait for the arrival of the boats. Phil perched where he could see, in the pale, ambient light, right down the cove to the open sea and checked his torch, ready to signal as soon as his watch indicated 0025, ready for the landing at 0030.

Chapter 20

They were late, not fatally so but enough to cause a problem. The companion MTB to the 'Flying Flea', unimaginatively known as MTB 46, had lost an engine two thirds of the way across the Channel. That still left her with two of her three engines firing but they had to be worked harder so for safety's sake and the desire to get everyone home at the end of the night, speed had been reduced by five knots, which added twenty minutes onto the crossing. Fortunately, they had been five minutes ahead before the breakdown, so by the time they lowered the dories into the water and headed for land, the deficit was only fifteen minutes.

Bud, in the bow, had spotted Phil's signal first, and replied as per orders with his torch. The simple codes tallied but the men readied to shoot, in the unlikely eventuality that Phil and Geraint had been compromised. Throttled right back for quietness, it took a further five minutes for the dories to reach the shore but finally they slid their bows up onto the sand. The tide would be coming in for the next eighty minutes, by which time the raid would either have proven to be a great success or a total failure.

The mortar team disembarked first, from Captain Ryan's boat, forming up silently on the sand. Once they were sure that all their equipment was in hand, and their sergeant having synchronised watches with Ryan, they followed Geraint at a fast trot, straight up the hill to their position.

Ryan himself quietly shook Phil's hand, 'Everything in order, PO? No nasty surprises waiting for us, are there?'

'Not that I know of, sir. This lady here', indicating Eloise, sitting quietly with her family, 'she is the cook at the target and she told me that the submariners had arrived as expected this morning, sir, and there's no change in the guarding of the building, as far as she knows. The only factor we didn't know about is that when we attack, up to half of the crew will still be up and about making merry downstairs. We had thought, sir, if you recall, that they would mostly be upstairs and in bed by then'.

'I do recall it, PO, I do. Damn! Well, it shouldn't make too much difference. You chaps with Sergeant Lane will be watching the doors anyway after you've clobbered the guards, it might just mean that you'll need to lay more fire into the ground floor. Your fella with the Bren', pointing at George, 'might come in very useful'.

Pierre was on the edge of the little group, keen to get the captain and his half of the raiding party on the move and into position, for time was moving on. One more handshake and Ryan and his men were gone.

Tom turned to Phil, 'You know the ground, mate, lead on and we'll follow you'. At that moment, Geraint returned from emplacing the mortar team and as the team formed up to move, Phil took the chance to have a final word with Eloise.

She looked up, smiling nervously as he walked the few paces across to her and bent down to speak, 'Stay here until the helmsman gets you on board and sit snug where he tells you, and I'll see you in an hour. The tide is coming in, so you'll be afloat by the time we get back'.

'I can't really tell you to be careful, Phil, can I?'

'Not tonight, Eloise, no, but I'll do my best'.

'Phil', called Tom.

'Sergeant', and touching her shoulder in farewell, he went to the head of the short line of men. Behind Phil was Tom, then Bud, Geraint, George and five commandos, all keyed up and ready to do their work. He took them off to the left, first scrambling up the rocks abutting the beach then within fifty paces, finding themselves dropping down into the stream bed. They had fifteen minutes to position themselves before the mortar group opened fire, so Phil moved quickly, gambling on the agility of the men behind him to avoid any clattering falls.

He was at the culvert in five minutes, diagonally across the road from the gate to the Manoir, with its two sentries, so quietness was even more critical. It would be difficult to maintain silence as they moved through the culvert, for the little tunnel was only a yard in height, and the clink of metal against stone would carry at night. Within thirty seconds of Phil arriving at the culvert's mouth, the others had joined him and he led the way.

He heard the odd scrape behind him as the rest followed but no noise that would have carried more than a few yards, and with seven minutes to spare, according to Tom's watch, they were all ready to move to their final positions.

George and Bud peeled off first, scrambling silently up the bank of the stream to road level. They were a mere fifteen yards from the main gate, with its gatehouse, and their task was to infiltrate to within striking distance and kill its occupants as quickly as possible, as soon as they heard the first mortar bomb leaving the tube. If it could be done silently, that would be a bonus, for even a few extra seconds for the others to take down their targets could make a difference. They would expect to find two men in the gatehouse, and there would be a minimum of another two patrolling around the main building. It could be four, but if Eloise was correct, it was more likely that two of the four would be stealing an extra couple of hours sleep in the stable with their mates.

Phil led the remaining seven men thirty yards further upstream then paused them there, while he climbed up to ground level, to determine their exact position. In the pale light, he could see that they were level with the rear of the house, as close to the rear entrance as they could be, with just the gravel drive between it and them. The stable block was visible to the left but another twenty yards further on, so Tom and the men designated for that part of the operation needed to advance that distance more in the stream bed before emerging, for it was vital that they took the shortest route to the soldiers' sleeping quarters.

A whispered instruction to Tom and he was on his way, taking Geraint and two of the five commandos with him, leaving Phil with the remaining three men. Phil's objective, after the mortar bombs had all fallen, was to prevent any of the men inside the Manoir from exiting the building through the back door, the front being taken care of by Captain Ryan.

As they waited in absolute stillness for the last couple of minutes to tick down, and as tension and apprehension rose within each and every man, occasional strains of music and laughter could be heard coming from the house. If any of them had cared to reflect, at that point in time, that they were about to slaughter as many unprepared partygoers in as short a time as possible, they might have hesitated but they were far beyond that. This was the enemy that they were hunting, not individual people, and the more that they killed or put out of action, the more likely their families and their mates would survive this horrible war.

George and Bud used the final two minutes to stalk closer and closer to the gatehouse, George using all of his skills as an ex-poacher to move himself silently and relentlessly forward, Bud stepping carefully in his footprints, scarcely daring to breathe. The crescendo was close.

Then, with a muffled 'whuump', distinct in the still night, the first mortar bomb was in the air. George instantly sped the last few yards, commando knife in one hand, pistol in the other and shouldered in through the partly-opened door of the guard hut. As he had hoped, the two guards inside were sitting down at a small table, the tiny room clouded with cigarette smoke as they took their leisure. Without a pause, he backhanded the knife into the throat of the guard to his left, while pressing the muzzle of the semi-automatic Colt into the chest of the soldier to the right and pulling the trigger three times. It was over in a few seconds and when Bud arrived, it was to see one soldier bleeding out rapidly on the floor while the other sat still and dead, slumped in his chair.

Outside, everything was happening. The first bomb landed short, in front of the house, and this had roused the two guards on patrol. One had been at the back of the house and as he moved forward to investigate, he saw Bud outside the gatehouse. He lifted his carbine to take a shot but was hurled to the ground as fire from Phil's section and from Bud himself overwhelmed him.

Tom and his three companions raced across the yard to the stable. They could hear movement and shouting in the building, but before any of the soldiers inside could come out to investigate, Geraint and one of the commandos had smashed the glass of the single wooden-barred window and emptied their Stens into the room. As their guns clicked on empty, Tom and the other commando opened the door just wide enough to roll in two grenades and duck back into shelter. The explosions, within a bare second of each other, must have been deafening inside the converted tack-room and shrapnel and debris smashed into the inside of the stable door. The remains of the window burst outwards into the yard, over the heads of Geraint and his companion who, having reloaded, emptied their guns once more through the cavity where the window had been. As they finished, Tom burst through the door, emptying his Sten around the room. There was no fire in return but Tom could just see the outline of a doorway and went to investigate.

As they were attacking the stable, the second mortar bomb landed and this time, it was a direct hit, detonating on contact with the roof of the big house and sending a shower of shattered stone tiles flying in every direction. It would be quickly followed by four more of high explosive, then four of white phosphorus, which would set the place ablaze.

Captain Ryan's team had commenced firing as soon as the first bomb had launched and were methodically raking the upper story of the old house. It was an ancient building with thick, stone walls, impermeable to the calibres they were using, so they were concentrating on the stone-mullioned windows, aiming to saturate the room behind each one with a storm of fire. The other sentry had been checking the front of the Manoir when the first bomb had dropped short, and although it missed the house, the shrapnel and the power of the blast had destroyed him utterly.

Despite the massive, incoming fire, at least some of the submariners were starting to organise themselves, and from the upper windows at the rear of the house, a few rifles and machine pistols were beginning to return fire. The man next to Phil, their Bren gunner, dropped with a grunt as a bullet smashed his arm, and he was hit in the head as he was pulled back into cover. Phil, thinking quickly, shouldered his rifle and relieved the man of his machinegun and magazines then, crouching behind a low stone wall, with the forestock balanced upon the top of the wall, he started to methodically strafe all the upper windows that he could see. His commando companion acted as his loader and between them, they kept up a heavy fire.

By now, the phosphorus bombs were dropping into the cavity of the roof, and through the clouds of thick, white smoke, tall flames were bursting into the sky. The roof beams of the old house, three hundred years old and thoroughly dry, shattered into kindling by high explosive, burned readily, making the destruction of the house inevitable. The upper floor, reasoned Phil, would have to be abandoned, and if the submariners attempted to evacuate the house from the ground floor, front or back, they would not get far.

Inside the stable, Tom had a feeling that not everyone in that little building had been accounted for. He could hear nothing beyond the open doorway, but the din of battle outside was so loud now that it was no surprise. Geraint had entered the stable now, seen in the light from the burning house, and Tom beckoned him over. This time, three grenades were rolled through the open doorway and exploded with a huge roar, followed by Tom, spraying fire around the room.

Again, there was no return of fire or movement and this time, Tom pulled a small, shaded flashlight from a pouch, revealing a scene of devastation. The second room had been a makeshift dormitory, with bedding thrown down in wooden stalls, and the three bombs had punched through the wooden partitions, sending shrapnel and splinters flying in all directions. It looked as though at least four men had been sleeping in here, and when the attack had started, they had roused themselves to investigate and defend the Manoir. Two of the men lay, eviscerated by the flying debris, while a third lay flat on his back in a spreading mass of blood, an irregular hole punched through his forehead. The fourth sat slumped against the far wall, one leg missing from the knee downwards and the other a mass of ruptured flesh and white bone.

Despite the horrendous and devastating pain that he must have been feeling, this soldier had somehow held onto his carbine and fired off six shots before a burst from Geraint's Sten killed him instantly. Those six shots proved costly, as Geraint's companion slid down the wall, blood pumping out between his fingers as he pressed his hand onto a gaping hole in his thigh, and even as Tom pulled out the man's field dressing and started to bind it over the wound, he shuddered and died.

There were no further rooms leading off the stable and the three men, leaving their comrade's body where it fell, moved back into the tack-room. If anything, the devastation in here was worse than in the dormitory. Five full magazines of automatic fire and two grenades had reduced the inhabitants to mere heaps of smoking flesh, their remains lying in a foul miasma of smoke and blood and burst entrails. It was sickening but the three men never paused, for their next duty was to help suppress any fire coming from the house. They passed through the doorway, to be greeted by yet another stunning sight.

The Manoir was well alight by now, and there was no more defensive fire coming from the upper rooms. The whole roof seemed to be blazing, and flames, greater than the height of the building, were illuminating the sky. Gunfire was being returned from the ground floor and before Tom and Geraint could find a position to fire from, a small group of desperate men burst out of the rear door of the Manoir, armed only with machine-pistols, spraying bullets wildly around the yard. Bullets ricocheted in all directions and at Tom's side, he felt someone stagger backwards under the impact of a round and drop to the cobbled yard. Along with everyone else focussed on the rear of the building, he fired as fast as he could at the desperate, advancing group, and it was as if they had walked into a solid wall, for in a matter of seconds, they were all shot down before they had made even ten yards from the developing inferno behind them.

Tom turned to the casualty beside him and was horrified to see Geraint lying on his side. He had been hit in the chest and was conscious, trying to apply his field dressing but unable even to remove it from its packaging.

Ripping his tunic open, Tom could see that it was a sucking wound, the bullet had entered his lung and now air was rushing in and out of the bullet hole as Geraint struggled to breathe. He could drown in his own blood in minutes.

Tom tied the dressing over the wound as securely as he could, but his friend really needed the earliest evacuation. He was about to send a messenger to Ryan when George came rushing into the yard from near the guardhouse and ran up to Tom, 'From Ryan, withdraw'. It was the correct decision, Tom knew, for the defenders had been decimated and more, their defensive fire had shrunk to almost nothing and the attackers' own ammunition would start to run short if they stayed much longer.

Tom shouted the orders and when he heard them, Phil came running over. He had seen Geraint fall and after checking him over, rushed into the tack-room, coming out a minute later with a door to use as a stretcher. Geraint was gently laid on it, and with Tom at one end and Phil on the other, they ran for the gate. George and Bud were at the road, pointing back in the direction of the village, and as Tom passed, he slowed down to speak.

'Hold them back for a couple of minutes, George, if they come after us, but no longer, and we'll see you at the boat'.

'How is he?' asked Bud, looking down at Geraint, pinched and still on the old door.

Tom could not reply, they just ran on, hoisting Geraint over the wall with great care and disappeared down the hill toward the beach.

The only noise now was the roar and crackling of flames as the conflagration that had engulfed the house consumed it. There was no firing from the house but then, Bud cocked his head as a different sound made itself heard.

'That's a truck, pal', he said to George and sure enough, within a few seconds, George could hear it too. 'It'll be from that chateau they told us about. We'll get out of sight'.

Chapter 21

Eloise and the others had stayed huddled together in their blankets after the soldiers had disappeared up the hill. She felt tremendous anxiety for Phil and Geraint and the others but also felt it for herself and the children and of course, for Gilbert and Clarisse. They had put their faith, and their lives, into the hands of these frightening British soldiers and only God knew if they would succeed.

As soon as the first mortar exploded at the Manoir, the helmsman of the nearest dory called them aboard. Danielle was handed across to him, still sleeping, and he stood there, rather sheepishly, holding her while the others clambered aboard. It took the combined efforts of Gilbert and Eloise to help Clarisse step up and over the gunwale, with Gilbert heard to murmur, 'No one could call you a light woman, my dear', and receive a sharp kick for his impertinence. He was not much more than skin and bone himself, and Eloise helped him over with ease.

They settled down to one side of the engine compartment but their attention now was wholly on the battle that was building up around the Manoir. They watched as the roof caught light and watched the spread of the fire, until it was the length and breadth of the building. The incessant noise of guns firing, the percussion of machineguns interspersed with the dull crashes of explosions, the roof at one end of the building collapsing in a fresh gust of flames and smoke. It was horrific and terrifying, even at this distance, and she understood for the first time what her dead husband, Henri, must have suffered before he died.

The din continued and continued then suddenly, it was gone. There was still the roar of the fire but the shooting had faded away. The first to return was Captain Ryan and his party, looking battered but elated. As they passed the first dory before climbing onto the second, he stopped for a quick word with the helmsman, and Eloise was able to overhear, 'Caught them with their pants down, Corporal, and it's not over yet, oh no!' He sounded triumphant, which she instinctively recoiled from but then, how was he supposed to feel? He had survived, and it seemed that the raid had been a success, so it was hardly surprising that he was happy. They were carrying one wounded man, who needed to be helped on board, but that was all. The second dory, already afloat, turned her bow to the sea but was held in position, waiting for Tom's half of the raiders to return. Ryan shouted across to Eloise, 'Your chum has pushed off home', meaning Pierre, she thought.

Within a few minutes, they could hear more men tearing across the hillside and clattering down the final yards of the little cliff. Several of them waited at the bottom and she watched as someone, attached to something, a door perhaps, was lowered with infinite care down onto the beach, then rushed across to the little boat. Now they were closer, she could see that the tall sergeant and her friend Phil were running across the final few yards of sand, then lifting one end of the door up onto the gunwale. As Phil leapt up onto the boat, leaving Tom to push the door, with its burden, further on board, she saw that it carried the young soldier with the blond hair, she had forgotten his name, and his skin looked as pale as his hair. He was having difficulty breathing, lying flat on his back and she quickly intervened, pulling him over onto his side. Within seconds, his breathing eased and she decided to stay with him.

While all this was happening, the sound of heavy firing broke out again from the direction of the Manoir. Eloise could see that at least two of the men were missing, perhaps more, so they must still be fighting. She saw the sergeant and Phil exchange a look before jumping back down onto the sand and scrambling back up the cliff, weapons in hand, they were going back for their friends.

Eloise was right, and the two men pounded back up the hill. The firing was heavy and judging from the flashes of tracer and the weight of fire, it was between a considerable force in front of the house and a much smaller force, two guns so it must be Bud and George, in the wood to the right. Instinctively, it made sense to approach from the left to try to catch the main force of shooters in a crossfire.

They paused before the final dry-stone wall and looked at the scene. A truck, and it had to be German, had stopped at the far side of the house and its load of troops had jumped out and to a man, were firing up into the wood. Both men knew that very soon, the German troops would outflank the two men in the trees, so they set up to fire, although only able to identify a few targets in the gloom. The best they could hope for was to cause the Germans to take cover, and hopefully that would give them a little to escape.

Tom was taking up the pressure on his trigger when, above and behind him, from the direction of the sea, an increasing, beating roar filled the sky. Phil looked back too, and they both spotted a huge, black shadow moving rapidly towards them in the night sky. Before it was over them, bursts of light burst out from its nose and wings and in a split second, cannon shells and machinegun bullets were hammering into and around the truck and lashing into the remains of the old house and the stable beyond.

There was a moment of stillness then an enormous crash as the truck exploded, illuminating the scene in blinding light. German survivors were marked out, as if lit by a searchlight, and the two men poured fire into them. It was close range, like a shooting gallery, and they could hardly miss, especially as the two in the wood were firing too. A few soldiers, led by a tall Unteroffizier, made to return fire but as soon as he went down, riddled by fire from both directions, the fight went out of the rest of them and they took cover.

It was as well they did, for by then, the aircraft had reversed its course and coming in from inland this time, it strafed the building and its surroundings once more. Tom and Phil had to duck down behind their wall as the bullets rattled into it, sending stone-chips flying. This time, the plane kept flying onwards and it disappeared into the darkness over the sea.

Tom, knowing that George and Bud would take the chance to withdraw, nudged Phil and they trotted back down the field, anticipating that their routes would intersect before they reached the beach. They did, but there was no backslapping or congratulations, time was short and the night was not yet over.

Both boats were turned seaward and as soon as the four of them had embarked, they were on their way. Eloise had Geraint sitting up, back against the gunwale, and she explained to Phil that his breathing seemed to be at its easiest in that position. He was conscious but in pain, just managing to crack a pale smile in his friends' direction before concentrating again at holding it at bay.

All the soldiers were immediately busy, thumbing rounds into magazines, as the dories worked up to their nine or ten knot maximum, slowed by the incoming tide. The baby still slept but little Adrien had woken again, after a short sleep and had spied Phil, shouting, 'Homme, homme', not satisfied until Gilbert had caught Phil's attention, and the little boy was rewarded with a wave and a grin before Phil turned his attention back to his work. He allowed himself a private smile, however, absurdly pleased that the little chap had remembered him.

The two MTBs were on station and as soon as their lookouts had spotted the dories, they swooped down on them, intending to hustle the men on board without delay. Tom's boat, however, took longer to discharge, with the children, the elderly couple and the prostrate Geraint taking time and patience to get on board. They were helped below decks and before they had even found places to sit or lie, the 'Flying Flea' was digging her stern into the water as the three mighty engines opened up and delivered their power. Their companion vessel, MTB 46, after some furious repair work, had three working engines again and followed them, on the starboard side of their wake. Both dories were sacrificed for extra speed, being holed and abandoned, rather than being hauled up on deck as usual.

They were three guns short on the 'Flea', having two commandos killed and Geraint lying wounded below. They still made a formidable group, together with the crew manning the twin Vickers in the stern, still not replaced with cannon, and further machineguns in the bows.

The 'Flea' had been making her thirty-five knots for an hour, and hopes were beginning to rise, when the look-out in the bow screamed out, 'Three points on the port bow and closing fast, two, no three bow waves!' The skipper, on the tiny bridge, lifted his binoculars and there, perhaps two miles away or more, were the shadowy shapes of three fast vessels, almost certainly E-boats, and with the MTBs in their sights.

He turned calmly to the signalman, 'Send this message, 'Enemy in sight, follow my turn, starboard thirty'. A change of course away from the E-boats would prolong the chase at the very least, and there was always the hope that there might be a friendly destroyer on patrol in the Channel which might help them out. The signalman, well-practiced on the Aldis lamp, sent the message off in seconds, then as soon as he shouted back, 'Acknowledged!' the skipper made the turn, gunwales awash.

Their pursuers had to turn too, but they lost no distance and in minutes, it was clear that the German boats were slowly overhauling them. The 'Flea' managed a couple more knots but the wind was beginning to get up and the E-boats, at almost twice the size, were able to manage rougher water more easily, and sure enough, the gap started to close more quickly.

Then, a shout from the signalman, 'Sir, message from 46, 'Engine fail Make home best speed'. The temperamental third engine in MTB 46 had let them down again. 'Make home best speed' was an order to the skipper of the 'Flea' to continue and it made sense, for if they slowed down too or tried to intervene, it would mean that both boats would be captured or destroyed, whereas if they kept running, there was still a chance that one vessel might get home.

The second MTB was obviously losing speed and rather than struggle onwards and be overhauled, the skipper had made the decision to make a 180 degree turn and attack the pursuers head-on. The turn was laborious, into the rising sea, but she made it and the skipper gave her everything from the two remaining engines. That probably meant ten knots less top speed but that would still give a closing speed of nearly seventy knots with the faster E-boats.

Captain Ryan must have brought all his men up on deck and soon, the crackle of heavy automatic fire came over the water. She would make a more difficult target at that speed and although the E-boats were firing back, nothing heavy was hitting her. Somehow, she made it through the German line without mortal damage, still firing hard, and two of the E-boats peeled off to follow her. The third, however, just ploughed on after the 'Flea', the German commander having made the sensible decision that two boats would make sure of the certain kill while the third tried for the other.

The sacrifice of MTB 46, for that was what it amounted to, had enforced some manoeuvring by the chasing E-boat and the distance had opened up by another half-mile but it would not be long before she made it up. The skipper's guess was that they would start firing their bow-mounted cannon soon, for they were within range, and the only bonus was that the wind-blown seas would make their aiming more difficult. On the other side of the argument, morning was not far away and the light was growing in the East.

Then, directly behind them, a white and red flash, right on the horizon, climbing into the sky, disappearing, then, endless seconds later, the boom of the explosion. It had to be the MTB meeting its end, it would never have prevailed against the larger German boats.

Then, as if on cue, the pursuing boat opened fire with its cannon. The first shell was in line but over, and the skipper flung her a few degrees to port, hoping to throw off the next shot too. He did, for although the shell landed level, it was off to starboard. She was not an easy target, small at seventy feet in length and in a broken sea, but the skipper knew that every evasive manoeuvre he made would bring the German boat closer. Tom had brought the men up on deck and they all found perches around the torpedo boat. George and Phil were the best shots and found positions alongside the open bridge, intending to fire over the heads of the stern twin Vickers.

The range continued to decrease and shells were coming closer and closer. How would their passengers be feeling down below, thought Phil, with all this turmoil around them. There were Carley floats to hold onto if they went into the water but would they even get the opportunity? How would they manage Geraint? What of the children and the old couple?

The E-boat was barely in range of their weaponry but the skipper ordered, 'Open fire!' They might be lucky in the few minutes that were left to them, so everyone let rip. It was a forlorn hope but they had to try.

The skipper had just ordered another swing to starboard when the stern lookout screamed, 'She's turning, she's turning', and of course, everyone looked at their pursuer and she was turning, turning hard to port until her course was reversed. That brought her rear guns into action and it was as much as the skipper could do to avoid any hits. Why had she turned away? No one could guess although as the skipper knew, E-boats were equipped with RDF, so perhaps they had detected something up ahead. He shouted down to the look-out, 'Jenkins, my granny could have given a clearer report than that, what should you have said, you miserable brute?'

The look-out was stumbling through a more conventional report as Phil dropped down into the cabin below. Geraint was looking even more pale, if that was possible, but was still sitting up, supported by Eloise. He explained what had happened then turned to Geraint, 'Hold on there, mate, something has scared them off so I reckon we'll make it. How are you?' it was a stupid question, he knew, but it took Geraint's attention.

He smiled painfully, 'I have been better, my friend but of course, Madame Beauchêne makes a better nurse than you. If she holds me tight at this angle, I find I can breathe. In fact, it was almost worth getting shot!' These few words took all his breath, leaving him gasping.

Phil looked around. Danielle had woken at last and was staring at him as she drank from a mug held by Clarisse. Incredibly, both Gilbert and the little boy were sleeping, laid out on the deck. It looked as if they might arrive in Britain after all.

Tom's shouted through the open door, 'Phil, come and take a look', and with a final smile to Eloise, he went back up on deck. Tom was pointing across the water at a grey-painted ship cutting across in front of them, guns continually training around.

He smiled wearily, 'Hunt-class destroyer, mate, single funnel directly behind the bridge. Four four-inch guns on the stern, one of ours, you can't mistake her for anything else. The white ensign's a good clue too'.

'Very funny, that's what the skipper said. He's signalled her, they have a surgeon on board, they'll take Geraint. They can treat him on the way in. They spotted us on their RDF, could see it was a pursuit. Skipper reckons the Jerry had RDF too, used his common sense and buggered off'.

'What about Captain Ryan, that was a hell of an explosion'. They contemplated the fate of the captain and his men in silence, knowing that the chances of any survivors would be small. The detonation had looked big, even at four miles or more, and the cold water would finish off any swimmers very quickly.

Two long hours later, they were threading their way past Studland and Brownsea Island, on the way in to the quay at Poole. Geraint had been hauled safely across to the destroyer, HMS Berkeley, tied into a stretcher and was whisked below decks to the sick-bay before the ship was underway. All they could do was to hope that he survived the journey to Portsmouth.

Eloise and her family were called up on deck for a sight of their new home, hopefully temporary, providing the Allies won the war. With Danielle in one arm, she hung onto Phil with the other and stared out at her new and unfamiliar surroundings.

'What will happen to us, Phil? What will your people do with me, and what about Gilbert and Clarisse?'

'I can't say for sure, Eloise. Major Barton, he's our commanding officer, he'll be waiting onshore and he'll know by now that you're all with us and don't forget, SOE, that's the people in London, they agreed that you should be brought back if you wanted to come, so they'll be expecting you'.

'And what about you, Phil, what will you do?'

'Me? Well, I'm under orders for the duration, so I suppose I'll go where they tell me to'.

'I did not mean that, Englishman! Will I see you again, after we land? In half an hour, I might be spirited away somewhere and you will forget me! You must excuse me, I am not usually as forward as this but our time together could be very short'.

Phil turned to face her, smiling, 'Then yes, you will see me again, I'll make sure of it'.

Chapter 22

Major Barton was waiting on the quay and greeted everyone solemnly as they disembarked. He took Tom to one side, 'Well done, Sergeant but it's a bad show about Captain Ryan and his men, bad show. Debrief later, of course, but was there any alternative to his decision to turn back and fight, eh, could you have done anything else?'

'There were alternatives, sir', answered Tom, 'he could have surrendered, especially after losing an engine but he would never do that, sir. We could have joined him in the attack but he ordered us to make our best speed home, I think he knew that we would have lost both boats if we had engaged alongside him. As it was, it's only luck and good seamanship that got us back, sir'.

'Quite, Sergeant, quite. Alright, there's a truck for you men, the young woman and her family can come in the car with me. The immigration and customs people need to check them out, Christ knows why, and we've agreed that they can do that at Anderson Manor, and I expect that your SOE chaps will want to see them too. Congratulations on the operation, of course, well done. The RAF will be sending over a plane to get a few photographs of the damage this morning'.

He had not mentioned Geraint, 'Any news about Lance Corporal Williams, sir? HMS Berkeley was heading for Portsmouth with him, sir'.

'Oh damn, sorry, Sergeant, I forgot to say, yes, he survived to Portsmouth and they were shipping him on to Haslar, that's the navy hospital there. The ship's surgeon managed to drain a lot of the blood from his chest but he's still bleeding of course so they'll be working on him today'.

'May I have permission to go and see him, sir?'

'You may, Sergeant, tomorrow. He will be out of it today, you need sleep and I need a full debrief. Now, get your men together and we'll be on our way'.

Tom thanked the MTB skipper for his efforts in keeping them afloat long enough to be rescued and commiserated about the almost certain loss of his friend in MTB 46. He agreed with Tom that Ryan had made the correct decision, although it had cost him his life.

They followed the established routine of quick debrief and breakfast, followed by much needed sleep and a long debrief later. Breakfast was enlivened by the presence of the two children, who seemed to have come through all the trauma unscathed and who filled the dining room with laughter and fun. Phil was noted to be very attentive to their needs and there was some friendly joshing in his direction. He took no notice and it was clear to Tom that once again, an intense, shared experience had pulled two people together, as it had in Crete with Elena and himself. How it would work through, who could say, but if they found a measure of happiness in the midst of all this death and destruction, who would deny them the chance? Good luck to them.

The long debrief was painful, because although the operation was judged to have been a great success, it had come at a great cost. They had suffered casualties before but never so many and it brought home the huge risks that his type of operation would always carry. Was it worth it? That would be for their masters to judge.

There were plenty of lessons learned that would be useful for the future; the French Resistance had been an invaluable source of accurate intelligence, and they would be used with more confidence in the future. Air support had been crucial and could have been useful again on their return run across the Channel. Cooperation with the Royal Navy, although accidental, had saved fifty per cent of the attacking force and some kind of formal arrangement should be explored with the Admiralty for future operations.

Finally, the loss of Ryan and his half of the force was discussed. The surviving skipper gave exactly the same account as Tom, and it was plain to everyone there, including Barton, that Captain Ryan had made a brave and necessary call. There was no doubt that his courage, and that of the skipper of MTB 46, would be officially recognised, not that it would be any consolation to their families.

Barton ended the meeting, informing everyone before they left that they were being stood down from duty for four days and given the losses, he did not foresee another operation for a considerable time. Tom was asked to wait behind.

'Sergeant Lane', began Barton, 'there are a couple of things that I need to tell you. First of all, congratulations are in order. You will forgive my shock, I hope, at losing so many men but you achieved every objective and the blow to the morale of their U-boat service will be enormous. My guess is that the 'powers that be' will push more resources our way and that there will be many more raids to come'.

He paused, then, 'However, you and your chaps will not be part of it, I'm afraid'.

Tom was stunned, what did he mean? Was someone looking for a scapegoat for the losses?

Barton, seeing Tom's shock, hurriedly continued, 'Sergeant, no one is blaming you for anything, if that is what you are thinking. As I said, the Brass are most impressed. No, on the contrary, SOE want you back for another operation elsewhere. We will be sorry to lose you but you were only here on loan, so to speak. You will be called to Baker Street in due course'.

That would be Smith's doing, Tom realised. Their shady handler would have further plans in preparation for them, God knows where, and he would have to decide whether to go along with it or to return to the Regiment. Perhaps Phil would want to go back to sea. He brought back his attention to Major Barton, who was still talking.

'They also want to interview your French woman, Sergeant, ah, Madame Beauchêne. Baker Street, the day after tomorrow, at least a day and maybe longer. Can you spare anyone to escort her, they can take a car'.

'I'm sure that I can find a volunteer, sir'.

'Anything else, Sergeant?'

'Yes, sir, Private Wilson', answered Tom.

'Private Wilson? The American? What about him, Sergeant?'

'Begging your pardon, sir, but he showed a great deal of aptitude for the work. A good shot, quick thinker, I was wondering, if he was to volunteer for SOE, would you stand in his way, sir?'

Barton was not pleased. 'Damn you, Sergeant, I wish I could! No, SOE has joint authority here and if they decide that they want someone, well, I have to go along with it, more's the pity. If he wants to tag along with you, then there will be no barriers put in his way'.

'Thank you, sir'.

'One last thing, Sergeant. You'll find twenty-five pounds behind the bar at the 'Royal Oak'. Get your chaps down there and celebrate what you've achieved, I have invited the crew of the 'Flea' too, they deserve it. No doubt, you'll drink a toast to Captain Ryan, eh?'

Phil didn't join the drinkers, he chose to sit with Eloise and the old couple in the Manor garden, enjoying the last of the evening sun. So much had happened in the past few days, turning their lives upside down, that none of them, as yet, had made much sense of it. So, they sat in the sunshine, playing with the children and hardly daring to believe that, for now, they were safe. They had no more than the clothes upon their bodies but for now, that would suffice.

Phil turned to Eloise, 'Our bosses want to see you in London, the day after tomorrow'.

Eloise paled, 'Me? What do they want with me?'

'They will want to talk to you, to learn as much as you can tell them about the Germans and how they are organised, that sort of thing'. He paused, considering if he should tell her, then decided, of course he should! 'They also have to be satisfied that you are not a Nazi spy, come to learn Winston's secrets'.

Her pallor increased, if that was possible, 'What will they do? Torture me?'

Phil smiled, 'No, just lots of questions, trying to catch you out in a lie. Just tell the truth and everything will be fine'.

'What if they ask me about Hans?' Now, thought Phil, that could be a problem. He could end up reprimanded or worse for endangering the raid, for there was no operational reason that justified ambushing the German orderly. No, he would not, could not, ask her to lie.

'If they ask, tell them. Nothing bad happened because of it'.

'How will I get to London, I have never been there before, I...'

'Sergeant Lane asked me to volunteer to drive you there. We could be away for two days or even three'.

'What about the children? How can I leave them?'

'Never mind the children', interrupted Clarisse, who was no fool and understood very well the attraction between the big sailor and the petite widow, 'they are used to Gilbert and me, they will come to no harm for a couple of days. Just as long as you don't forget that we are here when you finish having a nice time in London!'

The local pub, the 'Royal Oak', was used to boisterous groups of rough-looking men from the Manor but this lot, observed the landlord, were different from the usual. They were quiet, even subdued, to begin with but soon the local ale did its work and things became livelier, particularly when the crew of the 'Flea' arrived. Their shared sadness was put to one side and soon they were indistinguishable from the typical revellers.

Tom took George to one side, 'Mate, do you want to carry on with this?'

George grinned, 'Of course I do, Tom, there's twenty-five quid to get through!'

Tom laughed, 'Not the booze, you old tosser. No, I mean the work, with Smith and his spooks'.

'I knew what you meant, mate', answered George, 'yes, I reckon so. I'd rather be doing this than a lot of other things for His Majesty. You?'

'Yes, I reckon. I don't think I can sit back in Blighty and just wait for the war to end, can you?'

'We'll see what Smith has to offer, eh?'

'Barton gave me permission to ask Bud if he wanted to stay with us, we're going to need someone else with Geraint out of action, so I asked him'.

'What did he say?'

Tom looked puzzled, 'Well, he asked me if I was blowing smoke? What do you think he meant by that?'

'Not the foggiest, mate. What did you say?'

'I said, bugger blowing smoke, yes or no, and he said, the little sod, he said, does a one-legged duck swim in circles? I think that means yes'.

'He'll be an education, won't he', observed George, 'we'll all end up speaking Yankee in no time'.

The following day, Tom pulled in some favours and was given a truck and driver for the day. Tom and George, Phil and Bud, they all climbed into the back and travelled down to Haslar to see Geraint. They found him heavily bandaged but alert, and a delighted smile washed over his pale features as they entered the ward. Phil and Bud were immediately told to leave by the tigerish Ward Sister and told that only two visitors were allowed at one time, so they chatted to some of the other patients, all sailors, while they waited.

Geraint gave them the news, 'I have lost part of my lung, Sergeant, one lobe, as the nurse lady told me, and I have three broken ribs. She said that I was very lucky not to be dead, that the bullet was probably a ricochet or it would have gone right through me. I will be out of commission for three months, she says. After that, I hope that you will have some work for me'.

'There will be work for you, mate, never fear. How about I have a word with Smith when I see him?'

Geraint looked pleased, yes, he would like that and it would give him something to look forward to, something to work towards. The sister shooed them away far too soon, and Phil and Bud could only manage a few words with him.

'Soapy, my friend', whispered Geraint, short of energy even after this short talk, 'please tell Madame Beauchêne that she saved my sausages'.

'Saved your what? Oh, you mean saved your bacon'. He was well used to Geraint's imperfect grasp of the English language.

'That's what I said', snapped Geraint, a little peeved, for he was proud of his idiomatic English, 'tell her that the surgeon on the destroyer told me that she had probably saved my life, stopped me from drowning in my own blood. Tell her, please, that I am very grateful'.

The nurse was darting threatening glances in their direction, and they stood up to leave, 'Jeez, she's scary', commented Bud, but Geraint shook his head. 'No, not really. Elaine has promised to take me out to drink beer when I am strong enough, she is very sweet, I think'.

Phil looked down at him, wonderingly, 'I don't know how you do it, mate, I really don't. Be careful you don't bust your stitches'.

They came away, relieved, and promised to visit again, although they all knew that the war might make that an impossibility.

Phil and Eloise had an easy run into London, for at that time in the war, military traffic was not great in volume and most civilians used the train because of the shortage of petrol. They had a few hours before Eloise was due in Baker Street, so after a sparse lunch at a Lyon's Corner House, Phil showed her a few of the sights. The streets were all there, thought Phil, but so was the bomb damage and the missing shops, like gaps in a row of teeth. Eloise tried her best to be appreciative but it was difficult, for the war was still with them.

Phil delivered her to 64 Baker Street at the due time and was told to return the next day at midday, when either Eloise would be released or he would be told to come back at a later time. She looked scared as he left her, waiting in the foyer, and went off to find some accommodation for himself.

For the first time that he could remember, Phil felt lonely. How could he feel lonely in London, heaving with people from all around the around the world, and many of them only too willing to speak to a stranger? It seemed ridiculous but he did, and he knew why.

These hours with Eloise were precious, for as sure as the stars shone in the heavens, they would be separated soon enough. There would be orders and off he would go and might never see her again. It made a lot of sense to get through the war with no attachments but if it happened, what did you do? It had to be even worse for men like George, with a wife and children at home, waiting for him or waiting for the worst.

The evening passed, as did the night, spent in a Navy hostel. He was at Baker Street at midday but was crestfallen when he was told to return in two hours. There was more time to burn, slogging around the streets but his patience was rewarded, for at the appointed time, Eloise was waiting for him, and free to leave.

She was elated, there was no other word for it, and she hardly caught breath as she told him what had happened. 'Phil, they are letting us stay, all of us. Two men questioned me for six hours last night, six hours, but I just told the truth again and again and eventually they said, alright, go to bed. I think it was a cell I was sleeping in, I didn't sleep much and then they woke me at six for another three hours of questioning, the same ones over and over. They gave me a drink and some breakfast then told me that they believed me! They were interested in my languages and for the rest of the morning and after lunch I was taking language tests and solving puzzles, numbers and letters, that sort of thing. I asked them what it was all for and they wouldn't tell me but at the end of it, they said that they would like to offer me a job, helping to make sense of German messages and talking with the Résistance. They will pay me and help find a house for us all in London, what do you think?'

Phil smiled at her enthusiasm, 'That's great, Eloise, you can support the family and you'll be safe until the end of the war, congratulations!' He was genuinely delighted for her, how completely had her life turned around in a matter of a few days.

'Did they ask you about Hans?'

'No, they never asked, so I didn't tell'. Thank God for that, he thought, relieved, wondering how Hans had got on. His best guess was that he would have been found as soon as it was light.

She was hanging on his arm, looking up at him with a shy smile, and he realised abruptly and intuitively that this was one of those rare moments when his future was in the balance. He hardly dared to breathe as he waited for her to speak.

'Phil, do we need to go back to Anderson Manor tonight? The children will be fine for one more night with Clarisse, and I would like you to show me more of London'.

'We can do that, yes, I'll telephone the Major and tell him we'll be back in the morning, he was expecting it anyway, but I'll have to find a women's hostel or somewhere for you to stop overnight...'

'Stop teasing me, you awkward Englishman! No, you will find us a nice hotel and a room with a bath and there we will stay, together. Do you think that I would lose my matelot énorme when I have just found him?'

Chapter 23

The following morning, at the same time as Phil and Eloise were looking at each other over breakfast, and making some cautious plans for the future, Tom was summoned by Major Barton to his office. A civilian was sitting behind the Major's desk, chubby and bald and of course, it was Mr Smith, their SOE handler. Tom had guessed that a meeting would happen, but so soon?

'Sergeant Lane, what a pleasure to, ah, see you again. You have been busy, have you not?'

Tom had never taken to Smith, or whatever his real name was. His suspicion was that Smith used people such as he to do his dirty work and then claimed a large share of the credit and kudos. Tom had never taken kindly to being used by anyone, yet there was no doubt that Smith's judgement had been correct up until now.

'Good morning, sir. Yes, more or less busy since we left Cape Town, as I am sure you know'.

'Oh, I do know, Sergeant, I do know. I have been following your, ah, exploits very carefully and I am pleased to say that between you all, you have made a considerable contribution to winning this war'.

He must want something, thought Tom to himself, he's never usually this polite.

'Thank you, sir'.

'I was sorry to hear about Private Williams, Sergeant, or should I call him Lance Corporal?'

'That's right, sir, Lance Corporal and well-deserved'.

'I understand that he will be out of, ah, action for a few months, Sergeant. I have a mind to offer him some work translating, advising us about Kriegsmarine procedures, ah, that sort of thing. What do you think?'

'I think that would be just the ticket, sir, until he is fit again, and I thank you for the thought'.

'Good, I will visit him in Haslar. Now, I believe that you have a candidate to, ah, replace him'.

'Yes, sir, Private Wilson, Dorsetshires. He's an excellent soldier, sir, plenty of common sense and initiative, not frightened to speak up if he thinks something is wr...'

'Thank you, Sergeant, I will be the judge of that'. Ah, there he is, thought Tom, the pompous little shit.

Smith continued, 'The reason I am here is that I have another job for you, Sergeant. May I presume that you and your group are willing to remain, ah, attached to my organisation?'

'Yes, sir, you may, as long as Geraint is replaced to my satisfaction'. Put that in your pipe and smoke it!

'Alright, alright, Sergeant', answered Smith, his irritation surfacing, 'you can have your American, if you think that much of him. He's cleared anyway, working with the SSRF, so he's yours'.

Tom nodded, pleased that Bud would remain with them, he was a lad with a future.

'For your ears only, Sergeant, for now. You are familiar with the Kingdom of Yugoslavia, I am sure?'

'Up to a point, sir. I know that the Nazis invaded it around the same time that they invaded Greece, sir, not much more than that'.

'Well, that's a start, I suppose', commented Smith in his usual patronising fashion, 'what you probably don't know is that there is a Resistance movement there, very committed, hates the Germans but they're, ah, split, some of them support the King and the rest are communists. Churchill's orders are that we help whoever will fight the Germans, simple as that, royalists or communists, he doesn't care. Similar job to Crete in a way, Sergeant, training, weapons, planning. You with me?'

'Yes, sir'.

'Good. You will be based here for now, keep up your personal training and I'll send some chaps down who know the country, they'll brief you properly, that sort of thing, oh and you'll need to refresh your parachute tickets. It will be two to three months before the operation, so if you and your chaps want leave, I suggest you take it now. Shall we say seven days?'

'Thank you, sir, we'll take you up on that. May I ask you a question, sir?'

'You may, Sergeant, but I don't know if I will be able to answer it'.

'Sir', Tom hesitated, he felt vulnerable and maybe Smith would brush him off but he had to ask. 'Sir, had you heard anything from Crete before you left Alexandria? My wife, Elena Stephanidis, I left her fighting alongside her brother Yannis, with the andartes'.

'Ah, yes', answered Smith, looking down his nose at Tom, he had not approved of their union but by the time he had heard about it, they were married and it was too late for him to intervene, not that Tom would have allowed any interference.

'Yes, I did hear something', he continued, 'she left the group and went back to her village, I don't know why'. What neither man knew, and Tom would not know for another four years, was that Elena had become pregnant to Tom, following their one-night honeymoon, and as they spoke that very morning, she was nursing her new-born child, named Tomas, after his father.

'I have heard nothing since, Sergeant, sorry'.

Was she ill or perhaps wounded? Fallen out with her brother? Her hatred of the Nazi occupation was too strong to just fade away, so perhaps she had joined another group of fighters? The only option that he never considered was that she was carrying his child and had withdrawn from the conflict for the sake of her unborn baby.

It had been a small chance that Smith might know something more substantial but he felt that he had to ask and it was better to know a little than nothing at all.

Tom thanked Smith and went to tell the others about their leave. He was sure that they would all leave that day, eager to see their families, but he would stay. Probably he would keep a friendly eye on Geraint, recovering in hospital.

On that same morning in Brittany, Hans lay back in his hospital bed, content in the fact that he would be discharged within the hour and had been granted a short leave while his broken arm mended. He would not be able to warn Hilda, at home in Koblenz, of his arrival but they would be pleased to see each other and if the cost of his visit home was a broken arm and a stitched head wound, it was not that bad a bargain!

He had been discovered in the ditch on the morning after the attack, and although he had been thoroughly questioned by the Gestapo, at one point being accused of spying and treason, he had finally convinced them that he was telling them everything that he knew. He had escorted the cook off the premises and the next thing that he could remember was waking up, wet and in pain, in a ditch not a hundred metres from the guard-post. The assumption was that the cook, the Beauchêne woman, had betrayed him to the British or that someone had spotted him and that he was simply a target of opportunity. His story never deviated and finally they had released him to the hospital.

He kept to himself the shock of learning that Eloise spoke perfect German, and that she had probably listened to much of what had been said and discussed inside the Manoir. He had suspected that she was a German speaker but she had never let on, not until those final few seconds in the road. Had been spying for the British all the time? The Gestapo told him that her house, where she lived with an old couple and her children, was empty, so there was a strong likelihood that she was involved in some way. If she was, then she had been very successful, for only five ratings from the submarine crew had survived the assault. All of the officers had been killed, including the captain and first officer, both highly trained and experienced men and Dönitz must have been raging when he heard the news.

Hans kept his suspicions about Eloise to himself because he suspected that it would do no good to tell the Gestapo, they would only think that he was implicated somehow and this time, he might not be able to talk himself out of it. Another reason was his respect for Eloise; she had worked hard, without complaint, and had been facing the prospect of being separated from her children, in order that German officers could feast on her cuisine, so if she had conspired with the British, she had her reasons. It shocked him that she might have been complicit in the slaughter of so many young Germans but really, how surprising was it that the French people resented their invaders so much that some of them would rather join with the British in taking the war to their shared enemy? If this was the French Résistance, then it would only become stronger.

No, she was well out of it and he hoped that she had escaped alive. If she had, then she had done better than Unteroffizier Brauer, he had brought a truckful of troops to the Manoir immediately after the attack and had been shot and strafed to death in short order. Hans could feel no pity for Brauer, he was the worst kind of NCO, a swaggering bully who thought only of his own advancement. No one deserved to die but he could not say that Brauer was a great loss, either to the Wehrmacht or to the nation. In one sense it was better for him that he did die, for he would have made a marvellous scapegoat for the whole catastrophe. The Nazi hierarchy, all the way up through Dönitz to the Fuhrer himself, would outraged at the loss of virtually all of a U-boat crew, an experienced one at that, and their reprisals would be savage.

The Gestapo and Dönitz's security had descended upon the scene within a couple of hours and were viciously scouring the locality, looking for possible strays from the raid and arresting anyone who could possibly be a member of the Résistance, for there must have been local help to hand. Quiniou had given a list of suspects to the Gestapo and although he had been unable to provide proof of the involvement of any individual before he disappeared, the secret police had their names. Anyone who resisted was shot on the spot but little did they know that every summary execution would, over time, persuade more and more people to support the Résistance in any way that they could.

They came for Galou that afternoon. He was not at all surprised, having concluded that Quiniou would have written something down on paper, and that his name would be near the top of the list for sure. He could have left with Hervé and the rest but leaving France held no attraction for him. Since his wife had died, he had been waiting to join her, so dying here appealed more than living for a few more years in England.

He had picked up a discarded German semi-automatic carbine as he left the Manoir, together with a couple of pouches of ammunition. It wasn't much but it would be enough, he decided.

As the soldiers, with the two Gestapo agents, advanced watchfully up his roadway, Galou was in his loft, where the chimney pierced the tiles of the roof. He had carefully removed a short length of lead flashing and two stone tiles, leaving a hole in the roof through which he could poke his carbine, resting it on a wooden batten. Right up against the chimney, he hoped that his rifle would be difficult, if not impossible to see from the road, and that he would manage a few shots before he was overwhelmed.

The Gestapo, in their civilian clothing, looked to be the most valuable targets and taking up the slack in the trigger, he put two deliberate shots into the man on the right, knocking him off his feet, and one into his partner on the left, spinning him around as the bullet took him in the shoulder, then falling to the ground. The soldiers, very wisely, scattered, leaving the flic rolling in pain in the mud and Galou had time enough to finish him with another shot, before moving to the hatch in the floor of the loft and dropping through it.

His British wireless remained but with the valves and crystal smashed and anything on paper was just ashes in the fireplace. The Boche would know that he had been an agent but nothing else, no one but he would be compromised and, God willing, their search would stop here.

He tore down the stairs but as he ran through into the living room at the front of the house, glass shattered in the window and a stick-grenade came hurtling through it, landing on the rug in front of the fire. It exploded with a roar, peppering him with shrapnel as he dived behind the couch. It had deafened him too, and as the door burst open under the weight of two troopers, their machine pistols sweeping rounds all around the room, it was to the background of a roaring in his ears, like the sea beating against rocks in a winter storm.

From around the end of the couch, Galou gut-shot the first man in but as his aim settled upon the second, he was pummelled with the impact of a tight group of bullets in his chest and fell back, dead for France.

End-piece

The Special Operations Executive (SOE) was created in July 1940, after Dunkirk, to 'co-ordinate all action, by way of subversion and sabotage, against the enemy overseas'. One of their operational groups, in cooperation with 62 Commando, was the 'Maid Honour Force', named after the Brixham trawler that took a group of thirty men to West Africa in a search for German submarine bases, named 'Operation Postmaster'.

They were unable to locate any bases but they did find an Italian merchant vessel and a German sea-going tug in the harbour of Santa Isabel on the island of Fernando Po, a Spanish territory and therefore neutral. It took months for the British Foreign Office to give permission for the raid to go ahead, perhaps not surprisingly, given that it breached the laws of neutrality. The raid was a spectacular success, with no casualties on either side, and the Small Scale Raiding Force (SSRF) was expanded, under Combined Operations Command and Lord Mountbatten.

The history of the SSRF is short, disbanding in 1943 as commando operations became larger in scale, but was enormously successful for a small unit and sadly took significant casualties in many of its operations, for example, 'Operation Aquatint', when every commando who landed on a beach near Cherbourg were shot and killed.

Majors March-Phillips and Appleyard, along with Captain Hayes are three of the most illustrious members of the SSRF, none of whom survived the war, but perhaps the most well-known is Anders Lassen, a Danish merchant seaman who joined 62 Commando and took part in 'Operation Postmaster', for which he was awarded the Military Cross and was commissioned in the field, a very rare honour. He later joined the Special Boat Service (SBS) and the Special Air Service (SAS), undertaking amazing feats of soldiery, and was awarded two bars to his Military Cross and a posthumous Victoria Cross.

I have used elements of some of SSRF operations in this novel;

- 'Operation Postmaster', as described above.
- The attack on the Île de Vierge lighthouse (which still exists) is modelled upon the raid on the Casquets Lighthouse, west of Alderney in the Channel Islands.
- My 'Operation Alderman', attacking the signalling station in Normandy, is inspired by 'Operation Fahrenheit', a similar raid on a signalling station in north Brittany.

The attack upon the German submariners, 'Operation Nightjar', was not undertaken by the SSRF and is my own invention. However, U-boat crews from Lorient and Brest did sometimes take their leisure in the Brittany countryside and there is a record of the French Résistance passing information to the British regarding a manor house that was being used a centre for 'rest and recuperation'. It was attacked, but by the RAF only and not by ground forces.

I hope that I have given a reasonable impression of the courage and daring of the members of the Résistance who, in the earliest years of occupation, fought their invaders with little in the way of resources and support. They were powered by their own love of country and succeeded in causing considerable disruption and distraction for the German forces. They were subject to savage reprisal at times and they also had their own traitors to deal with, as in any other occupied country. Somehow, enough of them survived long enough to be part of a considerable force which made a great contribution when the Allies eventually invaded in June 1944.

"It doesn't matter if one man fights or ten thousand; if the one man sees he has no option but to fight, then he will fight, whether he has others on his side or not." Hans Fallada 1893-1947

Joseph Taylor April 2018

****
**

Coming soon

'Sergeant Tom 5: Partisans!'

44334374R00127

Printed in Poland
by Amazon Fulfillment
Poland Sp. z o.o., Wrocław